The CONGREGATION

A Jake & Amanda Bannon Novel

DESIRÉE BOMBENON

RIVER GROVE
BOOKS

This book is a work of fiction. Names, characters, businesses, organizations, places, events, and incidents are either a product of the author's imagination or are used fictitiously. Any resemblance to actual persons, living or dead, events, or locales is entirely coincidental.

Published by River Grove Books
Austin, TX
www.rivergrovebooks.com

Distributed by River Grove Books

For ordering information or special discounts for bulk purchases, please contact River Grove Books at PO Box 91869, Austin, TX 78709, 512.891.6100.

Design and composition by Greenleaf Book Group
Cover design by Greenleaf Book Group
Cover image: © Shutterstock/Jason Salmon

Cataloging-in-Publication data is available.

ISBN: 978-1-63299-047-1

eBook ISBN: 978-1-63299-048-8

First Edition

CHAPTER 1

JUMPING OUT OF A WINDOW ON THE THIRD FLOOR OF THE CHICAGO Cultural Center was not what Amanda had in mind this fine Wednesday morning. Smoke billowed up from the windows of the floors beneath her. A symphony of people screaming, sirens, and the crackling of flames accosted her ears. Fire trucks were lining up in front of the building as she looked down for the best place to land. There really wasn't a good place to hit the ground—after all, this was East Washington Street, Chicago.

Jake arrived, frantically scanning the area for Amanda. He saw her slight figure on the window ledge at the top floor and mentally tried to discourage her from jumping. Directly below her, firemen fanned out to try and catch her in case she fell. They beckoned her to hold on while they secured a ladder against the building.

Okay, one, two, three, jump. She encouraged herself, but she just couldn't do it. She sighed with relief as a fireman started up the ladder that was placed over to her left. Nearly reaching her, he beckoned her to grab on and start down from the ledge. Moving toward the ladder, she caught her left foot on the outer part of the ledge, which forced her to hike herself up and twist ungracefully as she slammed into the ladder and the building. Jake was already there at the bottom watching, as she slowly made her way down the ladder. Amanda trembled each step of the way. The fireman carefully watched her from a few feet below on the ladder. He encouraged her to continue down the remaining way until they were both safely on the ground.

"Is she OK?" Jake asked the fireman.

"I'm fine, Jake." Amanda coughed hard.

Jake continued his conversation with the fireman, ignoring Amanda's response.

"Looked like a lot of smoke. She must have taken some in."

"Yes, I think she'll be fine. But let's move her away from this building and over to the ambulance to check her vitals."

"Here, let me take her." Jake moved between Amanda and the fireman and gingerly put his arm around her shoulders while walking her to the ambulance.

As Amanda was being checked over, Jake watched the firefighters continue to work with the flames that now fully engulfed one side of the old brick building. Fine old Chicago brick . . . he had started thinking about how they got into this mess in the first place when the paramedic cut into his thoughts.

"No broken bones. Some scratches and bruises from the climb down. Not bad, but we are going to take her to the hospital for a few more tests just to be sure."

Jake surveyed Amanda's face, then her arms. His gaze hesitated on her lower left forearm—the scar still white against her skin—a reminder of their last adventure. They were involved in investigating the kidnapping of some friends on the Big Island in Hawaii. They ended up right in the middle of a very dangerous and disturbing situation. It was quite a harrowing experience, so why they had agreed to come to Chicago was beyond him. Of course, he had nothing to do with it. It was Amanda who said yes. It was always Amanda, and here they were about to go at it again . . .

CHAPTER 2

IT WAS ALMOST A YEAR SINCE THEY SOLVED THE CASE IN HAWAII and they were back home in Calgary—what some refer to as the oil capital of Canada. Hawaii was a very difficult time for both Jake and Amanda since the situation involved friends. In the end it didn't turn out that well. The teenage daughter of a close friend, Taylor Wright, hooked up with a psycho via an Internet relationship. That led Jake and Amanda through a frightening adventure to rescue Taylor and her family. People died. Taylor and her mother escaped, but not without permanent emotional scars. Taylor was only recently released from the psychiatric facility she was recovering in and was trying her best to lead a normal life. She had just turned sixteen. She celebrated her birthday quietly, with Jake, Amanda, and a few close friends. They all attended a private dinner that her mother Gail put on in their home.

"That girl will never be the same again," Jake mentioned to Amanda on the way home that evening.

"Would you be? At least she's alive. Besides, what doesn't kill us makes us stronger, Jake." Amanda was very defensive about the whole situation. Jake knew she felt she could have done more, although they did everything they could.

The next evening after dinner, they sat sipping the last of an exceptional bottle of Château Angélus, looking out over their beautiful treed acreage. It was late November and the sun had been down for some time. It was a clear night, and the snow on the bare branches of the trees glittered. The ground was covered in a new dusting, and it was pristine. None of the little animal paw prints tarnished the lot yet. The scene was right out of a Christmas postcard. Amanda suddenly blurted, "I need a vacation, but not Hawaii. I am not ready to go back there yet."

"Okay." Jake was amused. "Good thing I pay all those taxes to have a condo we don't use. So what's on the bucket list this time?"

Amanda ignored Jake's sarcasm. "Rome," she said without hesitation.

"Why Rome?" Jake's left eyebrow lifted in his telltale fashion. This was always one of two things, a sign of Jake's agitation or intrigue.

"The Vatican."

"Amanda, are you serious? You aren't religious, and you are totally opposed to everything the Catholic Church stands for. You preach constantly about the hypocrisy of the Church." Jake tried to sound incredulous as added inducement for Amanda to change her mind.

"I don't believe in organized religion. I am, however, spiritual, as you know. Besides, it's the history of the place, Jake. We need to know more about the beginning of civilization and all that."

"The history of civilization started well before Rome, my dear." Jake did little to hide his irritation.

"Well," she hesitated, "my mom received a letter from Cardinal Roland. She has a sick friend, and he is willing to bless a rosary and light a few candles for her."

"Oh, I see." Jake rolled his eyes as he leaned back in his chair. He was aware of Amanda's mother's almost fanatical belief in Catholicism. She was constantly praying for everyone, and although Amanda didn't agree with her mother's beliefs, she absolutely adored her mother. If it were for anyone else, Amanda wouldn't do it, especially with her strong agnostic way of thinking.

"So why not FedEx the rosary to the cardinal? It will save us a bunch of time, and no doubt the blessing would be just as authentic. Come on. Even God knows how reliable FedEx is."

"'Cause . . . I can't get a really authentic pizza or ossobuco via FedEx."

That was the end of it. Jake knew better than to argue with Amanda. He simply peeled himself out of the comfortable chair and headed over to the office to book their flight to Rome. A nice pasta dish with a great Italian Barolo sounded pretty good. He smiled as he thought about how tenacious his wife was—one of the many reasons she was such a survivor and why he loved her so much.

CHAPTER 3

THE NINE AND A HALF HOURS TO FRANKFURT WENT QUICKLY. It always did, flying with Amanda. She was a chatterbox and rambled on about everything and anything. Then, of course, she indulged in a few glasses of wine and passed out, allowing Jake to get some much-needed work done.

Amanda was comfortable in first class. Her small frame fit nicely into the pods. She wasn't at all upset that they were flying commercial. Their lifestyle afforded them the use of their corporate jets at any time. However, Amanda knew this was solely personal, and they would pay for the trip themselves. When Jake petitioned that they could pay and fly one of the company jets, she insisted they not tie one up for a non-emergency. He could barely stop himself from adding that her mother's wishes would never be considered an emergency, but he knew better.

Amanda knew Jake was disappointed, but only because he wouldn't have the opportunity to fly with the crew up front like he often did when they flew for business trips. He loved the chance to polish up his pilot skills. Amanda felt a bit guilty about not letting him take the company jet, but she knew he would get over it. Jake got over things quickly, which was one of his finest traits. Amanda gazed over at him, her eyes softening with all the years of affection and adoration she had for him. To avoid being caught looking like a lovesick teenager, she quickly looked away as Jake felt her gaze and turned toward her.

Amanda chastised herself and rolled over in the pod, pretending to sleep. Soon after, fatigue overcame her, and she fell into a deep sleep.

* * *

Amanda was hanging on the rock wall in the rain forest on the Big Island of Hawaii. She and Jake climbed the wall in a torrential downpour. The lightning flashed across her terror-stricken face. Then the tree above her exploded as lightning struck, and it burst into pieces. She screamed as chunks and pieces of the tree came tumbling down the wall toward her. She was reaching for Jake's extended hand—their fingers touched, ever so lightly—and then she was swept up in the tangled landslide of the tree parts. She was now part of the tree, as she spun uncontrollably toward the ground.

* * *

Amanda woke with a jump, as she tried to get her bearings.

"Hot towel?" The pretty flight attendant held out a steaming facecloth to Amanda. "We'll be landing in Frankfurt shortly," she said with a smile.

Amanda nodded, still frazzled from her nightmare. She took the hot towel and wiped the sweat from her face. Jake was staring at her with a concerned look from across the aisle. These new first-class pods were strange—like little fortresses—just you, the video screen, and an occasional visit from the flight attendant. However, right now she was rather relieved that Jake had not been right next to her; he could probably see her heart thumping right through her shirt.

She sent him a most disarming smile, and he relaxed back in his seat. At least it was just a nightmare and not a vision. Amanda felt her clairvoyance was the reason she and Jake tended to get into all kinds of trouble. It had been a while since Amanda had a vision. She was almost hopeful their last adventure had somehow sucked the power right out of her. That special gift she regarded as a curse.

Amanda had been born with extrasensory perception. She had on more than one occasion been very helpful to the local authorities in solving difficult cases by finding clues. In some cases she even found people. After their businesses were doing well, and they found great people to run them, Jake and Amanda had decided to semi-retire from everything, including dangerous cases that could put them in harm's way. After all, even though the children were grown up, they still wanted Jake and Amanda around. Often, when visiting, the kids would make comments like, "Sure glad you two have calmed down a bit. No more crazy adventures, right?"

*   *   *

They were pulled back into action last year while in Hawaii and felt they had no choice but to help, since it involved close friends. That last adventure nearly took both their lives. Since then, Amanda's abilities seemed to have gone dormant. She was not disappointed, since she found it extremely frustrating having these visions and sometimes seeing things she didn't wish to see. Her greatest fear was having a premonition one day that would involve Jake or their kids, and feeling helpless and responsible if anything were to happen to them. That would put her in the nuthouse. Even though she was determined not to get into any more of these situations, she also felt some kind of altruistic responsibility to use her skills to help others. After all, it was a rare ability—one that could save lives.

They had no trouble getting through customs in Frankfurt. Germans were generally efficient, and it seemed that was also true with their airport security. They boarded the small commuter flight to Rome. And before they knew it, they were preparing to land. Amanda loved Rome, but for some reason she couldn't help feeling a slight panic as they descended toward Leonardo da Vinci International Airport.

Amanda shook her head to dismiss these feelings and looked out the window of the plane to distract herself. Her heart leapt as the beautiful city appeared below her. *Ah, Roma, what a sight.*

* * *

Rome was warm for this time of year. It was just after 2:00 in the afternoon. When they landed the temperature was 19 degrees Celsius. In no time they had made it through the swarms of passengers and gathered their luggage. Waiting for them at the arrivals area was a well-dressed driver with a sign that read, "Welcome Mr. and Mrs. Bannon."

"You sure know how to treat a lady," Amanda said, smiling.

"Only the best for you, my sweet. But who's a lady?" Jake teased as he looked around, making Amanda laugh.

"I have to be honest with you, Amanda. It's the fact that I can't rent any kind of cool car here in Rome that we even have a driver. I guess the tires and parts somehow go missing very quickly in Italy."

"That sucks, but you can't be in the driver's seat all the time, Jake. Relax. Take a load off."

Amanda's grin was contagious. Jake laughed out loud as they headed toward the driver, who promptly reached for their bags.

* * *

They arrived forty-five minutes later at the Hotel Hassler, located at the top of the Spanish Steps of the Piazza della Trinità dei Monti. There was a bit of traffic on the way, but Amanda didn't mind gazing out the car window. She was absorbed in the ancient sights that created the city's core. Amanda found it exhilarating and awe-inspiring when she thought of Rome's role in history and its importance in shaping so much of the current world. Amanda enjoyed the ride next to Jake, taking sips from a cold bottle of water from time to time. They checked in and immediately had a shower and change of clothes. Jake wanted to lie down after all the travel, but he knew if he took a nap, he would get jet-lagged. So they went to explore the area around their hotel. They had stayed at the Hassler before and found that the old hotel transported them to another time, with its magnificent décor and breathtaking views. Amanda pictured staying at the hotel back in the early 1960s and running into Audrey Hepburn. *Why hello, Audrey. I loved you in* Breakfast at Tiffany's. *It's one of my favorite movies of all time!*

There were some very nice shops around and so many streets snaking off in every direction. There was always something new to explore in this old city. Jake wasn't surprised to find Burberry and Gucci very close by. Amanda was checking out a light spring jacket in Burberry. It was simple, creamcolored, with only a patch of the well-known Burberry signature design on the cuffs of the sleeves showing. The exchange in US dollars showed the price at $2,750. She left it and moved on to browse the watches at the counter. Jake had seen this movie before. Amanda wasn't a shopper, so if she took more than thirty seconds to look at something, he knew she really liked it. But he also knew, although generous with others, she wasn't about to pay $2,750 on anything for herself. He waited until she had her back to him, browsing through wallets, to ask the sales clerk to wrap the jacket. He handed over his American Express Black Card, and the clerk, understanding what Jake was up to, quickly rang it through and had it bagged in under two minutes. Meanwhile, Amanda moved on to the signature scarves. He walked up behind her and kissed her on her neck.

"What do you think, Jake? You'd look good with this scarf. Very European." She picked it up and displayed it for Jake.

"Already have one. The kids gave it to me for my birthday last year, remember? Anyway I already bought myself something." He held up the bag.

"Wow, that was quick. Whatcha got there? A fedora in a big bag?"

"Nope, I got myself a cute little jacket for you to wear."

Amanda tilted her head to the side and peered under the tissue to see the jacket.

"Can't get anything by you, can I?"

"Nope, and you should really stop trying."

She went up onto her tiptoes and put her arms around his neck. She gave him a deep and passionate kiss, to the utmost delight of the sales clerk, who looked away to give them a moment alone.

"You'll get your present later," she remarked, as they moved to leave the store.

"Mmm, sounds good. Now, how about an early supper?"

"Great! I'm starving!" Her eyes lit up.

"Of course you are." The only thing bigger than Amanda's curiosity was her appetite.

Walking back along the cobblestone lanes toward their hotel, they found a little pizzeria on the corner of a courtyard. Jake asked in fluent Italian if they were open for customers. This never ceased to amaze Amanda, no matter how many times it happened. Jake spoke five languages, and Italian was her favorite. She loved the melody that seemed to come from the language. It wasn't spoken as much as it was sung.

* * *

The dinner was amazing. The staff seemed a bit miffed they were having dinner at 6:00 p.m., as most restaurants wouldn't have dinner guests arriving until much later. This was Europe after all. They ordered the *casa speciale* pizza, which started with a thin crust that was drizzled with olive oil, then sprinkled with fresh basil and oregano leaves, and topped with thinly sliced tomatoes, arugula, and fontina cheese. Jake and Amanda watched the pizza being made and cooked in a stone oven. The smell was fabulous, and their mouths watered as they anticipated the hot pie. While they waited, they ordered a *fiasco*, a bottle of Chianti Reserva that came in a little straw jacket. They were pleasantly surprised at the quality of the wine, since they couldn't find a bottle costing more than a few euros on the menu. Jake wondered about fontina cheese on a pizza, but then he took his first bite. The expression on his face said it all.

"I think we better order another . . ." he said through a full mouth. All Amanda could do was nod while she stuffed the remaining piece in her mouth.

They ate quietly over the next half hour, caught up in their own thoughts, sipping intermittently on the Chianti. Jake broke the silence. "Any visions, Amanda?"

"Nope, and I don't plan on having any."

"Not even the lottery numbers?" he asked slyly.

"Why? Because you need the money so badly?" Jake knew Amanda thought they already had more than they deserved. She made a point of making sure he knew how fortunate they were on occasion. Although they both did their best to help several charities by serving on boards and through their foundation, to Amanda it was never enough.

"No, I was thinking of giving it all to the Catholic Church," he retorted, while Amanda stuck her tongue out at him and then continued to eat.

CHAPTER 4

AMANDA COULDN'T HELP STARING—DARK HAIR, SMOKY GRAY EYES, and very tall—he had no right being married to the church. Amanda could feel the heat of Jake's stare on her, but she ignored him. The priest was stunning.

"Amanda, shake your head; your eyes are stuck," Jake whispered as the cardinal made his way over to greet them.

"Well, I was just thinking—" Amanda was saying when Jake interrupted her.

"Please, Amanda. Only you would think of corrupting a man of the cloth."

Earlier that morning they had made an appointment with the church secretary who said that Cardinal Roland would expect them, and would 3:00 p.m. today be convenient? The cardinal had arranged a special tour of the Cappella Sistina. A car would arrive to take them to the side entrance of the Vatican, leading through the Apostolic Palace. Amanda was thrilled. It wasn't about religion. It was about art and history. Having a private tour of the Sistine Chapel was indeed an honor. Amanda loved art. Though Jake was not as passionate about it, he was appreciative of the work of the greats, especially Michelangelo and Sandro Botticelli, so he, too, was pleased at the thought of the tour.

"Welcome, *buon pomeriggio!*" Cardinal Roland smiled and extended his hand to Amanda as she admired his perfect teeth.

"Good afternoon to you as well, Cardinal," Amanda said, beaming. "I must say, we weren't expecting this special privilege. We are grateful for the opportunity to tour the Sistine Chapel with you."

"It is my very humble pleasure, and good afternoon to you, Jake. I am hoping you are enjoying Rome so far?" The cardinal spoke now in his regular American accent.

"Buon pomeriggio, Cardinal." Jake shook the cardinal's hand firmly, "Well, it is our honor to be allowed this special admission, and I am certainly a fan of the Renaissance."

"But not of the Church," the cardinal said with a smile, and continued as Jake lifted an eyebrow.

"Oh yes. I was speaking to your mother-in-law who prepared me for your arrival. But not to worry; the Church of today understands the individualism of spirituality. We can only hope that light finds its way to all. We are not the Church of the past, Jake. We all need something to believe in." Cardinal Roland's manner was so gentle and kind. It was tough to come back with any type of argument without looking like a bully, so Jake just nodded.

"Allow me," said the cardinal, and gestured for Amanda and Jake to follow him as he led them through to one of the most magnificent sights within the walls of Vatican City.

Although they'd visited Rome on occasion, they had never had a chance to view the Sistine Chapel. To be able to take in its splendor without a crowd to work around was so much more enjoyable.

"Wow. I am speechless," Amanda gasped upon entry to the Sistine Chapel.

"And that's saying something. It takes a lot to silence her," Jake responded. Cardinal Roland nodded as if he knew what Jake meant. Then he peered up and around. "It takes my breath away no matter how many times I see it." The cardinal whispered almost to himself.

Amanda and Jake walked in awe through the chapel, noting many of the famous fresco pieces. However, what got their attention was the piece taking up the entire back altar wall.

"The most talked about piece in the chapel, *The Last Judgment*, took Michelangelo four years to finish, from 1536 to 1541. He started this piece some twenty years after finishing the ceiling of this chapel."

"No doubt," Jake mused. "I am surprised he took the job at all, after all the work he did on the ceiling."

"Oh, back then, you really had no choice. To be a great artist was an honor and a curse."

Amanda quickly thought about her special abilities. She could relate to the honor and curse bit. Suddenly she felt a pang of sorrow for the great artist Michelangelo, and the others who spent their lives creating these masterful pieces, being exploited for their talent and never being able to truly enjoy their work for what it brought to them personally.

"It seems so deep and dark."

"Yes, Amanda." Cardinal Roland stepped up behind her to view the wall. "It was said to be a dark time for Michelangelo. He was in his late sixties when he finished this painting and wasn't happy about being commissioned to do the work. In fact, he wrote a poem reflecting that. You are looking at a restored version of the original. Much of what you see here in the area of nudity, specifically, had been covered up after Michelangelo's death in 1564 by Daniele da Volterra, when nudity in religious art was condemned by the Council of Trent."

"I remember hearing about the restoration, starting in 1980, right?" Amanda questioned.

"That's right, and during the restoration the censorship that created the so-called fig leaf campaign was removed, so to speak, revealing the artist's true depiction and, really, the struggle and pain he felt during the project years."

The rest of the tour seemed to go by quickly. Amanda and Jake were both surprised when the cardinal concluded, "Well I certainly hope this added to your trip. It is nearly 6:30, and I have a service to attend."

"It was magnificent," Amanda almost sang. "Cardinal, about the rosary . . ."

"Oh, yes. I haven't forgotten. I will have it properly blessed and ready for you to pick up tomorrow. How long will you be in Rome?"

Jake slipped into the conversation. "Unfortunately we are here for only a few days more. We have some business next week in Chicago and must be back for that. But knowing Amanda, I am sure we will get back to Rome very soon." He smiled at the cardinal. "Amanda loves this city, but mostly for the food!"

The cardinal's eyes suddenly clouded over, and Jake mistook this as disapproval of his last comment, "Forgive me, Cardinal. I meant no disrespect about Rome . . ."

Cardinal Roland was shaking his head and put up his hand to stop Jake's apology. "No, Jake. Your comments are welcome, and I understand Amanda's appetite. I speak to her mother often," he said jokingly, but it came across without the intended humor. Something was bothering the cardinal. "Your business trip to Chicago reminded me of a dear friend I have from my days at the seminary. We both graduated from the University of Chicago Divinity School."

Amanda and Jake remained silent and waited, as it seemed the cardinal needed to get something off his chest.

The cardinal sighed heavily and continued. "While I evolved in my career through service and was eventually elevated to cardinal priest, my dear friend asked to be kept in his position in Chicago to continue to serve the community there, feeling that this was what God intended for him. We continue to keep in touch, and I fear he is struggling very much of late." Cardinal Roland's downcast look was almost more than Amanda could bear. It seemed disproportionate to the situation; there had to be more.

"Go on," Amanda encouraged, feeling the cardinal needed to finish something important.

"I hear such sadness in his voice when he calls, like he has lost all his faith. I just wish I could go there and offer him support. We used to collect old religious relics, whether Christian or other, anything the church or museums didn't want or need for their collections. I have one that I wanted to give to him, to remind him of our mission, and at the same time personally check up on him. Unfortunately, my duties here keep me in Rome for another month at least."

The words were out of her mouth before Jake could intervene.

"Cardinal Roland, can we take it to him for you? I mean if getting it to him more quickly would help him . . . would that make you feel any better?"

Amanda caught the shadow that crossed Jake's face and cringed internally, knowing the scolding she would hear on the way back to the hotel.

The cardinal's eyes lit up. "If you could do that, I would be very grateful. I truly believe it will give him strength, if nothing more than a reminder of the past. I hope it will help him get through this difficult time. We all have our spirits tested at some point."

"Yes, we do. Don't we?" Jake spoke softly and turned to Amanda, who knew exactly what he really meant. She heard it loud and clear.

"If you will come by the Vatican clerical offices tomorrow after 10:00 in the morning, I will have it along with the rosary and contact information. Father Kristofferson, that is my friend, will be so happy to see you in Chicago. In the meantime, I must be going, and again thank you so much for offering and your kindness. It was great meeting you both."

"Our pleasure, Cardinal." Amanda smiled politely.

"Wasn't that exceptional?" Amanda started the deflection as soon as they stepped out of the building and into the street.

"Don't even start, Amanda." Jake waved down a taxi, and they got in. Jake spoke to the driver, "Hotel Hassler."

The driver nodded at Jake, and they entered the early evening traffic.

"Okay, but it's a good deed we are doing, Jake." Amanda refused to let it go without getting Jake's buy-in.

"Really, Amanda. Don't you think we have enough to do? By the way, you are dropping off a trinket, not getting baptized. This doesn't buy you any points. You are still going to hell, no matter what you think."

"Very funny . . ."

"Amanda, you know how I feel about all this religious mumbo jumbo, and we have work to do in Chicago . . ." he trailed off, but the anger had already diminished. He would acquiesce, like he always did, to Amanda's spontaneity. He left it at that and focused on the amazing Amarone wine he planned on having with dinner that evening, something to take the edge off.

CHAPTER 5

THE NEXT MORNING CAME EARLY FOR BOTH JAKE AND AMANDA.
They were groggy from too much of that fine Amarone. Amanda rolled out of
bed, remembering that the rosary and relic would be ready to go by 10:00 a.m.

"We should have stuck to one bottle." Jake scowled, dehydrated and
irritable.

"Yeah, well it seemed like a good idea at the time, and I don't recall you
protesting too loudly."

"I'm surprised you remember anything at all."

"Quite the pithy comeback this morning, lover boy . . . you okay?"
Amanda popped an Advil and held the bottle out to Jake, knowing full well
he didn't like to put any chemicals in his body, or "temple" as he referred to
it. Just for a second he looked like he would take it. Instead, he walked over
to the in-room fridge and cracked open a San Pellegrino.

"Mmm, nectar of the gods." Jake downed the bottle in just a few
swallows.

Roma was old and beautiful. From the window of their room they could
see a group of performers gather to sing at the top of the Spanish Steps. And
just to the right and below they could see the vast expanse of lovely historic
structures, rich with history, the history of the world. Amanda could actually
see the St. Peter's obelisk in the distance, brought in from Egypt in 37 AD by

Emperor Caligula and erected in the center of St. Peter's Square in 1586. The dome-shaped roofs of the many basilicas were scattered throughout the city, highlighted by the glints of sunlight reflecting off their coppery lids.

After picking up the rosary and the relic left for them at the Vatican offices by Cardinal Roland, Amanda and Jake made the walk through the Pantheon, the most well-preserved building in Rome. Although "Pantheon" was Greek, meaning "a temple consecrated to all gods," it was mainly used as a tomb. Both Amanda and Jake were intrigued to find that some great artists, including Raphael, lay among the kings of Italy. The square in front of the Pantheon was flooded with tourists. It was even more impressive once you got into the building, which was a rotunda hidden behind the rectangular façade on the front. It still stood as the world's largest unreinforced concrete dome. "Quite impressive," Jake remarked while walking through it.

The Colosseum was just as impressive, although Jake thought it even more so because of the remarkable engineering for a building whose construction started back in 72 AD under one emperor, Vespasian, and was completed in 80 AD under another, Titus.

"Jake, really. They used to slaughter people in there. How can that be impressive?"

"I am talking about their ability to build in the hypogeum. Can you imagine the massive brain trust that went into creating two levels of underground networks for the gladiators and animals with all their props and cages? And what about the aqueduct? How ingenious was that? So they could flood the coliseum and reenact wars at sea!"

"Yes, Jake. But truly who would want to reenact callous blood-spilling episodes from their wars of past? Don't you think that is a little morbid?"

"All right, but you have to admit, even today it would stand as a great feat in engineering accomplishments."

Amanda's mind reeled back to the days of gladiators fighting other gladiators, lions, and all sorts of other animals. *The games—how little we have learned, how little we have evolved since those days. We still take human life for granted, and it's always a competition. The strong will survive.*

Just then Amanda had a strange sensation. She saw, swimming in front of her eyes, like air that is too hot, shimmering in thick waves, the words from Matthew 5:5: *Blessed are the meek for they shall inherit the earth.*

The words slowly melted in front of her. Amanda figured she'd been out in the sun too long. But she felt uneasy, because the sensation she got in the pit of her stomach was the same one she had experienced many times before when having a vision. It was fleeting and it passed. She chalked it up to a Sunday school memory from her childhood.

Amanda reminded herself there was also the influence of being here in Rome, Vatican Square, surrounded by churches. At one time, this city was the center of the world. If nothing else, you felt a very real spiritualism, and even if you didn't believe in God, you almost wanted to. She convinced herself that the vision was nothing more than a manifestation of her exposed senses.

Jake managed to move the meetings in Chicago, so they could spend a bit more time in Rome, which they enjoyed thoroughly. Chicago would definitely be fun. But the weather in December could be treacherous, although all reports he checked showed the city was unusually warm for this time of year. He was happy about that. The only thing he wasn't happy about was Amanda's promise to visit Father Kristofferson. Jake wasn't clairvoyant like Amanda, but he did have gut instinct, and his gut was telling him that something wasn't quite right.

CHAPTER 6

CHICAGO. "I LOVE THIS TOWN!" JAKE BEAMED; HE WAS IN HIS element. Chicago, with all the hustle and bustle along with everything else you could hope for. Great restaurants, theater, music, and the overall vibe made it a great city.

In recent years, it had become a more carefree and safe environment. Chicago was just a cool place to be. It reminded Jake and Amanda of a larger version of their hometown of Calgary. The people were friendly, and the city was clean and charismatic. Chicago was a big city with small-town values— their kind of place.

"What's for dinner tonight?" Amanda was excited about trying some new restaurants that were recommended to them.

"Well, thank goodness they have pretty good fare here. After Italy I was concerned Chicago would be a letdown for you." Jake was kidding, of course. He knew Amanda was happy eating anywhere. She was a real foodie. But how she kept so slim, he would never know. All that yoga and stuff, he guessed.

"I heard we should try The Girl and the Goat on Randolph, but it's difficult to get into." Jake winked. Amanda knew that Jake would have already made a reservation and would have gone through some of his connections to ensure a great table with the best server and maybe even a pre-planned menu, so she spoke causally with disinterest.

"Well, I was thinking we would order room service, watch a good action flick, and get caught up on some sleep—get on the right time zone, you know."

Jake looked hurt. "Well, if you really want crappy hotel food." They were at the Waldorf Astoria, and Amanda knew the food would be great at the hotel, but she was excited for a new experience, so she squeezed Jake's arm, who now was pretending to not care at all. "Well, what about this girl and the goat thing? Is goat on the menu?" She wanted to play this out.

"Well, if goat isn't, maybe the girl is," he said, looking devilish. Amanda rolled her eyes with exaggeration. "Oh, is this one of those places?"

"Nope, but they have amazing oysters. Will that work?"

"Works for me! Let's go!"

CHAPTER 7

THE HOLY NAME CATHEDRAL, LOCATED ON SUPERIOR STREET IN Chicago, was an amazing structure. The only cathedral in Chicago, it had a history of survival since it was established as the Chapel of Holy Name in 1846. It was destroyed in the Great Chicago Fire in October 1871. And only through the perseverance of many, including Bishop Foley and Fryer McMullen who crossed the country raising awareness and funds to rebuild the church, was the Holy Name Cathedral saved.

Even after all its hardships, in 2006, part of the roof fell, and once more funds were raised to renovate it, only to have a fire destroy it again in 2009. It seemed like the church was doomed from the beginning of time. Yet the cathedral still stood and served a growing congregation of diverse people from across Chicago.

This was one of the reasons he visited—the tenacity of this church, the hope, the strength, to stand within the walls and feel all that it has overcome. Being there helped with all the other pain and hardship. Father Kristofferson realized he had been holding his breath and let it out slowly. He quietly wondered, "Why am I here? Why do I come to Holy Name? What am I looking for?"

This was not the first time he had visited the cathedral. His small parish was located in Old Town. He simply started walking and arrived. This time of day few others would be at the church. He needed the cathedral to remind him of his obligations, of the reasons for his faith. Most of all, of the devastation that had happened over and over to this tough old church, and how it still stood, tall and ornate, larger than life.

*   *   *

It was time to get going, and Amanda insisted they take a cycle rickshaw to the restaurant. "Come on. We can't just show up like everyone else, in a black car."

"Yeah, but a pedicab? Come on, Amanda. Do you know how far it is from the hotel to the restaurant?"

"Yes, I do. Google Maps, my friend, states it is 2.2 miles and about twenty-five minutes in a cab through traffic. But the cyclist can do it faster, because he can go around traffic. Besides, they do it for the exercise!"

"No, they do it for the money, and it's freezing out. If I have to get out and help this guy push his bike, you are going to be in big trouble . . ." Jake tried his angry face, but Amanda wasn't buying it, so she just grinned and hopped into the buggy, grabbing the warm blanket lying on the seat and pulling it up to her neck.

Fortunately there was no snow, which was a good thing. They made it in twenty minutes, which even surprised Amanda, but she didn't hesitate to rub it in. "Hope that wasn't too long for you, Jake . . ."

"Traffic was lighter than I thought, and the pedaler was buffer than I anticipated."

"Oh, I didn't mind." Amanda's eyes were teasing. "He's really cute. Give him a big tip, okay?"

"What tip? Like don't eat yellow snow?" Jake snapped. "Or steroids make you fat?"

Amanda punched his arm, and Jake quickly picked off an additional ten-dollar bill and handed it to the grinning hunk.

Inside, the restaurant was bustling. This was the new, happening spot.

It was tough to get into without knowing someone, and the ambience was just what Amanda enjoyed, casual and earthy. Take simple and make it fun and inviting, and it became a place you could start a conversation that ends comfortably four hours later. Then you had yourself a hot restaurant.

Their table was completely surrounded by others, making the most of the space; yet it was strategically set up to make them feel like they were alone somehow. Looking at the menu you knew there was nothing permanent about the choices. Most menus at good restaurants were not stagnant. They offered what was freshest and most bountiful during the various seasons of the year. Oysters seemed to be the in thing everywhere right now, and Jake could eat them by the truckload.

"I see you have the Shibumi oysters on the menu." Jake was already at it with the server, a pretty redhead who was maybe twenty-three years old. "What do you have that's not on the menu?"

"Well, the Shibumi is an amazing oyster . . ." she started, and Amanda looked down at the table, knowing what the poor girl was in for.

"Yes, I know. Washington. Puget Sound, right? I believe the southern part." The server was nodding as Jake continued. "They are very succulent, great cucumber flavor with a hint of smoke to it. The problem is, they are a little small for me."

The server's face grew flush. *A little out of your league perhaps,* Amanda thought, feeling sorry for the girl.

"Well sir, we do have some that came in just earlier today from Eastern Canada. They only come at certain times of the year."

Jake jumped in. "Bras d'Or? Yes! I love them. It's the right time of the year. These oysters marinate for three years in that beautiful Atlantic brine. I will take a dozen. Amanda?"

Amanda, feeling like she needed to give the server a bit of a lift after Jake's oyster snobbery, ordered. "The Shibumi oysters sound amazing. I will take half a dozen, 'cause I would like to have more than just oysters tonight."

The server gave Amanda a grateful smile. "Anything to drink at this time?"

"Oh, yes. Two Grey Goose martinis straight up with a twist, please, and a fresh pepper mill." The redhead's eyebrows went up as Amanda added the pepper mill request, but she knew better than to ask. These two were characters.

"Did you have to make the poor kid feel so bad? I think she's gonna quit tonight after her shift is done."

"Why wait?" Jake laughed. "Hey, she'd better learn her oysters; especially in a place like this where people are connoisseurs, not just foodies. At least I didn't quiz her on species."

"Do you know ...?"

"*Virginica* for the Bras d'Or, and I believe *gigas* for the Shibumi."

"Of course you would know," Amanda said, rolling her eyes. "Where the hell is my martini?"

CHAPTER 8

JOSH NEWMAN WAS BEAUTIFUL, OR SO THOUGHT ALMOST EVERY girl and most of the boys at the Gathering, on those evenings when he chose to go. Many of the teens who attended the Gathering had met Josh during one of his years at private Catholic school in Chicago, either St. Clements where he attended middle school, or later at St. Ignatius College Prep School. Josh was brilliant. He was an honor student, and his teachers loved him. He was also athletic without being intimidating. He was an all-around great guy, and everyone wanted to be in his circle.

His father was well respected and ran a financial brokerage firm, catering to many of Chicago's elite. His mother was a community volunteer who went out of her way to step up and help as many causes as she possibly could, while still getting dinner on the table by 6:00 p.m. when Josh's father, Stanford, came home. Elise was short and frumpy, and people often wondered what Stanford saw in his wife. He was wealthy and handsome, tall, with dark brown hair and dark eyes that were almost black. Josh seemed to have gotten all his looks from his father, except for his eyes; those were his mother's. Elise had large stunning eyes, the color of slate with azure highlights that brightened in the daylight but could darken when her mood changed. The combination of those eyes, with Stanford's looks, left most people gawking when introduced to Josh.

As always, when he showed up at the Gathering, a small crowd formed around him. And he greeted them warmly. Josh had gained a status with the young group. There were kids as young as twelve and as old as twenty-two, but Josh, at nineteen, had power over them all, and he planned on using it.

*   *   *

Cardinal Roland paced the floor of his room at the Domus Sanctae Marthae, a hospitality residence based at the edge of Vatican City. The residence was built in 1996 when Pope John Paul II felt the cardinals should be housed in more comfortable quarters during the conclave when a new pope is voted to office. Prior to the roomier residence, the cardinals slept on small cots located in stuffy rooms next door to the Sistine Chapel where the voting takes place.

His thoughts flew about his head, and it gave him no peace standing on the holy ground of Vatican City. He knew what was coming, and it wasn't clear how he was going to stop the chain of events. His only hope was that Amanda and Jake would somehow figure things out and, by handing over the relic, connect those things to his lifelong friend. They would understand then. They had to.

What would become of him after would not matter. He would most likely be removed from his new position, and he might even have to disappear. No matter how much time goes by, history always seems to repeat itself: We are bent on destroying ourselves, over and over. We never learn how to stop this flywheel from spinning. He could hear the thump-thump of something. *What was it? A drum outside?* He listened and realized it was his own head. It felt like it would explode. The migraine was so sharp that he stumbled into the chair in his room. Holding his head with both hands, he put his elbows on his knees and stared at the ground. Then he closed his eyes tight, trying to squeeze the pain out. *This can't be happening*, he thought. *But it is*. He remembered back to the conversations ten years earlier.

* * *

"What about after, Michael? We have to prepare for it. If we do this, you know we can't just go through with it and leave it. We have to let them know why. It has to have meaning, or it is done for nothing."

"They don't care. This isn't about the people, or God, or anything. This is about money. The Church has been corrupt since the beginning of time, taking advantage of the fact that people have to believe in something, anything. Would God allow the atrocities that have happened over the history of our world? Of course not, but we blame Him just the same. God is just part of all of us, the part that wants us to do the right thing, the part that wants us to save ourselves, to forgive others, and to live good lives. God cannot stop what is happening on the other side, because the Devil is in all of us as well, pushing God to the back and prioritizing our lives by what we have, what we can take, and how we become numb and apathetic to everyone and everything else."

As usual, Michael was right, Sam decided. "Okay, but this is so big. It's bigger than us, and surely we can't get away with it. Don't you think we need help? Will we get caught?"

"Sammy, we will get caught. That's the point, and if we lose everything to expose the Devil, don't you think we should expect the worst?"

Samuel nodded. He adored Michael, and it's not like he didn't know what he was getting into. They had been planning this for nearly seven years, and they knew they would have to be the ones who set the wheels in motion. December 12, 2012. That's still a long time away, he thought. Maybe things will change. Maybe everything would be all right, and they could put the plans away.

* * *

Cardinal Roland woke with a start. *Michael* . . . his young face floated away, leaving the cardinal hazy and adjusting to the late-afternoon light that angled into the window of his room. He wondered, "How long have I been sitting here? What time is it?" His thoughts drifted back to the old days, the days when there was time, lots of time. How quickly a decade can pass, how agonizingly quickly, with no way to stop it. Michael had built his team over the years. Samuel didn't know a lot anymore; just that the plans had changed. It was no longer just the two of them. The plan was out of control. The cardinal looked out at St. Peter's Basilica, the sun warming his face, as the tears rolled slowly down his cheeks.

CHAPTER 9

AMANDA WAS PECKING AWAY ON THE COMPUTER WHEN JAKE walked out, freshly showered, wearing a towel around his slim waist. Amanda peered up admiringly and wondered how he managed to keep so fit when they were constantly traveling.

"Good genes," she muttered under her breath.

"What was that? What jeans?" Jake asked inquiringly.

"No, I meant you have good genes, as in G-E-N-E-S. I was admiring your youthful physique, for such an old man."

"I didn't hear you calling me old last night." Jake strutted over to the closet and pulled the door open.

"Yeah, well, you also had a dozen oysters supporting your efforts, didn't you?"

"Whatever! I am ready to go again. Come on. I will dispel any belief that it was just the oysters from last night."

"Keep it in your pants, buddy. It's already almost 9:00. Let's head out and get some breakfast and then see if we can find this Father Kristofferson."

Amanda was giggling. Suddenly she felt a bit giddy and closed her eyes. She could see St. Peter's Basilica clearly, like she could reach out and touch the building.

Jake was beside her. "What is it, baby? What's wrong?"

"Something about . . . I could see St. Peter's . . ."

"Well sweetie, we were just there, in Rome, only days ago. It makes sense—"

Amanda cut him off. "No, Jake. This is different. This is now. It's not right, and I think Cardinal Roland may be in trouble."

"Don't say stuff like that Amanda. It's not a good thing when you say stuff like that."

"I know, Jake. I don't like it either. I wish I could just stop it from happening, but I can't. Damn!"

Amanda was clearly upset, and Jake knew to leave her alone. It must be such a helpless feeling, and even scary, when you're clairvoyant. Amanda had been living with this all her life. At first, Jake would disregard her visions as lucky guesses or even great intuition. But after so many episodes where she was able to say something significant, and he watched it happen either later the same day, or at some point in the future, he finally gave in to the fact that she did have a gift.

He couldn't imagine how difficult it must be to not have any control over when and where you would see something that could be instrumental or even life-changing or, worse, life-taking. He felt bad for her many times. However, a lot of good came from Amanda's gift. She had been the sole reason that a few unsolved mysteries were now solved, and if it weren't for her visions during their time on the Big Island of Hawaii, they would not have saved their friends. So, although it was a burden, Jake admired Amanda's attitude and courage to carry this with her and use it as best she could.

Amanda was breathing softly. "Well, I can't get any more of it right now . . . I just hope I can get clarity soon. I feel like Cardinal Roland is in some kind of impending danger."

She thought about the small item in her handbag, the one that the cardinal asked her to deliver to Father Kristofferson. "Jake, I wonder if that relic we have has anything to do with my vision?"

Jake thought for a second. "Well, let's see if we can find an expert before we go see the priest. Someone in this town must know something about religious relics, right? This town has a lot of churches and history, too. Not quite like Rome, of course . . ."

"Right." She went to Google on her MacBook Air and started searching for experts in the Chicago area.

*   *   *

The object was not spectacular in any way. It fit in the palm of Amanda's hand, and it was in the shape of a hexagon, six equal sides, with some unique markings on the top. It was made out of a dark wood. Mahogany was Amanda's guess. And if polished up, it would be quite beautiful.

She sat admiring the item in her hand while she and Jake waited in an obscenely messy room. Amanda had found the small office on Google, and the reviews from visitors about Professor Orloff were interesting and positive. Apparently, he knew what he was doing, but his office was certainly not an indication of his abilities, or at least she hoped not. Books lay in piles all over reception area tables and most of the chairs. Books were also scattered on the floor, along with some industry magazines. Where you could see the carpet, it was stained with coffee. Well, Amanda thought it looked like coffee anyway. Layers of dust covered it all. By the look of things, the dust could have been there since the late '70s.

They had squeezed in through the front glass door, trying not to trip over the items on the floor. The glass on the door was so dirty you couldn't see through it to the front office. It could be a great deterrent to burglars for sure. A short, older woman, in her mid- to late sixties, looked up from a tiny desk surrounded by boxes, books, and what looked like scrolls, and asked only with her eyes, "Well, what do you two want?"

"Hi," Amanda blurted, "we called earlier . . ." Her eyes scanned the small desk for a phone and realized the phone must be buried.

"Oh, yes. You want to see the professor about an article of interest." She seemed quite professional. "I will let him know you are here. He stepped out for a Danish at the bakery next door."

Amanda felt her stomach growl. They didn't get the breakfast they discussed before her vision, and now she was starving. She felt worse for Jake who spent a tremendous amount of energy the night before and must be famished.

The woman pulled out a cell phone from her pants pocket. *And so there's the phone*, Amanda thought.

"Professor? Yes, that couple, uh-huh, yes, yes, they have it with them . . ." she said as she looked at Amanda inquiringly. Amanda held the relic up, while the woman nodded into the phone. "Yes, I will advise them."

They continued to wait. The older lady told them that the professor was held up for a bit at the bakery, speaking to an important client, and would be back soon.

Jake was perched on the end of his chair, looking as if he feared he would catch something from the seat. Amanda smiled up at him hopefully, from the stack of books she sat on. There was nowhere else for her to sit without having to move a lot of stuff, so she plunked herself down on the nearest pile of books she could find. Jake raised an eyebrow, giving her the what-have-you-gotten-us-into-now look, so she quickly turned away and was relieved when the door opened and the receptionist announced, "Professor, Amanda and Jake Bannon are here to see you."

Professor Orloff matched his office perfectly. He was unkempt, his hair was straggly and sticking out in several directions, and his clothes were wrinkled so badly that Amanda wondered how he was able to get into them. He had on a pair of dark-rimmed glasses with lenses so thick, you could count the gold flecks in his magnified hazel eyes. His shoes were a scuffed and battered pair of Hush Puppies, no doubt from the '70s, Amanda guessed. But his hand, as he stuck it out toward Jake, was smooth and young, and there were no lines on his face. Amanda was shocked. Professor Orloff couldn't have been more than forty years old, maybe younger.

"Oh, thanks, Mom," he said, winking at the older woman while he took Jake's hand. "Pleasure to meet you, Mr. Bannon."

"Um, call me Jake, please." Jake was clearly amused at the whole situation: a young professor with a shop of horrors, manned by his mother of all people.

Amanda was already getting ready to take the heat about this one when she suddenly got the distinct feeling that she kind of liked this unlikely professor. She gave him her best smile, and the professor's large eyes twinkled as he politely lifted her hand to his lips. "Mrs. Bannon," he said, sounding quite sophisticated as he gently released her hand.

Jake almost burst out in laughter, but he caught himself at the last possible minute and coughed into his fist instead.

"My boy is such a charmer," his mom slash receptionist giggled, beaming from the back of the room. "Why don't you go into the conference room for your discussion?"

Conference room? Amanda had not noticed any space in this tiny office for a conference to take place. Her gaze followed the professor's to a door—more like a slit in the wall—that led to another room at the back of the office.

"Oh, yes. Please follow me." The professor led them around some stacks of books and stepped over a box, carefully moving around the small desk where his mother sat, mindful not to disturb any of the books or any of the dust. Then he seemed to disappear into the wall where the opening was. Amanda shrugged her shoulders at Jake and followed.

The conference room was surprisingly larger than she expected. It had a dark wood table with six chairs around it. There was a computer desk in the corner with a MacBook Pro and what looked like a state-of-the-art digital camera sitting neatly on top. The room was spotless compared to the front room. It was as if you had entered some kind of time machine and stepped out into a different year and place.

"Nice camera." Jake was all over it. "Nikon, D-SLR, right? The 7000 model."

"Yup. I keep the high-tech stuff in here, although that's not really the high-tech stuff. My mother would be upset if she thought I actually had to use things like magnifiers and intensifiers to distinguish real items from fakes. She thinks I am a genius and can tell you everything by scanning it with sight alone. You can see that my eyesight is not all that it should be, and it makes her feel better thinking I make my living by using my eyes. They have been pretty much useless since I was a kid. I think she feels like my poor eyesight is her fault, but it was just bad luck, and a nasty bout of the measles."

"Wow, that's interesting. I thought you could get sore eyes from measles, but I didn't think it could really harm your eyesight that much," Jake remarked.

"Normally not. The fact that I had vitamin A deficiency and the measles at the same time, resulted in a corneal ulceration that could have left me blind. Frankly, I consider myself quite lucky." He grinned and behind those goggles Amanda saw a kindness that instantly solidified her early impression. She liked Professor Orloff. He seemed to take things in stride and didn't blame anyone for his condition. In fact, he made the best of it.

"Well, I am sure you didn't come all the way out here to listen to me talk about my childhood disease, so let's have it." He extended his rather large hand, palm up, toward Amanda.

"How did you know I had it?" Amanda wondered as she slowly walked over and placed the object gingerly in the professor's hand.

"Lucky guess," he said, grinning. "Now, let's see . . ." The professor walked over to the wood table and slid his hand underneath. A soft click could be heard. Suddenly, a portion of the wooden table slowly slid open. Rising up on a separate shelf, something appeared that resembled a microscope out of a sci-fi flick. There was a monitor hooked up to it and a camera, and the glow of LED lighting all around it. Next to it was a tray with all kinds of tiny tools like what you would see at the side of a surgeon's operating table, but with brushes and tiny magnifying glasses, too.

"Is that a 19-inch monitor? Cool setup," Jake commented.

"Yeah. The eyes . . ." The professor placed the object under the lens of the microscope and switched on the monitor. The three of them gathered around to take a closer look. The ambience of the room transported them from the old-fashioned office they originally entered into a secret high-tech lab.

CHAPTER 10

ELISE FINISHED DROPPING OFF HER BAKED GOODS AT THE ANNUAL home Is Where the Heart Is bake-off that she entered each year with her neighbor, Carol. She didn't particularly like Carol—maybe because Carol was a good-looking, thin blonde, and everywhere they went together men were openly eyeing her up and down. *No, that's just a small part of it*, she thought. *Mostly it's because Carol has her independence.* Elise knew she shouldn't dislike Carol for it, but whenever they did these charitable errands, Carol drove. It's not that Carol wanted to do the driving, or that she didn't trust Elise to drive. Elise just never drove. Carol assumed Elise was paranoid or wasn't a good driver, so she asked Elise if she could pick her up every time.

Elise would love to drive just once, if she were ever allowed to take the car.

"Did you see Patricia Redford's cake?" Carol interrupted Elise's thoughts and was looking sheepishly over at her. Elise was used to the constant stream of gossip that came from Carol during these trips. She shook her head no.

"I hadn't noticed." Elise tried to look as disinterested as possible, hoping that Carol would move onto something else, or just shut her big trap for once.

"Well, it's that same one she just did for the kids' cancer bake-fest. I heard the Hansons, who bought it last time, threw it out after one bite. It was absolutely horrible. Ann Hanson said she wouldn't even feed it to her dog." A smug grin played on her lips as she continued. "Rumor has it that nobody is going to bid for that cake this time, and they are hoping Patricia gets the hint. Do you think she will?"

"Maybe the Hansons are just too picky, Carol. They bought the cake as part of a charitable donation. So what if it wasn't up to their fucking standards? What about buying the cake for the right reasons and not so you can gorge your fat face on shitty sweets and gossip about the people who are trying to do something nice, for a goddamn change?"

Elise hadn't noticed that Carol had pulled over. She turned to see Carol's eyes were wide like saucers. "What the heck has gotten into you?" Carol managed to sputter.

Elise just realized she had said more to Carol during this conversation than she had in any other since the two had met nearly ten years ago. And she never ever cursed in the presence of her or any of their friends. Elise hung her head low as Carol pulled the car back onto the road.

They pulled up to her house, and Elise nearly jumped out of the car while it was still moving. She had apologized about twenty times, as they drove the remaining fifteen minutes to her home. Even with Carol's assurances, Elise was afraid. *What if she tells Stanford? What if she gossips to everyone else about me?*

Elise's large slate eyes were brimming with tears. She had begun to swear profusely as she stumbled up the walk, fumbling for her keys, finally opening the door, and slamming it behind her without looking back. At the end of the walk, Carol sat in the vehicle staring, bewildered, at the closed door.

Elise and Stanford Newman moved to the Lincoln Park area of Chicago when they were newlyweds. Old Town in Lincoln Park was well known for younger couples or new families, and they spent many years there before Stanford became amazingly successful with his brokerage business. When they were able, and Josh could move schools with little disruption, they bought a home on the Gold Coast.

Stanford justified this move by stating that most of his clients lived in and around that area, and he wanted to ensure he could meet with them conveniently whenever they required his expertise. Elise couldn't stand the Gold Coast. Sure, it was beautiful and upscale, but Old Town was more real, authentic. She was out of her comfort zone now more than ever, even though she had never actually been comfortable in her life with Stanford. She wondered what her life would be like if she hadn't married him, but then Josh wouldn't have been born. She thought about that and wondered if that would have been better for both of them after all.

Elise had baked the cupcakes that morning for the charity event. And like always, she only took half to the auction; the other half she kept hidden in the bottom drawer of the fridge, where Stanford would never see them. He loathed her cravings for sweets. She took one beautifully iced cupcake and took a large bite, munching away as her nerves settled from her earlier outburst.

Stanford never allowed that kind of food in the house, except once a year for Josh's birthday. She could bake a cake, and they were able to each have one piece. Stanford would take an obligatory bite, rustle Josh's hair, and then throw the rest of his piece in the garbage along with the entire remaining cake. On those occasions, Elise would rummage through the garbage later that night when Stanford was in his office working, pull the cake out, and stuff handfuls of it in her mouth. She hated Stanford.

CHAPTER 11

JOSH HEARD HIS MOTHER ARRIVE HOME, SLAMMING THE FRONT door hard. *That's unusual, but whatever.* His mother was a strange duck. He didn't think of her one way or another; she was simply there. He had been reading up on the history of Catholicism, which, in his mind, has been a brutal and bloody power struggle over the weak-minded. When he attended St. Clements Middle School, he purchased the book *God Is Not Great* by Christopher Hitchens and soon became confused by the constructs he was surrounded by, both in his home and externally. After that, he read several interesting books that countered everything about the religion he had been brought up to respect. *The God Delusion* by Richard Dawkins was the book that held his interest for the next few years and through his time at St. Ignatius. Now he was researching all the historical data, armed with his new belief that religion of any kind is an evil created by man to instill fear, because it is only the unknown that causes fear. Once you feel no fear, nobody can control you.

Josh graduated from St. Ignatius with honors and had his choice of several colleges and universities that his mother had applied to on his behalf, but he had not yet decided which, if any of them, he would attend. His father had agreed to one year off, to reflect and decide. With their money and his grades, a generous donation to the school of his choice would almost certainly guarantee his entry. He lay on his bed with his iPad, going over the St. Bartholomew's Day Massacre and thinking about last evening at the Gathering.

It was definitely growing. Each time he attended, there were at least four or five new faces he had not seen before. There was that girl from school. He remembered seeing her practicing once with the theater club in his last year. She had glanced up at him from the stage, as he watched the rehearsal. In that brief moment, he felt her gaze pierce him, and he walked away.

What was she doing there last night? Who brought her? What was her name? He was thinking that maybe he should have gone over and introduced himself, but the orators had already started their rants, and the crowd had hushed to listen and learn. Besides, she had not noticed him and that might have been a good thing. His plans were well beyond the small-minded whining and bitching that went on at the Gathering. His future endeavors would be the beginning of an evolution. He pulled out the letters, thirty-three total. He would head to the mall to drop them in the mail. He had been writing and sending these letters since he was fourteen years old. He had originally started with just one . . . to a priest in Chicago's Old Town.

* * *

Amanda and Jake left the object with Professor Orloff. He was fascinated with what he deemed "very interesting markings," and he wanted the chance to research and get the correct information on them. Amanda trusted that the professor would do just that. In the meantime, she asked if there was anything they could do to help out. He didn't think so, but since Amanda mentioned visiting a church in Old Town, he suggested visiting the Chicago Cultural Center. The center was built in 1897 and held some of the most interesting information that could be found about the history of Chicago and the area. He said it would give them something to do while he did his work. The professor was not very clear, but Amanda thought it would be interesting to do follow up on his advice, since they had never been to the center in all the times they had visited the area.

Jake had been at one of the business meetings they had scheduled. That was the original intent of their trip to Chicago. He was to meet Amanda at the cultural center right after he was done. He arrived to the chaotic scene of smoke and panic, with Amanda on the third floor getting ready to jump, just as the fireman showed up with the ladder.

After chatting with some of the police authorities at the hospital and being checked fully for smoke inhalation, Amanda was released. Her wounds were minor. However, they were wondering what she was doing in the third floor administrative offices while everyone else was at lunch. She explained her interest in finding out where she could get more historical information on Chicago and that she was looking for someone she could speak directly with about the topic. She avoided mentioning that her real search was geared toward the background and history of the churches, and one specifically in Old Town. The police had no reason to hold her. They let her know they would be investigating further and asked if she would be in Chicago for a while.

"Probably another week or so. If not, you have all my information and know where you can find me."

"Yes, but you are Canadian."

"Not to worry, I didn't start the fire," she said as she winked at the officer.

The officer nodded. "Yes, ma'am. We'll be in touch."

"Well, at least the fire didn't cause too much damage." Jake was walking Amanda to the parking lot. "Apparently it was mostly a lot of smoke and very little actual flame. It started in the restroom on the second floor, so some of the areas of the second floor will require restoration."

Amanda frowned. "How do you know all this?"

"From one of the investigative staff working the scene with the firefighters. I chatted her up."

"Her?" Amanda's eyebrows shot up.

"She was explaining it to the senior officer on the scene while you were on the way to the hospital. One of the reasons they are questioning you is because, although the fire was started with a substance that caused a tremendous amount of smoke, there seemed to be no real intent to damage anything or hurt anyone. It was done during the lunch hour on the administrative floor while almost all staff were out. It took place on a day that was not very busy for tours, when none of the meeting rooms were booked. Looks like an inside job, to send a message."

"Oh, and why do you think a message was the intention, Sherlock?"

"Because apparently someone knew you were there and waited until you were in a spot that would force you to take notice, but you missed it."

"Missed what?"

"When the smoke cleared, written on the wall of the Claudia Cassidy Theater was the verse from Matthew 5:5, 'Blessed are the meek for they shall inherit the earth.'"

Amanda was stunned. She remembered the vision she had while they were in Rome, and she had dismissed it as nothing when she told Jake about it over dinner that evening after too much Amarone. Now she feared they were in for something much more than they had expected. And worse, she could tell by Jake's expression that he thought so, too.

"Don't worry. I didn't snitch to the cops about your vision. Not that they would have believed me in the first place."

"Gee, thanks, honey. Did you get anything else from this investigator chick while I was suffering in agony from smoke inhalation?"

Jake laughed, "Not a damn thing. How about you? Did you find anything pilfering through the admin files while I was hard at work trying to secure some business, so we can live?"

"I wasn't pilfering. I was borrowing, and, in fact, I did." Amanda pulled out her iPhone and grinned. "I will go through the pictures with you once we get back to the room. In the meantime, where are we going? Cabs are out front."

"Well, since we were going to be here for a while from what I could tell anyway, and the weather is amazing, I decided to rent us something a little more civilized. I was afraid you were going to get me to ride in one of those rickshaws again."

Amanda's eyes lit up as Jake pressed the unlock button on the key fob in his hand. There was a quick beep, and the lights blinked on a beautiful black Mercedes SL63 AMG, one of Amanda's favorite cars.

"What happens when it snows?" she asked.

Jake smiled. "We trade it for the ML63."

CHAPTER 12

FATHER KRISTOFFERSON WALKED THROUGH THE GARDENS AT THE Lincoln Park Zoo, as he often did midweek when he had time. It helped him to clear his mind and focus on what he had to do over the next few weeks. He often used the time to write down notes for the sermon he would give during the weekend services. They didn't do weekday services anymore; he didn't have the staff or the interest. The church would be packed on Sunday, as usual. He scoffed at the thought of all the good people attending church. The service ended in time for the congregation to rush out ritualistically and blanket the family restaurants in the neighborhoods that surrounded his small parish in the Old Town district. Everyone was famished after a morning in church. After all the lessons were learned and all their sins forgiven, then bellies were filled.

He stopped to look at the stunning contrast between the beauty and solitude of the area before him, and the tall, hard structures of downtown Chicago. He was so close, he felt he could reach out and touch them. He realized he had his arm and hand stretched out to do just that, as a young couple walked by holding hands and giggling. He quickly moved his arm down to his side and closed his eyes.

The zoo was mostly empty today, although it was a warm, welcoming afternoon. He thought the young couple might be skipping school, or were they out of school? Everyone looked so young to him now. Why wouldn't they come here? So many people took advantage of this spectacular zoo— forty-nine acres of prime real estate on the lakefront and only minutes away from the core of the city. The most amazing thing about this zoo was that a quarter of its annual operating budget was provided by the Chicago Park District. The rest was funded through donations and revenues from its programs and gift shops. The admission was free, and that made it one of the most visited attractions in Chicago. After a moment's reflection, the priest opened his eyes and found a place to sit.

* * *

The letters will be out, they will all make their way to the intended receivers by next week, and so we begin . . . He thought then about his call to Samuel.

His mind drifted back to when they first made the deal, when they agreed they would expose the whole lie of God, of religion, of the Church. They were turning twenty that year. Both of them had been accepted to divinity school a couple of years earlier and became best friends through a buddy program. After two years, they knew that they could not be apart from each other. They fell in love. Understanding the situation and the times back then, or really even today, they knew the Church would not tolerate a gay relationship, so they kept their love affair secret.

They were both respectably handsome, although Samuel was so much more outwardly attractive. Women flocked to him wherever they went. The fact that they were studying to be priests helped to deflect the onslaught of admirers, but every once in a while Michael felt that pang of jealousy. Samuel always put his mind at ease quickly, with a wink, or a slight touch to remind him that they belonged to each other.

Then that day happened. Their house of cards so painstakingly and lovingly built, came tumbling down. They knew their relationship was fragile and special. That one day changed their course in life forever.

CHAPTER 13

JOSH RODE HIS DUCATI DIAVEL DARK, THE ALL-BLACK BIKE, dressed in his all-black armor, and streaked through the bright daylight at breakneck speed. He felt fortunate that they had very little snow so far this year, and the roads were dry. He was one of the few who would ride his motorcycle any time the roads allowed it. In his backpack the letters were stamped and ready to be mailed. This time it would be the mall. He chose a different drop spot each time, something he thought would make things more difficult to trace. At the end of it all, when everything finally went down, it wouldn't matter anyway. He was already resigned to his fate, and it made no sense to hide from it.

Earlier, on his way out of the house, he had to go through the kitchen to get his bike keys. He had left them on the counter after he got home the night before from the Gathering.

"Oh, hi, Josh. I didn't know you were home." His mother shyly looked up at her six-foot-one son.

"Hi, Elise." Josh referred to his parents by their first names. He had stopped using "Mom" and "Dad" around the age of eight, when he felt that neither could be described as real parents. Elise didn't care that he called her by her first name, and Stanford put up with it, because it was Josh.

"Elise, you have cake all over your face." He picked up his keys and left.

As he careened around corners at speeds far beyond the legal limit, he seemed oblivious to the danger of a potential accident or endangering others. For some reason he had been able to avoid both since getting the bike. His thoughts drifted to Elise, his pathetic mother. He knew all about her binge eating, and in some ways he didn't blame her, but he also didn't feel sorry for her. She accepted her life as it was, and she had to live with that.

Josh knew she had to live with a lot more, too—with a psycho husband who treated her like shit, a man who called her names on occasion, and told her how worthless she is regularly. *One of the reasons she spends so much time doing useless work for charitable organizations,* he thought. *Well, if it makes her feel better to auction cake or whatever, and she believes that will make a difference, she may as well go for it. She, like everyone else, lives in a pre-programmed world of bullshit and hope. They hope the more they give and do for others the less likely they will suffer. What goes around comes around. It's just another survival tactic in today's society, where the new trend is social responsibility, and everyone wants to play.*

"Social responsibility, yeah, right," he muttered out loud, the sound of his voice echoing inside his helmet, startling him. "What about fixing the outside issues by starting with the inside ones. The ones nobody ever talks about."

He parked in the no parking area of the mall lot. He knew that his bike would be left alone. The parking attendants were less than accountable for what they got paid to do, and it was too cold for them to walk around and properly monitor the lot. Besides, the parking lot was packed with holiday shoppers, and it would only take him a few minutes to finish his errand and leave.

The mall was buzzing, mostly with older shoppers. Being midweek and past the lunch hour, the school kids who hung out were back in class, and everyone else was at work. Or playing hooky. It was such a nice day today. He should just take off on his bike and ride, maybe just keep going and never turn back. The thought was very appealing, and it wasn't the first time he had it. Then he remembered the letters in his pack. He had more important work to do, and it wouldn't matter after that. He would be free in other ways, and, more importantly, he would be freeing others from known oppression, snapping them out of the hypnosis they have been under all of their lives.

Josh had just finished pushing all the envelopes down the slot at the post office when he got the sense that someone was standing right behind him. He quickly turned around, his slate eyes dark and smoldering.

"Olivia," she said and stuck out her hand. "Olivia Bennett, remember? We went to St. Ignatius together." She was still standing there with her hand thrust out at Josh, who slowly took it and gave it a quick shake, as his expression softened. She was very pretty. She had long, wavy, dark hair, full red lips, and dark brown eyes that shimmered like pools of melted chocolate.

"Yes, I remember," he almost mumbled. He wasn't normally ever this shy when meeting someone. Stanford had always encouraged him to speak clearly and to look directly into the person's eyes when conversing.

Josh straightened to his full height. "I saw you at the Gathering last night . . . I didn't know you were interested in all that."

"Well, I am, sort of. I mean, one of my good friends told me I should come out and listen and keep an open mind. It's difficult, as you must know, coming from a 'Christian' background."

"I don't find it difficult at all." Josh's eyes were now on fire. "In fact, I think it makes it easier, being embroiled in the teachings all your life, you know, to find all the holes and discrepancies." He realized he was getting worked up, so he stopped there.

"I guess that's one of the reasons I started attending." She shifted her gaze to the mailbox. "That was a shitload of letters you dropped in there. Do you drop off for your entire neighborhood or something?"

Josh flushed but maintained a steady voice. "No, actually, my mother is quite the community activist. She is involved with a lot of charitable work." He shrugged nonchalantly. "I help the old lady out every once in a while." He then put on his most brilliant smile, and he could tell it had the right effect.

Olivia's eyes fluttered. "A little cold for a bike ride, don't you think?"

Josh held up his helmet. "Yeah, I'm a bit of a rebel."

There was a chime, and Olivia looked quickly at her smartphone. "My mom just texted me. She's waiting for me over in the food court. We took a mom and daughter day today to shop for gifts."

How sickeningly sweet, Josh thought, but instead grinned. "Well, maybe we'll catch up at the next meeting."

He could almost see her heart leap out of her chest and instantly regretted the complication. *I don't need to give her any hope.*

"Sure, that would be awesome! I think probably tomorrow night. See you then." Her last words came out in a breathy rush.

Josh winked at her and then turned and walked off. *Nice move, asshole. Ugh. What am I doing?* He shook his head as he made his way back to the parking lot.

CHAPTER 14

NEWMAN AND ASSOCIATES WAS LOCATED ON THE SEVENTY-FIFTH floor of a 100-floor high-rise on Michigan Avenue in downtown Chicago. There was no expense spared in creating the ambience of stress-free wealth. Stanford Newman had started in a small office on the seventh floor twenty-five years ago and slowly transformed his one-man financial management firm into 35,000 square feet of glass and wood, housing nearly fifty employees. He was still considered boutique in size, but he didn't mind. The fees charged by his firm and the select clientele made him the envy of most large competitors. He had the business without the headaches of the larger entities. The interior offices were stunning, decorated with modern pieces of art by sought-after local artists as a show of community support. The floor-to-ceiling windows boasted views of both Chicago's brilliant city skyline and the lakes on the other side. Along with the employees' offices and workstations, the floor contained two kitchens, seven training centers, and four conference rooms. Stanford specifically renovated and converted two full offices into a meditation room that he used as often as four times a week. The full fitness facility and spa on the third floor of the building rivaled some of the world's best. On the main floor were two five-star restaurants and a cigar lounge that resembled Hemingway's Lounge at the Ritz in Paris, but much larger.

Stanford's office had a brilliant view of the city. His soul was uplifted by the sight of the tall concrete jungle around him. The heart of his success beat in and around those towers. He sipped his decaf coffee—no sugar, no milk—and skimmed through the paperwork sitting on his desk. Marie, his executive assistant of fifteen years now, had everything tabbed with colors of priority. They had worked out the system years ago, so that he knew what to look at first and what could wait if he ran out of time before heading out to meetings or home. Today was rather low-key: He had two yellows (low priority) and one blue, which meant FYI only.

Stanford preferred silence in the mornings. A typical day had him completing most of his work by noon, then heading to the gym for a workout. He would then stop for a to-go salad at one of the two restaurants downstairs. He generally switched back and forth between the two, so he was a good client to both. Of course, any requirements he had for office meetings or customer appreciation events were catered by one or the other. He knew the importance of building strong relationships with both clients and vendors. He booked most of his meetings after lunch and ensured they were finished by 4:00 p.m. Then he would take thirty minutes in the meditation room to help bring clarity to the thoughts and discussions processed during the meetings. Finally, he would scan his email (color-coded the same way by Marie) before he left for the day. He had good people working for him. They were well trained to handle most situations. There was rarely a red flag, meaning urgent, and therefore very few days where he needed to stay past 5:00 p.m. He was expected to be home on time for dinner with Elise and Josh.

Stanford finished his coffee and spent the next two hours going over paperwork and signing off on a few requests from his second-in-command, Tim Fletcher, a shrewd financial wizard who had managed to keep them afloat through the recent economic crisis. Stanford was a master at surrounding himself with efficient and smart talent. If more business leaders would let go of their egos and allow companies to run as they should, Stanford would have more competition. He smiled, knowing that key success factor would be difficult for others to adopt. Too many CEOs needed the kudos and the control. He was happy to just reap the rewards of their lack of self-confidence.

He quickly checked his email for any red flags. He only did this once before lunch and once at the end of the day. He had seen many great business leaders waste valuable time hitting Reply All and Send that could have been spent on building their companies.

He placed his pen in the top drawer of his teak desk and stopped to gaze at the soft brown leather of his father's bible, a keepsake from so long ago.

His father, John Newman, or Johnny, as his friends called him, was a British immigrant who arrived in Chicago in 1948 at the age of seventeen with his mother. Stanford's grandfather had immigrated two years earlier. Once he had established himself, he sent for them both. Johnny married a neighborhood girl he became smitten with against his parents' wishes, and they disowned him and his new wife. Stanford allowed his fingers to touch the well-worn cover, as he remembered the hardships his father endured trying to raise a family without any education or help from his family.

Johnny worked for the Wilmington Coal Corporation and spent many days in Braidwood, outside of Chicago, coming home only every so often for a few days' rest.

Johnny became ill with cancer. Years of smoking and poor working conditions from mining contributed heavily to his condition. He was also a heavy drinker, which added to his list of ailments. He spent each evening sipping a bottle of Jim Beam while he read the small, leather-bound bible to Stanford.

Stanford rubbed his forehead. He felt a headache coming on and had the urge to visit the meditation room early. He did not like thinking of his father, because it brought back vivid memories of his mother. His mother was not an immigrant. She was born to white trash in Chicago, and this was one of the reasons his grandparents did not approve of the marriage. She was known as a "loose girl" around the neighborhood, and they felt she pressured Johnny into the marriage. However, Johnny had gotten her pregnant and was determined to do the right thing by her.

They were poor. Stanford could remember vividly his mother sneaking off at night when his father was away at the mines. She would stumble back in at all hours of the early morning. One time she arrived home, and Stanford could clearly hear her giggling and the voice of a man saying, "Come on, Helen. Let's go for one more round."

"Shh . . . we don't want to wake the kid." Her words were slurred. Stanford pretended to be sleeping, but she came into his room and whispered, "I know you're awake, you little shit. If you tell your father anything, you will be out on the street. Do you hear me?"

Quite often Johnny would come home to find his son kneeling on the floor in front of the picture of Jesus hanging on the wall of their front room. His arms were outstretched, palms up, and two heavy books balanced on his hands. His arms were shaking and the tears were flowing. The red marks from a leather strap were visible on both arms—the result of dropping his arms at any time during the punishment. Whenever Johnny found his son like this, he would rush over and push the books off, pick Stanford up, and carry him out of the house.

"What was it this time?" he would ask as he rubbed Stanford's arms, which were burning from the intensity of holding up the weight of the books.

"She said that if I were a better son, you would be a better father," he responded, his voice small and meek. At only seven years of age he hated his mother and could not comprehend what he continued to do wrong, or why she didn't love him.

The next year Johnny lost his job after missing too much work due to sickness. With no health insurance or family they could call upon, there was little that could be done. Two weeks before Christmas he died in his bed, unable to continue the battle. They had no money for a funeral, so Stanford stood by and watched as some men came and took his father's body away. Stanford had hidden the bible his father read to him under his pillow, so it could be close to him and in a way keep his father's spirit near him, too. Helen had no job of her own and never wanted the responsibility of a child, so after withdrawing the small amount of money they had in the bank, she abandoned him, leaving him at the door of a neighbor with a note, stating she had moved back home, with no indication as to where that might be.

* * *

Stanford spent the next ten years in an orphanage. He grew up with the intention of never having to suffer the same lifestyle as his father. He would have money, a nice home, and a healthy mind and body. He especially would find a wife that would take care of their home and their children, and would obey him.

He realized that he had been deep in thought for some time. He quickly checked his watch, a beautiful Patek Philippe Golden Ellipse. He chose this watch specifically because it was a masterful piece, but not flashy. Its simple brown leather band and white gold face was unassuming. And except to those who were real connoisseurs, nobody would know the whopping price tag that came with it. Stanford noticed it was 1:45 p.m. He would have to skip the workout and lunch today. He pulled a protein bar out of a box he kept in his drawer and closed it, concealing the bible and his past.

CHAPTER 15

THE SL63 WAS AN AMAZING MACHINE, SLEEK WITH LINES CUT IN just the right places. It was a triumph in the line of luxury sports cars.

"Stunning and racy, just like you." Jake winked at Amanda as they sped through the streets leading back to the Waldorf.

"Yeah, whatever." Amanda refused to take compliments well. "At least it has high-performance winter tires on it."

"Not just any. These are Pirelli Scorpion ice and snow tires."

"Ha. Too bad there's no ice and snow," Amanda shot back. "And I am pretty sure that you can't just rent one of these at any of the rent-a-wreck locations, so . . ."

"Correct, so . . . I chatted with a buddy who knows the owner of a dealership here, and he happened to have just one that was allocated to their store."

"And you made it sound like you were a potential buyer," Amanda jumped in.

"Well, aren't we?" Jake looked hurt. "He told me to take it for a few hours. I told him we would be here for a while, and if my wife liked it . . ."

"Does he know we are Canadians?"

"Of course, and with the US dollar trading so low, it's a bargain to buy down here."

"Okay, as long as you know that if you break it you buy it." Amanda was concerned about the possibility of this entire situation getting out of control. She thought about the fact that the fire was intentional, so who knew what they were getting themselves into.

"Jake, what do you make of the scripture from Matthew 5:5 on the wall back there? Do you think it is just a coincidence that they chose today to make their point?"

"You know I don't believe in coincidences. I think someone was trying to tell us something. Who besides Professor Orloff and Cardinal Roland knows about us being here in Chicago?"

"Well, I would think that Father Kristofferson would know. Wouldn't Cardinal Roland inform him that we would be coming by with the trinket?"

"You're right, Amanda. Let's head over to Old Town and pay a visit to Father Kristofferson. Perhaps he can shed some light on this for us . . ." Amanda was nodding in response to Jake's comments when he turned to her. "And who uses the word 'trinket' anymore? Really, Amanda."

She managed to give him the one-finger salute before saying, "Can we stop by the hotel on the way? I need to change these clothes. They smell like smoke."

"No problem. I suggest you have a shower and maybe brush your hair," he said, grinning. Jake had put the top down on the convertible. It was only fifty degrees Fahrenheit, still unusually warm for December, but cold for a convertible ride. Jake bragged that the neck scarf and heated seats of the SL63 would keep them warm. He was right. However, Amanda's hair was now a tangled mess, and although he made fun of it, Amanda knew he secretly loved the look.

While Amanda showered, Jake ordered two hot chicken sandwiches, a fruit and cheese plate, and a large bottle of San Pellegrino with slices of lime. He knew Amanda would be starving and now that all the excitement was over, it would hit her hard that she had nothing in her stomach since the oatmeal at breakfast.

He put a rush on the food order. Amanda would be in a hurry to see

Father Kristofferson. Chances were that the fire and the father were not connected. In fact, there might have been no connection at all except the vision Amanda had while in Rome. But that could have just been her second sight letting her know there was danger pending. This all still could be a wild goose chase, but he knew Amanda wouldn't let it go until she knew for sure.

She came out of the bathroom. She wore a towel around her body and her hair. She looked refreshed and frankly quite sexy.

"Are you sure you want to get going right away? Maybe we should take advantage of this really great room and the fact that you are naked?"

"I'm not naked. I have my super-protective, high-tech towel on that has been fitted with an electronic sensor that will zap anyone who tries to take it off. Only I can dislodge the towel by placing my thumb precisely on a spot that only I am aware of."

Jake's eyebrows went up appreciatively, "Wow, that's some towel, but I think I can disarm the sensor with relative ease . . ."

Jake jumped up off the bed and raced after Amanda. She let out a short squeal and ran back to lock herself in the bathroom just as there was a knock at the door.

"Room service," the muffled voice said from the other side of the door.

"Saved by the bell," Jake announced. "Please get on some clothes before you come out and excite the hotel staff."

Amanda waited until she heard Jake finish with room service and then came out to get her clothes from the closet. She quickly dressed and gasped with delight when she saw the spread of food Jake had laid out on the table.

"Lunch is served, Your Highness."

"Jake, sometimes you really are worth all the trouble." Amanda skipped over to the table and picked up the chicken sandwich, taking a bite that was far too large for her mouth. Jake laughed as her cheeks bulged and her eyes rolled up with delight as she devoured her sandwich.

With a full belly and feeling much more herself, Amanda watched the scenery fly by as Jake headed toward Old Town where Father Kristofferson had his parish. It was such a warm and sunny day in Chicago, and they decided to drive along the lakefront to take full advantage of the convertible. Amanda had tied her hair back in a ponytail so that it wouldn't be too messy when they met Father Kristofferson. Unfortunately, they wouldn't have the relic to give to him, which was still with the professor, but they could tell him about it, and at least find out how he was doing for Cardinal Roland.

Amanda loved visiting Chicago. She never had the opportunity to spend time in Old Town proper though, and she was very excited that their adventure brought them to this part of town.

Entering the district, and seeing the wrought iron sign for Old Town, Amanda was fascinated. It was lovely. The architecture was mostly Victorian from what she could tell. The word "quaint" popped into her mind immediately. The holiday lights were up, and although it was daytime, they still added to the festive look of the area. This was a part of Chicago she could actually see herself and Jake living in. All that was missing was the snow.

Jake could tell Amanda was enjoying herself, so he drove slowly through the picturesque area, giving her time to take it all in. They made their way past shops and historic homes built on cobblestone streets, and finally came to a stop outside a rather small parish church. Nothing like the Holy Name Cathedral or St. Michael's, also located in Old Town.

"Well, there certainly is a difference between where Cardinal Roland ended up and Father Kristofferson chose to stay." Jake was moving around to Amanda's side of the car to get the door. She admired Jake's manners, which even after all these years of marriage surprised her. He insisted that a real gentleman always treat a lady like a lady. There had been times where he literally raced over and brushed her hand away, when she tried to open the car door herself. It was tough for Amanda, who was very independent, to give way to this. But she knew it was part of Jake's personality. Many women had commented on how lucky she was to have a true gentleman for a husband. Chivalry was not dead, at least not in the Bannon household.

The church was brightly lit from the sunlight streaming in through the stained glass windows. At the front, mounted high on the wall, was the usual sculpted depiction of Christ nailed to the cross. Below it were the altar and standing podium that would be used for sermons and readings during Mass.

Amanda always felt strange stepping into a church, as if she would burst into flames because of her nonbelief. Jake didn't look any more comfortable than she felt. She noticed the frown on his face as they walked in. The church pews were completely empty, and some of the pews at the back were a little dusty, looking like they had not been used for some time.

"Is there a doorbell or something we can use to summon the priest?" Jake said as he scoured the room.

"I'm not sure. And by the way, who uses the word 'summon' anymore? Let's take a look in the back rooms. There should be some administrative offices."

They were making their way to the right of the altar toward a side hallway, when a young man emerged from the darkened area. At first he was visibly startled to see Jake and Amanda. But he calmed immediately, flashed a genuine smile, and spoke. "Hello there, can I be of any service to you?"

"Yes, you can." Amanda beamed while feeling uneasy. His smile was appealing, but there was something hidden behind it. "We were hoping to see Father Kristofferson today. Is he here?"

"No, I am very sorry. I hope you didn't come a long way. He is out for his walk at this time. He usually goes to the zoo and generally gets back late in the afternoon."

"Oh. Well, do you think we can make an appointment to see him? I think he may be expecting us. It's Amanda Bannon and my husband, Jake. Cardinal Roland—"

Amanda was cut off by the young man. "Oh yes, that's right. Father said you might come by one of these days, but he wasn't sure when. He will be disappointed that he missed you today. He seemed very eager to meet you both. Father Kristofferson doesn't make appointments, but he will be here first thing tomorrow morning. In fact, he sleeps here, at the church, so you can catch him early."

"Oh, do priests still live at the churches they service?" Jake was surprised.

"Not usually, sir, but Father Kristofferson always has."

"Thanks so much. We really appreciate you letting us know. We'll be back tomorrow then." Amanda quickly grabbed Jake by the hand and pulled hard. Jake gave her a quizzical look and nodded to the young man. "Thanks. I guess we are going."

The young man watched as Amanda half dragged Jake out the door into the sunlit day.

"What the heck, Amanda—"

"Jake," she cut in, "did you see his left hand?"

"Umm, no. I wasn't looking."

"He had the design, the same one as on the relic. It looked like it was tattooed on the back of his hand."

"How did you even see that from the angle we were at?"

"The silver vase on the table near the door. I saw it in the reflection. It was a bit blurred, but I am almost certain that's what it was."

"Okay. Again, that is too much of a coincidence, but what does it mean exactly?"

"I don't know," Amanda said halfheartedly, "but I thought it was better just to get the heck out of there and talk to Father Kristofferson tomorrow. It kind of gave me the creeps."

"This whole thing is starting to give me the creeps." Jake's voice sounded far too ominous as they stood looking up at the run-down church.

CHAPTER 16

THE HOME GYM DOWNSTAIRS WAS ONLY USED BY ELISE. STANFORD always worked out at the office gym. She was on the elliptical trainer and sweat was pouring off her brow. She was watching the show *Ellen* on the flat screen mounted to the wall in front of her. Ellen was chatting it up with Halle Berry. They were laughing about whatever and then talking seriously for a bit. Elise wasn't listening. She hated the drab conversations of the "hardships" endured by these beautiful, perfect people. It was quite pathetic that they pitched their difficult ordeals to the public and expected people to actually feel sorry for them, when the very next day photographs of them suntanning on their yachts in the Bahamas would be spread all over the most popular magazines. *Such a tough, tough life* . . . "Poor baby," she growled at the TV.

Well, she could say the same about her life. She knew that when she helped out at the homeless shelters and walked in wearing her Armani scarf and Gucci boots, the workers there were thinking similar thoughts about her. She tried to dress down, but Stanford wouldn't have it. He would remark that if she couldn't do her volunteer work being who she really was, then she should stop volunteering. He often remarked that those people didn't even know the brands she was wearing and to stop being so self-absorbed.

Well, she wouldn't stop volunteering! If she stopped volunteering, she would lose her mind. She would be completely useless then. So she did as she was told but remembered to at least take her jewelry off before she left the house. Her five-carat yellow diamond ring generated a lot of attention. This was the ring Stanford gave her after making his first million. It replaced the original half-carat, pear-shaped diamond he proposed with.

She had been on the elliptical for an hour and was in the cooldown session when she heard Josh return home. She knew it was Josh because Stanford never stepped through the door before 5:30 p.m., and it was only 3:20. She looked up at the screen in time to see Ellen and Halle hugging at the end of their talk. She gave them one last dirty look, then clicked the Off button on the remote and stepped down from the machine.

She walked over to use the steam room. She loved going in there after her workout. Stanford never used it, and Josh said it was unsanitary. She would drift off in her own dark world and masturbate, something Stanford would not approve of, she was sure. She hesitated. It was already getting late. If she got caught up in the steam and dinner was late, she would be in very big trouble. She skipped the steam and climbed the stairs in her workout gear to the main floor. She popped into the kitchen to grab another bottle of water. Josh was sitting at the counter, taking a bite of a sandwich. He stopped mid-bite and gazed at Elise with disgust. "Elise, you stink."

"Sorry, Josh. I am just trying to stay in shape. It doesn't come as easy for me as some people."

"Well, you may want to switch it up from cake to lettuce then."

Elise looked hurt, but Josh didn't seem to notice or care.

"Well, don't eat too much, Josh. Dinner will be ready soon."

"No dinner for me. I am going out tonight. You might want to let Stanford know. I will be pretty late."

"Where are you going tonight?"

"Elise, you know that's none of your business. I just wanted to inform you. Although you have never stayed up and worried about me, Stanford does."

"Well, believe it or not, I do worry about you, driving around too fast on that bike in the dark. What if something happens to you?"

"Yeah, what if something happens to me?" Josh posed the question at Elise who knew exactly where he was going with that comment. She shuddered at the thought.

"Just be careful," she mumbled and turned to head upstairs. She needed a shower. Talking to Josh was just as exhausting as being on the elliptical.

"I will be gone someday, Elise. You'd better get prepared. Stop being such a coward and fight for yourself. There isn't much time left. At least end it with some dignity."

Elise was shocked. She hadn't heard such emotion in her son's voice since he was a little boy. She turned back to Josh, wanting to look into his eyes, her eyes, but he had gone back to eating his sandwich, head down.

She made her way up to the bedroom and undressed, all the while thinking about Josh's words. "There isn't much time left; at least end it with some dignity." *What did he mean? Time left for what?* Whatever it was, she knew Josh was serious. He had been this way all his life, and she knew to take his word seriously. She stepped into the hot shower, as thoughts came to her from the past. When had she first realized she had lost control of her own life?

* * *

They had been married for less than a week when Stanford starting imposing the "rules" of the house. They met in college at the Booth Business School at the University of Chicago. Stanford had been accepted at both Harvard and Stanford, but he thought Harvard too elite and that it was somewhat narcissistic to attend a school that was his namesake. His father had chosen the name for him hoping that someday he would go to a great university like Stanford. Booth Business School was regarded as one of the best in the United States, and he was more than satisfied with it and the fact that he was able to go to school in the city he grew up in.

Elise Cunningham was a very pretty, petite girl with long, thick, flowing red hair—not the coppery red that gets you picked on at school with nicknames like "Ginger"—but a deep burgundy that intensified her large slate-colored eyes. Her Scottish background was fascinating to Stanford. The two of them debated England and Scotland's long history often. Their favorite discussions always led back to the famous William Wallace. Elise insisted that her ancestry was linked to that famous leader of the Wars of Scottish Independence, and Stanford would laugh at her, saying he couldn't picture her family being among the Guardians of Scotland. She would punch him in the shoulder and laugh along with him. Years later when the movie *Braveheart* came out, Elise would watch it over and over. Although highly fictional, she didn't care. She used it to give her strength to get through some of the tough times, reminding herself that she had the blood of Wallace running through her veins. Somehow, that didn't fix much, if anything, of her life with Stanford.

Stanford, who was two years Elise's senior, graduated with an MBA, concentrating in finance. They were both admitted using scholarships and were in the top 5 percent of their class. Stanford continued to see Elise while he established his small financial services firm. And that next summer, he proposed to Elise. She had a year to go to finish her MBA, but Stanford insisted he wanted to start a family right away and have her look after their new home in Old Town. He said she could always finish her final year and get her masters if she really wanted to later, after the children were older.

Elise, coming from a large family, understood Stanford's excitement to have children, and got caught up in the thought that this would be her fairy-tale life. Little did she know that her life would change almost immediately after she quit school and married him, and not in the way she had hoped.

* * *

Elise returned from her thoughts and jumped out of the shower. The water had turned cold, and she hadn't even noticed. Now she shivered a bit as she reached for a towel. She hoped she had not been daydreaming too long, but her gut feeling told her otherwise. She seemed to be falling into these mind-wandering episodes more and more often lately. She guessed it was some kind of coping mechanism, but then she wasn't any kind of psychologist, was she? She was smart enough to know something was going sideways, though. Toweling off, she studied her fingers that were wrinkled like prunes. *Too long.* She ran over to the bedside clock. It was 5:05 p.m. She hurried and dressed. She had to do her hair and makeup before Stanford got home. He didn't like anything to be out of place. She worked as quickly as she could, applying the slightest bit of makeup. Too much, and he called her a whore. Too little, and he looked at her with disdain. She found the floral dress he liked, the one that fit nicely over her breasts but didn't have too deep a neckline. Then she slipped on her low slingback heels and headed downstairs to get dinner going.

Josh was just heading out the door, helmet in hand.

"Elise, you look nice," he said as he opened the door to leave, "but you know you're late . . . good luck with that."

She stared at the door for a minute after he closed it behind him. She turned slowly to look at herself in the hallway mirror. She looked terrified.

CHAPTER 17

WHAT AN IDIOT. SHE'S GONNA GET HER ASS KICKED. JOSH WAS swerving in and out of his lane, pretending he had the Ducati on the switchbacks of some tight Euro trail, when he noticed the flashing lights in his side mirror. *Nice. Fight or flight. You could easily lose the cops.* He decided it wasn't worth it tonight. Especially if they did manage to keep up, he would have to miss the meeting or lead them right to the Gathering. Probably wouldn't make him the most popular guy, so he slowed the bike down and pulled over to the side.

He kicked the stand down and leaned back as he undid his helmet. He slipped his head out and turned to see a female officer standing beside the bike. *My lucky day.* He smiled his most charming smile.

"License and registration please." She seemed to be the no-nonsense type. He unzipped his pocket and pulled out his documents, at the same time asking, "What's the problem, Officer?"

"Well, you seemed to be swerving a little erratically, especially since you are on a straight road. Have you been drinking today?"

"Nope, not a drop. Unfortunately, I was a bit bored and was pretending that I was on some wicked back road having a great ride. You know, trying to stay warm riding a bike at this time of year."

"Well, you're not on some wicked back road. You are in a Chicago suburb, where we like everyone to drive safely."

"Yes ma'am, and I am so glad that I was pulled over by, as far as I can see, one of Chicago's finest." He looked her over admiringly.

She seemed amused by his comment, and a slight smile played on her lips. Was this kid that smooth? "You also probably know that December is not a month for motorcycles. How long have you had this bike?"

"Not long at all," he replied and winked as she handed him back his items.

"Well, I'm going to let you off with a warning. I can see how a young guy like you would want to ride this bike all year long if you could. It's a beauty, but safety first." She made the remarks in a stern voice. Josh could only assume she was trying to reprimand him in some manner for his actions. "Take it somewhere you can let some steam off every once in a while. Get it out of the city and out of your system." Then she winked at him, turned on her heels, and headed back to the police car.

That was easy. He took his time getting his helmet back on and waved as the cop car drove past him. He waited until the vehicle was out of sight and then turned in at the next street. He looked at his watch. It was 5:30 p.m. The sun was setting, and he still had plenty of time to make the 6:00 p.m. start at the park. His thoughts went back to his mother. Stanford, well, he should be getting home any minute. *Poor Elise*. He felt a slight twinge of compassion for her. He didn't allow himself to feel anything beyond that. It didn't matter. She didn't matter in the grand scheme of things. She was a pawn, expected to play her part in the world of losers. He had a key role, expected also to play his part. *The letters were sent. Let the games begin.* His grin widened as the bike leapt forward into the late day.

CHAPTER 18

"YOU HAD VISITORS TODAY."

Father Kristofferson was startled by the voice, as he walked into his room at the back of the church. Sitting at a desk, a dark figure played with a pen, spinning it around and around on the blotter.

"The Bannon couple?" the older priest managed to croak out, then swallowed hard as the dark figure stood.

"Yes, and they will be back tomorrow. I highly recommend you be here and clear things up and move them on their way. We don't need any trouble."

"Oh, I don't think they will be any trouble. They are simply looking in on me for Samuel. They have no idea, and why would they?"

"While you were out frolicking at the zoo, I did a bit of research on them. This is no ordinary couple. Did you know the woman, Amanda, has assisted in a number of investigations and has helped the police solve several cases?"

Father Kristofferson looked down at the floor. "They know Samuel. I don't really know much about them. They are simply dropping off a relic. We collect them. Samuel and I have done so for years. They won't be a problem."

"They'd better not be. If they are, you will be the one to deal with them." The man pushed past Father Kristofferson and headed out toward the hallway and the front doors of the church.

Father Kristofferson picked up the phone and dialed Samuel Roland's cell phone number. It was 12:30 a.m. in Rome, and a groggy voice answered. "Hello . . . hello? Who is it? Michael?"

"Sammy . . ."

"Michael, what's wrong? What is it?"

"Why are the Bannons here?"

"Because I am worried about you."

"There's nothing to worry about. I told you!"

"Then why is your voice quavering, and why are you calling me in the middle of the night here?"

"I want you to call the Bannons and tell them that everything is fine. They don't need to come by and check on me."

"I will do no such thing. And anyway, they have something for you, for the collection."

"What is it? What did you find, Samuel?" He was afraid that Samuel had found out he was unable to call off the original plans, that in fact they would move forward. It was no longer his to control.

"You will know when you see it. It's a reminder that things change. Michael?"

"Good night, Samuel."

Cardinal Roland put the phone down slowly. Something was wrong. Something was very wrong. Cardinal Roland could hear it in his voice. Perhaps not everything was going as Michael informed him. He would not stop Jake and Amanda from looking into it. In fact, that seemed to be his only hope. If things were indeed going sideways, they might be able to stop it all from happening. Whatever was going on now seemed to be eating Michael up inside, and Samuel wasn't going to stand by and let that happen. Something had to be done.

For some reason he felt hopeless, as if he were a small part of a much bigger puzzle, and he had no idea how any of the pieces fit together anymore. And now he wasn't sure that the Bannons could handle this either. He sat on his bed thinking for some time. Finally he decided that he had to step in. It was time to go home.

CHAPTER 19

"JAKE, I THINK WE SHOULD CALL PROFESSOR ORLOFF AND SEE IF HE has anything for us." Amanda was restless while they drove to dinner.

"Please, Amanda. What is the difference between now and tomorrow morning? Give the guy some time to work on it."

"I don't know. I feel like something is going on, all around us right now. Kind of like a tornado, and we are in the middle of it . . ."

Jake was saying something back, but Amanda couldn't hear it. She saw his lips moving but no sound. Then her stomach started to feel queasy, and she bent over. Flashes of light danced in front of her eyes. As she closed them tight she saw flames and burning crosses. The relic with the markings floated in front of her eyes. Then there was darkness.

Jake was wiping her eyes with a tissue. "It's okay, Amanda. Shh, shh . . ."

She slowly opened her eyes. Jake had pulled off the road into a back alley parking lot. Her face felt hot and wet. He was dabbing gently at her cheeks as she looked up to face him.

"How's my mascara . . ." she managed to say in a small voice.

"Oh, looks a bit like Ozzy Osbourne on a good day," he said and smiled gently at her. "Seemed like you had quite the internal show going on. I didn't know if we should drive straight to a local exorcist or what."

"Yeah, Linda Blair I am not."

"So . . ." Jake said. He didn't want to push, but he knew the best thing was for Amanda to explain it out loud, right away.

"So, it was a lot of fire and brimstone. Yeah, I know. It sounds 'out there,' but that's what it was. Burning crosses and the relic. It was floating around all of it and changing, like a Rubik's cube."

"Wow, that's not normal. Usually you get a better picture than that. I think maybe we should go have a drink and see if anything else comes to you."

"I don't know if a drink is a good idea right now, Jake."

He closed his hands over hers to stop them from shaking. "Oh, I think a large martini is just what the doctor would suggest right about now."

"And . . .?" she said, pleadingly.

And . . . I will call Professor Orloff, as you suggested, and see if he has something now, sooner rather than later."

Amanda broke into a huge smile and that was worth more than anything to Jake. He knew how hard it was for her to experience the physical part of having visions. And then there was the emotional side on top of that, but Amanda never complained.

He gave her a quick peck on the cheek and pulled out of the alley. Amanda tried her best to clean up the streaks of mascara, while making a mental note to purchase waterproof mascara. "And it's Alice Cooper, Jake," she said out loud.

They zipped off down toward North St. Clair Street where they had managed to get a last-minute reservation at Tru, which had an award-winning wine list and an unorthodox style of French cuisine. Amanda let her thoughts settle by picturing a wonderful dinner with Jake and not the disturbing thoughts of destruction that lingered at the edge of her mind.

CHAPTER 20

THE GATHERING WAS HUMMING TONIGHT. SMALL GROUPS HAD formed, and there was a definite excitement among the chattering circles. Josh walked between groups, making his way up closer to the front, where there was some kind of natural space created for speakers. There was no soapbox, stand, or stage, just a simple spot under a big tree. He wasn't exactly sure of the type. It could have been a walnut tree, but it was older than the park being named.

He wondered if the people here knew they were gathering so close to a graveyard. It wasn't anymore, of course, but it had once been the shallow graves of smallpox and cholera victims. Lincoln Park began as a small public cemetery on the northernmost boundary of the city. The bodies were exhumed at one point, because they posed a health threat to the city, and the cemetery was converted to parkland in the 1850s. In 1860, Lake Park was created using a reserved area of sixty acres of parkland. Then, shortly after his assassination, the park was renamed Lincoln Park in memory of Abraham Lincoln.

Oh, great. Josh stopped mid-stride as he spotted Olivia with the last rays of the evening sun. She was leaning against the large tree and turned to stare right at him. He knew he couldn't pretend that he didn't see her, so he walked straight up to her. His eyes darkened as he stopped only inches away from her. He heard her catch her breath, but he said nothing. They seemed to be standing that way for a while to him, yet it had only been seconds. He wanted her to wither under his glare, but she seemed to enjoy it instead. Neither of them moved or dared to blink.

"Hey, what's going on here?" A plump blonde pushed her way between the two of them. Josh recognized her immediately as the mouthpiece in one of his past English classes.

"Oh, Angela. I was wondering where you went. Josh, this is Angela Garner."

Angela looked up at Josh. "Oh, I know who Josh is, Olivia. Who doesn't? Let's see . . . captain of the debate team, first-string quarterback, most likely to succeed without trying, and so on . . ."

Olivia shot her friend a stern look but that didn't seem to register. Josh cut in quickly, "Hey, I thought you said you were coming tomorrow night, not tonight?"

"What I said was that I thought the next meeting was tomorrow night, but Angela said there's a special meeting tonight." Then she looked at him quizzically. "Which is why you are here, right? But you didn't say anything when I mentioned it earlier." Josh thought she looked hurt, but he dismissed it.

"This meeting is special. I wasn't sure how much you knew about the speaker tonight. He's, well, let's say, he doesn't hold back, and you kind of have to understand what's going on."

"You think I won't get it?" She seemed offended.

"No. In fact, what I am worried about is that you *will* get it."

She was about to say something further when they realized everyone had become quiet. There were a few *shhs* here and there and then silence. Moving out from behind them through the crowd came the speaker for the evening. The path opened up before him as he walked past them to the speaker's area. He was wearing a black hoodie and the hood was pulled up over his head. Although it was difficult to make out his face, Josh knew what he looked like. He had seen his face many times before, along with the tattoo on the back of his left hand, the one that matched the one Josh had on the back of his left calf.

"12 12 12. Today is the day. Today we will move forward as citizens of the new world. We all know that the social leaders of our time have been blinded by greed, by self-serving traditions, and by using religion as a way to instill fear. This way is no longer a belief; it is now a disease. We can see it when we ask them to give of themselves. They do, but not in a selfless way. It's to make themselves look better, not to truly make a difference. If they wanted to make a difference, they would give up what they have to ensure equality among every man, woman, and child on the planet." His voice was not loud, yet it was heard all the way to the back rows of the now-seated crowd in front of him.

"Why do we let this continue? It's because we didn't think we could fight the machine of the Church, the largest business and profit-making machine on earth. Things have changed." He scanned the group, as if waiting for someone to speak, but everyone remained still. "We are no longer too small, and we are no longer going to stand still and be oppressed by those who weaken all of us by using the beliefs of others as an instrument of control. We will be the ones to make the difference and start the change." He turned directly toward Josh off to his left. Josh nodded at him and stood up. Then the man turned and walked back the way he came, through the park, and he was gone.

The crowd slowly began whispering among themselves in their small circles. Then the voices got louder until everyone was chatting amicably as if they were at an outdoor party and not a secret meeting.

It was fully dark, and it was starting to get pretty cold. Most of the group was bundled up nicely. Josh knew it was his role to meander through the crowd and listen. He listened to catch bits of conversation, to figure out who might be right to bring into the Inner Circle. Many of these kids came here just to hear someone speak out against authority, others to get high and ponder the bigger picture. However, a few came here for the same reason Josh did his very first time—to do something about the blackest, darkest cult around, the Roman Catholic Church.

CHAPTER 21

STANDFORD PULLED INTO THE GARAGE PRECISELY AT 5:45 P.M., AND immediately noticed Josh's Ducati was gone. He wondered where Josh went off to these evenings. He was now gone more nights than not. He didn't blame the kid. Why would he want to sit in this house alone or, worse than alone, with his mother?

He stopped to pick a piece of paper off the ground. No, not paper, an envelope addressed to someone in Florida, and in Josh's handwriting. *Weird. Don't all kids use Facebook and Twitter these days?* There was this new thing called Instagram as well now. Stanford didn't pretend to know anything about these social media connections. He couldn't give a shit actually. He stuck the envelope inside his briefcase. He would ask Josh about it tomorrow. He knew Josh would be late. He generally snuck in around 11:00 p.m., thinking no one would notice, or care, because Stanford and Elise were in bed by 9:30 every evening. The truth was that Stanford liked to watch the late edition of the news in bed and wait until he heard Josh come in the door. He would mute the TV to hear Josh get a glass of water, meander up the stairs, and close the door to his room. It was pretty much the same routine each night. Some nights, he would hear Josh grab something to eat from the fridge, but that was rare. Josh, like Stanford, looked after himself and rarely ate after 7:00 p.m. Once he heard Josh moving about his room, and only then, would Stanford turn the television off and roll over, away from Elise.

Elise was at the counter ripping up kale for a salad and chopping tomatoes. Her hands were shaking. She had a salmon on the counter, but it had not been dressed yet, and the oven was still heating up.

"Dinner is not on yet?" His gaze was piercing.

"I got tied up with the bake sale, and Carol was late running me home, because . . ."

"That was this morning," he cut her off, "you would have been home hours ago. Do you want me to check the cameras?"

Oh, God. The cameras. She cringed. "No need to check. You are right. I should have had time to get everything going."

"Damn it, Elise!" he slammed the briefcase down on the counter, and she jumped, dropping the knife, the sharp edge barely missing her toe.

She bent down to pick up the knife, and Stanford was next to her in a flash. He grabbed her by the hair. She squealed, and he turned her head slowly to face him. "Shut up! You sound like a little pig. Why do you sound like a little pig, Elise?" She tried to shake her head no, but he had too tight a grip on her hair. "Because you are one," he spat out through clenched teeth. Tears were welling up in her eyes, but she kept quiet. She knew from experience that it could only get worse if she made any noise now. He pushed her, and she landed on her hands and knees, knife still gripped in her fist.

"Dinner should have been ready," Stanford fumed. "It's not, but you are going to eat it anyway. Why waste a perfectly good salmon, right?"

She pushed herself up and back on her knees, keeping the knife in her hand. For a brief second she thought of sticking the knife right through him, pulling it out and then stabbing him over and over. The vision was overwhelming and her heart was pounding, but she was a coward and he knew it.

"Drop the knife, Elise."

She did as she was told, and the knife dropped with a clang inches in front of her. Stanford pulled up the legs of his perfectly creased trousers and squatted in front of Elise. He picked up the knife with one hand and gently cupped Elise's chin with the other and lifted her face up to look at his. He brought the knife up and, just an inch away, pointed it directly at her right eye. She started to shake. "Stop shaking! Nothing has happened to you, has it?" She mouthed the word "no." "Do you want something to happen to you?" She shook her head slowly. His hand was eerily still. She felt faint, as if she could fall forward and end up piercing her own eye with the weight of her falling body. He dragged the salmon off the counter and dropped it on the floor in front of her.

"Dinner's ready," he sang playfully. "Now eat!" Stanford moved the knife away from her eye and pointed it at the salmon. He held it so tight that his fist was turning white from the strain.

Elise knew better than to plead, or beg, or run. She picked up the raw salmon and started chewing on it. She was not a salmon fan. It was Stanford's favorite, and she chose it to please him tonight, hoping to mitigate his anger about dinner being late and all. She hadn't even had time to skin the thing, so the black scaly coat now rubbed harshly over her bottom lip. She couldn't stand sushi, and she gagged as she pulled the raw fish apart with her teeth.

"Be a good girl and finish all your dinner, and you won't have to go to the dark room, okay?" Stanford almost sounded concerned, like he used to sound, back before they were married, back when he cared, before Josh.

She closed her eyes and continued to chew and swallow. She kept telling herself that this was normal. So many people eat raw fish. It's good for you. Stanford pulled up a chair from the nook table and sat, watching her, his eyes and thoughts somewhere else, a different place and a different time. She let her thoughts drift far away as well, away from where she was. She remembered when Josh was little, everything— how she fed him, how she bathed him— was about Josh. It all had to be perfect. If he got diaper rash, it was her fault. She was a bad mother. If he got sick, she had to take him to the doctor day or night, even for a minor cold. Stanford would rock Josh when he was a baby, for hours, singing to him, coddling him, even when Josh couldn't sleep during his teething months. She wasn't allowed to breast-feed Josh. When they found out she couldn't have any more babies due to an infection she caught during Josh's birth, Stanford became more protective of Josh, even though it was she who almost lost her life from the infection. Many times he told her that they, meaning Josh and he, would have been better off if she had just died from the infection. Now she was just an infection living in their home.

She wondered why she stayed. She used to be such a strong person, but something died in her many years ago, when the abuse started. She thought there must be something wrong with her and that she could make the change that would make the difference. Then she realized something was wrong with Stanford, and she had to help him. She would bring Stanford back to his old self. However, after many years of trying, it didn't make a difference, and instead she lost who she was. She kept saying, once Josh was out of high school, was a young adult and able to look after himself, she would go. Now here she was eating raw salmon off the kitchen floor with her abusive husband hovering over her, a sharp knife in his hand.

"Hurry up, you cow. I don't want Josh coming home and seeing you like this. You embarrass him enough." She had eaten all the meat off the half-pound piece and only the skin remained. She held it up to him to show him.

"Tsk-tsk, Elise. You left the best part. Finish it." This was not a request. His words were ice. She started to plead with him, and gag, but he kept shaking his head "No, no, no. You started it, remember? This is your fault. Now face the consequences. Do you have to constantly disappoint me, Elise?" She slowly put the fish skin in her mouth and closed her eyes. While chewing, she heaved and threw up most of what she had eaten up to that point.

Stanford stood and kicked his chair out of the way. It flew dramatically across the floor and skidded into the wall. He walked up to Elise and threw a hard backhand across her face. Blood gushed from her nose. She put her hand up to stop it and saw the blood leaking through her fingers.

"Clean this mess up! You're lucky I don't make you eat your wretched vomit. What a waste of food! With all the charity work you do, you must be aware of how many people don't have your luxuries. Your sense of entitlement is really rather pathetic, Elise. When you are done, clean your-self up and meet me in the dark room."

"No, you, you promised," she stammered, crying and trying to hold her nose to stop the bleeding.

"No, I didn't promise. You fail again, Elise. Stop whining and deal with it. I will give you five minutes. Do you understand me? Five." He held five fingers in front of her face.

She nodded and raced to get the mop and bucket, with her face held back, choking on the blood running down her throat.

CHAPTER 22

"WELCOME TO TRU. I'M ROB, AND I WILL BE SERVING YOU THIS evening. Can I get anyone a cocktail to start?"

"I don't know about anyone, but you can get us two Grey Goose martinis, straight up with a twist." Jake made the order sound regal.

"Right away, sir." The young man turned to go when Jake held him up. "Wait a minute, Rob. Don't you want to know what the lady will have?"

The server's eyebrows went up, and Amanda laughed. "He's just kidding. He thinks he's funny." The server nodded and gave her a knowing look, then went off, no doubt, to tell the bartender he has another one of *those* customers.

"I am funny." Jake looked hurt.

"Yeah, funny-looking, not funny ha-ha." Amanda loved to banter back and forth with Jake. She waited for his next line. Instead, he took out his cell phone.

"Forget to call off the date with the other chick?"

"Nope. Just keeping my promise to this one." He hit Send.

"Professor Orloff? Yes, it's Jake Bannon. Amanda was wondering if you had anything on the relic yet. Yes, I know it's only been a few hours." Jake rolled his eyes at Amanda, and she squirmed a bit in her seat.

"Oh, really? Well that's interesting. Quite interesting . . ."

Amanda was now bouncing in her chair. She wanted to hear the other side of the conversation. Jake mouthed, "It's nothing."

It was Amanda's turn to roll her eyes at Jake. He stuck out his tongue and continued, "Okay, Professor. Yes, we will. Yes, first thing. Around 8:30 a.m.? Sounds good. We will see you then."

"Well, what was so inter-es-ting?" she said, exaggerating her words as she leaned over the table toward Jake.

"Get back on your side of the table, girl. It was nothing. He said that the markings were nothing together, but separately they do have meaning. He didn't know if they were purposefully put together that way or not. He also said the relic was not a relic. The wood was older, probably from the 1800s, but the markings were fairly new. He wants to study it a bit more and talk to us tomorrow. Sounds like it is more of an ornament than a relic, but Cardinal Roland would have known that, right?"

"Did he tell you what the markings were separately?"

"Yes, he did." Just then Rob, waiter extraordinaire, showed up with the iced martinis.

"Yummy." Jake licked his lips.

"I'll be back in a few minutes to take your orders, if that's okay?"

"More than okay," Jake said and winked at Rob, who seemed to cringe at the act. Rob managed an "enjoy" before he disappeared.

"Don't even think of taking a sip of that until you tell me what those markings meant." Amanda's eyes were on fire, and her lips did not move. Although Jake heard her perfectly well.

"Oh my, I am really scared now," he said as he slowly pulled the drink across the table close to him. "And how did you do that ventriloquist act just now? Do you practice speaking without moving your lips? Were you part of a carnival act or something when you were a kid?" He placed his lips on the edge of the glass.

"Jake, don't you dare!" Amanda's eyes pleaded.

"Whoa there, crazy lady. Okay, okay . . . when you pull the markings apart, there are two symbols. One is a Christian symbol, an early form of the monogram for Christ. There is a much more complicated explanation that the professor rattled off, but that was the gist of it."

"Okay, that's no big deal. After all, it's supposed to be a Christian relic, so that makes sense. So what was so interesting? It must be the second part."

"The second symbol is the Greek letter Omega."

Amanda thought about it for just a second, then took a large drink of her martini.

"Hey, you forgot to 'cheers' me," Jake protested.

"You know what that means, don't you, Jake?" Amanda was very serious now.

"Yes, Amanda. The burning crosses in your vision are starting to make sense now. When you take the symbol for Christ and cross it with Omega, someone could interpret that as meaning the end of Christ or the end of Christianity." Jake then tapped his glass against Amanda's and took a big swig of his martini, downing half of it in one gulp. "Salut."

CHAPTER 23

JOSH MOVED STEALTHILY WITH AN AIR OF CONFIDENCE AMONG THE young people. He made eye contact with a few who were already part of the Inner Circle. They went about casually conversing through the groups, asking questions, not showing too much interest, yet waiting and watching to see who would fit in and be the next one chosen to join.

Josh had left Olivia and her chubby friend sitting by the tree. He had no time for them, and Angela was too much of a blabbermouth. She did not fit the profile for the Inner Circle. His thoughts flickered back to Olivia. *Hmm, I wonder . . .* Then he dismissed the thought. She was too innocent. She had nothing she could give to the group. She seemed to be close to her mother, so family life was not an issue like in the rest of the group. She wouldn't have a clue what a dysfunctional life or traumatic experience was, never mind how to cause one. No, she would have to be left out, and he would have to stop thinking about her. "No distractions" was one of the core rules of the group. They could not care for anything or anyone, except each other, lest they start to feel an emotional tie, or start to empathize. Then it would all fall apart.

He met up with Ryan, a short stout fellow about his age.

"Hey, Josh."

"Hey, Rye." Josh held his hand up in a half salute but didn't shake Ryan's hand. No touching. That was also an unofficial rule. Touching just seemed wrong, especially since Ryan had been sexually abused from the time he was six years old by an uncle who babysat him while his parents traveled the world. Ryan had been part of the Inner Circle since he was fifteen. He had left home shortly after telling his parents about the abuse. They didn't believe him, even after he asked them to take him to a doctor to show them proof. He ended up on the streets and joined a gang. Living in various places, he stole car parts to feed a drug addiction. He was 117 pounds at five foot nine and barely able to walk when Father Kristofferson found him passed out on the grass at the Lincoln Zoo.

Father Kristofferson gave Ryan a room, fed him, and helped him to fight off his addictions. Although he still smoked cigarettes, he was clean of other drugs and alcohol, and he would do anything for Father Kristofferson, just like all the rest of them. Father Kristofferson encouraged them to join groups such as AA and follow the steps associated with those groups. It was a good foundation for recovery. All the Inner Circle kids knew that Father Kristofferson was the rock behind them when things went off the rails. And for that, they would be forever in his debt.

The Inner Circle was now fourteen strong. Josh wasn't the oldest, but he was decidedly the leader among them. Pete was twenty-four, and Ryan was twenty. The rest were younger than Josh, ages twelve and up. The one thing they had in common was that they had nothing to believe in, until now. The Inner Circle was started by Father Kristofferson to help young people—from bad homes, whether abusive or neglectful—cope with life. He seemed to understand what it was like to be taken advantage of and used. Josh figured this was due to his working in the Church for so long and realizing that nothing in the world was changing for the better. In fact, things were growing steadily worse. The rich were getting richer, and the poor were ignored. In a world that had enough food and the means to feed every man, woman, and child in every country without issue, why did children still die of starvation every day? That was just one of the many discussions within the Inner Circle.

Father Kristofferson reviewed the information with them regularly to show them what we were doing to each other, what we were doing to the planet, and how this was all connected to the greed of people and organizations, the most devious of which being the Catholic Church. How he had been tricked into believing that sacrificing his life to the Church would somehow help. He shared how it was all a sham, convincing those who had nothing and those who had everything to give it all to the Church for a shot at eternal life. "This is the only life we have," he would say, "and this is the only time you will be able to do something about this ongoing treachery. If not now, if not us, then who? This plague will go on infinitely."

"Find anyone interesting?" Ryan was gazing up at Josh who suddenly snapped out of his daze.

"Nope. You?"

"Well, I was hoping to get a chance to talk to that Olivia girl. Angela has brought her along a few times. I wonder what her story is."

Josh felt a flush rise to his cheeks. He didn't know why he felt strange when it came to Olivia. He managed to go on nonchalantly, "I don't know her story, and I don't think she has one. I saw her at the mall today with her mom. You know, shopping. I don't think there is anything there. No chip on the shoulder. No reason to wanna fight the system."

"Yeah, we don't want to have any weak links on the team. Whatcha think of the speech tonight?"

Josh was only half-listening. He was watching Olivia make her way through the crowd toward them. "Oh, the speech. It was okay. I've heard him so many times, I know the spiel by now."

Olivia was now ten feet away, and he could see the appreciative glances she was getting from a few of the guys as she pressed through.

"Josh, here comes that Olivia chick now. We can check her out a bit."

"You can. I've had enough. I have to go meet FK." FK was the Inner Circle's nickname for Father Kristofferson, and Josh wanted to move as quickly as possible. He walked in the opposite direction away from where Olivia was pushing through just in time to hear her ask, "Wasn't that Josh Newman . . . ?"

He started to run, and he didn't stop until he was in front of the church. He bent over, hands on knees, and tried to catch his breath, which was visible in the cold air. He gazed up at the old church. The moonlight caught parts of the stone, and the wind suddenly picked up. The dry leaves on the ground danced in front of the old stone steps leading to the door. They beckoned him to dance with them. Come home. This was his home away from home. No, this was his only home.

CHAPTER 24

THE DARK ROOM WAS ONE OF TWO LARGE WALK-IN CLOSETS IN THE Newmans' master bedroom. It had taken Elise just over six minutes to clean up the mess on the kitchen floor, and then wipe the clotted and dried blood from around her nose. It was still bleeding, but not enough to worry about it dripping onto the beautiful beige carpet of their bedroom. She unsteadily made her way up the stairs, carrying her pumps in one hand and dabbing a Kleenex at her nose, with the other.

She stopped as a dizzy spell hit her half way up the stairs. *How long did it take me? It wasn't five minutes, was it?* She got to the top of the stairs, took a deep breath, and headed into the master bedroom. The door to the dark room was open, and she could sense Stanford was inside.

She dropped the pumps on the floor, stuffed the Kleenex up the sleeve of her dress, and walked in. It took a few seconds for her eyes to adjust to the darkness, and she shivered inadvertently when she heard Stanford's voice next to her ear.

"You're late."

"Sorry, Stanford," she said flatly. "I tried my best. I didn't look at the clock. It felt like it was less than five minutes." She knew there was no use arguing or making up excuses, so she just waited.

"You know the drill." He seemed bored, like this was a complete inconvenience to his day. All he wanted was to come home to a nice meal, a clean house, and a good wife.

She got on her knees. The rustle of the plastic sheet beneath her was familiar as she put her arms out, palms up. He stacked two encyclopedias on her outstretched hands. He closed the door behind her and then they were in total darkness. He switched on the flashlight and aimed it at her face. She flinched as the light hit her eyes. The books remained steady. They were heavy, but she had done this many times and knew she could hold her arms up for a good amount of time. It would depend, of course, on Stanford and how upset she had made him.

"Late dinner and then late clean up. Let's give it fifteen minutes."

Her eyes started to well up. The longest she could hold the books would be for around seven minutes before her arms would give out. This meant more punishments each time her arms failed her, and they would drop more and more often due to fatigue. Her arms were hurting already just thinking about it.

She closed her eyes and went to that place inside her head. The time she spent the summer in Paris with her friend Tia. They ate so much that summer she gained five pounds, but it was easy to lose weight back then. Not like now. She couldn't lose any of the weight she gained no matter what she did. That summer she laughed so much. She was so young and carefree . . .

She was startled out of her reverie by a loud thud. *Oh no.* She had dropped one. She wondered how long she had lasted.

"Only four minutes. You are weak today, aren't you?"

Elise clenched her fists and braced herself just in time to feel the lash of the leather come down on her back. She heard the rip of cloth as the second blow came harder across her shoulders. His math was simple: fifteen minutes of punishment, minus four minutes, equals eleven lashes. The dress wouldn't make it. She hoped she wouldn't make it either, but she wasn't that lucky.

Hot tears streamed down her face, but she made no sound. It would mean a more severe punishment. She could feel the tiny drops of blood running down her back, the hot sting that came with the lashes. She counted silently to herself. *Eight, nine, ten . . . last one.*

Stanford was breathing hard. Then sighed, "Will you ever learn? You are a bad wife, and a worse mother. Say it . . ."

"I am a bad wife and a worse mother," she choked on the words as they came out.

He hung the strap on a hook on the wall. The room was completely bare except for the strap, a rope, and a bucket. The bucket was there in case she had to use the bathroom, because a visit to the dark room was an all-night event. There was a light switch, but Stanford had removed the bulb long ago.

He calmly walked out, softly closing the door behind him, taking the small beam of light from the flashlight with him. Then she heard the familiar click of the door being locked from the outside.

She slept on the plastic. She knew in the morning that it would be smeared with her dried blood when she woke. She would remove the plastic and throw down a new sheet the next day. Stanford always disposed of the old sheet. She didn't know how or where, just that he took it with him when he left in the morning. She kept all her dresses. She hung them back neatly in the closet, torn and tattered, as a reminder that she was a bad wife and a worse mother.

She hung them at the back end. If Stanford knew, he didn't care. He ignored the dresses and surprisingly never asked her to throw them out. She sensed he was pleased with this unofficial count of her inadequacies and her incompetence.

CHAPTER 25

"IT'S GETTING LATE. WHERE IS HE?"

"He'll be here, Gavriel. He is dependable, that I can assure you." Father Kristofferson spoke confidently, because he trusted Josh, and Josh and never let him down. He remembered meeting Josh long ago, when he was one of several priests to visit St. Clements. Almost a year later he received a letter from Josh, a letter filled with questions about the truth about the Church. Father Kristofferson had met with Josh several times after that, along with Gavriel, one of Father Kristofferson's altar boys, and they formed the beginning of the Inner Circle group. They didn't know it at the time. At least it wasn't intentional at the time. How many years ago had it been? Finally, they were ready for all their plans to come together. Destiny. *Soon, very soon, Samuel . . . we will have our closure.*

His thoughts were interrupted as they heard the large wooden doors at the front open, and a few seconds later a shadow followed by its owner, Josh, entered the back room.

"Father . . ." Josh walked in. He recognized the other figure in the corner opposite the priest and nodded. "Good speech tonight."

"Thank you, but just good?"

"I guess that depends on what your goal was this evening. We haven't been too inspiring lately. Both Ryan and I didn't think there were any new connections."

"Perhaps you're not trying hard enough?"

"Perhaps . . ." Josh shot back equally, his slate eyes growing dark.

"Okay, boys. Let's get past all this and focus on what's important here." Father Kristofferson stepped in to ease the discussion. "The letters?"

"Done earlier today, Father."

"Where was the drop?"

"At the mall this time."

"Did anyone see you?"

Josh didn't know whether he should mention Olivia or not but decided it was best to disclose that encounter. "A girl that I went to school with, Olivia Bennett. We had a brief conversation."

"Anything we need to worry about?" Gavriel's dark eyes were piercing.

"Nothing that I can tell, although," Josh said, hesitating for just a second, then adding lightly, "she was at the meeting tonight."

Gavriel shot a quick, uneasy look at Father Kristofferson who then turned to Josh, his eyes soft and kind. "Josh, there is nothing going on between you and this girl, is there?"

"Father, honestly, no. I think she has a crush on me. We went to the same school."

"And you?" his eyebrows went up inquiringly.

"And me, I have no feelings for her whatsoever. I am focused."

The priest nodded in satisfaction. "Gavriel, shall we brief Josh then?"

"Of course we can." But as he spoke, Josh could feel that Gavriel wasn't 100 percent sure. But he continued regardless. "What we have started today will be impactful, and we must be careful. Josh, use the back entrance from now on, please."

CHAPTER 26

"I FEEL FAT." AMANDA SAT RUBBING HER TUMMY AFTER FINISHING the last bit of her compressed pineapple and banana parfait from the menu's Chef's Collection.

"Yeah, you look fat, too." Jake sat mocking her. "Look at those arms. Sausage links is what they look like. And what is that . . . two? No, wait . . . three chins?"

"You really know how to make a girl feel guilty."

"You started it. Besides, who was the one who wanted to go all out with a nine-course meal?" Jake made a few snorting noises, while Amanda looked around the room, embarrassed.

"Jake, please. I just wanted to see if I could do it."

"Yeah, well, you did good, my girl."

"Well."

"Well, what?"

"You did well, not good," Amanda corrected him.

"Listen, English is not my first language, and you are not an English teacher, so why don't we switch to French or Italian?"

"Okay, okay. Settle down, cowboy. Let's get the bill. It's getting late, and we have to go see the professor early." The thought of sleeping in was far more attractive at this stage. A belly full of good food and some leftover jet lag was leaving Amanda feeling a bit fuzzy.

"Why do you think Cardinal Roland gave us this piece? He must know that it's really not a collectible. He does have some experience with these things, doesn't he?" Jake was naturally suspicious, but his thoughts were not far off from her own.

Amanda was wondering the same thing. "I don't know, Jake. This is starting to make less sense the more we get into it."

She leaned over the table conspiratorially. "Here is what I am thinking so far. Cardinal Roland is worried about his friend, Father Kristofferson. They have known each other since they were quite young. They went to school together, started these collections together, and so on. One of them is promoted, or whatever you call it, through the ranks and the other one isn't."

She stopped to take a breath. "What I don't get is why send a piece that is not real with us to the other priest? What does it do, and how does it help Father Kristofferson?"

"Perhaps it's some kind of message from Roland to Kristofferson. Something he doesn't want to say over the phone or in email." Jake was just throwing stuff out there, but suddenly Amanda's eyes lit up.

"Jake, you're a genius."

"Well, yes. I like to think so, but what exactly have I uncovered?"

"It's a message, but maybe not for Father Kristofferson. Maybe it's a message for us. The fire today may be connected to all of this somehow. I don't know why or how, but I just have a feeling."

"Great." One of Jake's eyebrows shot up. "Amanda, I think we need a new hobby." He waved to the server who came right over. Jake handed him his Amex card. "Take care of it, please." Rob headed off to run it through.

"Just think about it, Jake. There is something going on here, and it has to do with these two priests, and the fire, and Matthew 5:5. It has to do with this object that symbolizes the end of Christ or Christianity."

"Okay, Amanda. I get it. We need more though. We can't tie the fire to anyone, except maybe *you*." Amanda rolled her eyes at him. "Let's see what Orloff has to say about all this. Maybe he will have uncovered more by now."

Rob showed up with the processed bill and Jake's card. As he signed the slip, Jake noticed the date at the top of the receipt, 12/12/12.

CHAPTER 27

THE GATHERING HAD ALREADY STARTED TO BREAK UP. RYAN AND A
few others made their way back toward the church. The Inner Circle meeting usually started about an hour after the speaker finished. Not everyone
from the Inner Circle attended the Gathering. They had already been initi-
ated and had bought into the program long ago. Only a few attended now
to seek other like-minded individuals. Lately there were few to choose from
and even fewer who would be invited. It seemed the Gathering had become
more of a social event than a political platform. Young people showed up
alone and left with new friends, generally hitting the bars if they were old
enough. If not, they'd head down to the river to sip on booze stolen from
their parents' cabinets at home. Nevertheless, the Gathering had served its
purpose over the years, and a solid group had formed, one that planned to
make a difference. The message sent today with the fire indicated the start
of nine days to when the Mesoamerican Long Count calendar would end its
5,125-year cycle on December 21, 2012.

Gavriel had been going on now for nearly an hour while Father Kristofferson paced around the room. He looked at the small clock on his desk and
noted it was coming up to 8:00 p.m. The Inner Circle would be forming soon.

"Well, do you have any questions?" Gavriel made it sound like a rhe-
torical question.

Josh shook his head. "No, not for you." Josh looked over at Father Krist-offerson who was scanning the floor. "Father, are you good with all of it?"

Father Kristofferson looked up. "Yes, of course, Josh, not to worry. Gavriel and I have discussed all this at great length. You know we have been working at this for such a long time."

Josh couldn't help but feel the tiredness that came with the words Father Kristofferson was speaking. His body language, slumped shoulders, and ashen face all seemed to indicate his reluctance, yet he seemed 100 percent behind Gavriel.

"Whatever you want, Father. You know the Inner Circle is here because of you. We would do anything for you."

Josh swore he saw tears in Father Kristofferson's eyes as he turned away toward his desk and whispered, "It's time for you to go, Josh," as he slid his finger under the desk and hit the switch. The panel in the wall behind Josh unhitched. Josh slid it open just enough to squeeze through. Gavriel and Father Kristofferson could hear the click as the panel was pushed back in place from the other side.

*   *   *

Josh pulled the lighter from his jacket pocket and flicked it. There was barely enough light to see the stone steps, but he had descended them so many times he could have made it down in pitch black. There were eleven steps, and he counted them in his head each time he descended, even though they never changed. The long skinny corridor went under the church and the back lot until it widened in three directions. The left track led to a wooden ladder going up to the shed floor to the far left of the church's back lot, and the right went for a very long way, finally coming out at a small dirt hole near the gathering spot in Lincoln Park. This was the path that Gavriel had referenced when he told Josh to take the alternate route when coming to the church, one that would ensure he wasn't seen. The middle track led to a small stone room with pillows, sleeping bags, some nonperishable food and water. At the very back of this room was another tunnel that opened up into a cavernous maze with drops that went down hundreds of feet to sharp stalagmites that formed on the cave floor.

This small stone room was where the Inner Circle of Father Kristofferson's Congregation met to learn about their next steps to salvation— true salvation—others might call it heresy, but that was just another way to deflect the truth. Nobody wanted to face reality if fantasy was available. Fantasy was so much less stressful, and there was no accountability.

They were already there, sitting on the floor, some on pillows, some wrapped in the blankets. Candles were lit, and the rest of the group waited quietly for Josh to arrive.

Ryan and Pete were standing at the back, as usual, signaling they were longtime protectors of the group. Josh looked at this group. *Were they really going to change the world? The fourteen of them?* The youngest was Kendra. She would be thirteen in a few weeks but joined when she was just twelve. She was Pete's younger sister, who now lived with him. Their story was tragic but unfortunately not unique.

Pete's mother was a crackhead. Pete had raised his younger sister since she was born. His mother lost her job and hooked up with a dealer who would feed her habit when she couldn't afford to buy it. Pete's mother was basically a whore for the junk. Pete, who was sixteen at the time, was making minimum wage at a part-time job after school in order to feed himself and Kendra. When Pete refused to hand over his pay to his mother and her dealer, he was kicked out of the house. He was devastated as he looked at his little sister, just four at the time, and wondered what would become of her without him. He fed her, dressed her, took care of her, and, most importantly, he loved her.

Kendra clung to his leg as he was leaving. She was crying and would not let him go. Their mother grabbed her roughly by the arm. "No, Kendra. Bad girl. Let him go . . . doesn't belong here." Her words came out in a slow, almost inaudible slur. It was a language they had come to understand because being high the majority of the time affected her motor skills, including her speech.

"I will be back for her," he uttered under his breath. But his mother, stoned from her last fix, just stared at him glassy-eyed, with no emotion.

Josh was glad that Pete had finally found Kendra. He tracked her down through social services. She had been placed in foster care. When he was twenty-one and had a good job, he legally took custody of his sister with the help of a kind social worker. By then, Pete had been part of the Inner Circle for four years. Kendra was ten when she came to her first meeting. But she only became a member at twelve, per their rules. Now, at nearly thirteen, she was considered senior. Josh glanced over at her, the candlelight flickering over her young, solemn face, and he started the meeting.

"We have a 'go' on the plan." There was delicate but appreciative applause. Everyone knew the seriousness of what they were about to embark on. It was not taken lightly.

"The fire earlier today was the signal. December twelfth. We are nine days out. The letters were mailed today. They will all have orders for the night of the twenty-first. It is time. So speak up if any of you have second thoughts or want out."

Silence filled the room. Determination was all he saw on the thirteen faces in front of him. So much determination that, for the first time, Josh felt a pang of anxiety. Not for himself, but for the group he had nurtured and inspired for all these years. So many young lives, each about to change forever. *Could this all be a mistake? Focus. It's too late now.*

CHAPTER 28

THE CHICAGO LATE NIGHT NEWS WAS PLAYING ON NBC. ELISE COULD hear the muffled sounds through the door in the dark room. Stanford always watched the 10:00 p.m. edition. She must have fallen asleep. She moved to stretch and froze as she felt the searing pain of the cuts on her back. She gingerly curled back onto the plastic sheet.

Except for the occasional bloody nose or hard slap across the head, Stanford generally kept any cuts or bruises confined to Elise's back—never the legs or arms or anywhere someone might notice or that might cause suspicion. Elise hadn't been to the doctor for many years. The last time she went was to do more tests after the bad infection she contracted when giving birth to Josh. The doctors did say the chances of having another child were slim to none. Elise and Stanford had planned on having a large family. The news was devastating to her but more so to him.

She remembered Stanford was adamant and angry. He had said, "Josh needs support. He needs brothers and sisters. I don't want him to grow up alone."

She had done everything. She even suggested in vitro fertilization or surrogacy, but Stanford wouldn't have it. If she couldn't do it naturally, then she was just incapable.

"A real woman would be able to have her children naturally. What does that make you, Elise?" His words always stung. However, they seemed to be directed at more than just her. He never spoke much about his past, and she knew he grew up in an orphanage. *Did they even have orphanages anymore?* She wasn't sure, and she imagined it would have been a hard life for him. What was inside the man that created such hate, she did not know. She just wished she had seen it before they were married. Whatever it was, he hid it all too well, until it was too late for her to realize and get out.

Elise spent her time in the dark room often justifying why her husband was the way he was. She thought about Josh and how strange he seemed. He was very bright, and even as a baby he never seemed like a child to her. He always seemed to know things. She knew he was aware of Stanford's abusive ways, and when he was younger Josh often defused Stanford's anger by running into his arms and hugging his father. This was the one thing Elise knew for certain about Stanford—he loved Josh more than anything, definitely more than he ever loved her, if he ever did love her.

The last time he had touched her in a loving way was after Josh was born, in the hospital. He said, "You did well, Elise. He is beautiful." Then he kissed her forehead. After years of trying unsuccessfully for a second child, he never touched her again, except in anger. They did not sleep in the same bed. She had a cot in the corner of their room, and there was the dark room. She realized the more time Josh spent away from home, the more time she spent in here.

It was suddenly quiet. Stanford had shut the television off. It must be 10:30. Josh would be home soon. She closed her eyes and felt the plastic sheet against her left cheek. *When Josh goes, I go. What did he say today? "I will be gone someday, Elise. You better get prepared. Stop being such a coward and fight for your life. There isn't much time left. At least end it with some dignity."*

She fell asleep thinking about ending it, although she was sure it wouldn't be dignified at all.

* * *

After the meeting, Josh took the right tunnel back to Lincoln Park, where it came out in a small grove covered by grass and shrubs. He climbed out and dusted off dirt and dead leaves. It was late and nobody was around. It was also cold. He walked past the place of the Gathering. It was empty. Everyone had gone back to their simple lives. He wondered what that was like . . . having a normal childhood . . . where you went to parties, and took trips over the summer months, or went backpacking through Europe. His father would graciously pay for anything he wanted to do with his year off, but he explained to Stanford that he just wanted to "veg" this summer, to collect his thoughts. His father nodded in his knowing way. *What do you really know, Stanford? How to terrify Elise and how to suck up to clients?* He made his way through the park and back to where he had parked his bike earlier that night.

A thin layer of frost had formed over the bike. It started without a problem, though, and he hoped the roads wouldn't be too slick tonight. He needed to make it home safe, if only for nine more nights . . .

His thoughts drifted back to Elise, and he wondered what she had to put up with tonight. He knew she was late with dinner and that would mean Stanford would be upset. Whatever it was, it would be done by the time he got home. Nothing ever happened in front of him, but he knew . . .

He arrived shortly after 11:00 p.m., a little later than usual, but Stanford would be okay with that. Stanford would be okay with anything Josh did, and Josh was aware of this.

He pulled into the garage and parked his bike up at the front side where he normally did, careful not to scratch Stanford's SUV, a black Cadillac EXT, in mint condition even after three years of Chicago winters.

He slipped off his boots and made his way upstairs quietly, although he knew Stanford was awake waiting for him to come home. Josh closed the door softly, but ensured it made a noise so that Stanford could get to bed. Tomorrow was a big day, and the next few leading up to the twenty-first would be what they had all been planning for. The thirty-three letters with instructions were sent. The world would be on fire, or, more specifically, the Christian world.

CHAPTER 29

JAKE WAS BLEEDING. THE BLOOD GUSHED FROM HIM, AND AMANDA was screaming. She was trying to get to him, but someone was holding her back, grabbing her arms, crushing them against her body. She tried to fight. She was struggling as hard as she could, but she couldn't get to Jake. She could hear him calling her, "Amanda! Amanda!" She closed her eyes and screamed.

"Amanda!" She opened her eyes, and Jake's face was an inch away from hers. She looked from side to side. They were in their hotel room. Jake had his arms wrapped tightly around her.

"Amanda, it's okay. Wake up." He shook her gently, and she relaxed in his arms. He let go of her and got up, poured a glass of water, and brought it to her. She took a small sip.

"You were bleeding. I couldn't get to you."

"It was just a bad dream, honey. I'm okay."

"Jake, you know I don't have bad dreams. I have bad visions. I don't want you to come with me tomorrow."

Amanda was visibly shaken, and Jake stroked her head softly.

"I am going with you. You can't stop me. And by the way, you don't always have bad visions. You have good ones, too."

"Yeah, like when?"

"Um, let me see. Remember the time you said you had a vision we would be eating caviar and drinking Dom for New Year's? And we did?"

"That wasn't a vision. That was a craving." She giggled and snuggled into his chest. "I couldn't stand it if something happened to you. It would be my fault."

"If something happens to me, it will be my own fault. And you seeing me bleeding doesn't mean that something bad happened to me." She looked up at him disbelievingly.

"It means something worse happened to the other guy." He grinned down at her.

Amanda smiled, but inside she felt sick to her stomach. She looked over at the clock on the nightstand. It was 4:00 a.m.

CHAPTER 30

THE 11:00 A.M. DIRECT FLIGHT FROM ROME TO CHICAGO ON British Airways was on time. Operated by American Airlines, the flight would land at approximately 3:00 p.m. Chicago time. *What time is it there? That would make it 4:00 a.m. in Chicago right now,* Cardinal Roland thought, as he squeezed into the window seat and prepared for the long plane ride to Chicago. He managed to get a last-minute seat on the only nonstop flight that day.

He was wearing dark jeans and a black casual jacket from Armani Exchange, with a crisp white polo shirt. He had already won the admiration of the flight attendant and several female passengers nearby. He helped the young lady next to him put her carry-on in the overhead compartment and immediately regretted it, as she leaned into him and asked him where he was from.

He answered her in Italian and felt a pang of relief when she looked at him and said, "Sorry, I don't understand you." He shrugged, smiled warmly, and turned toward the window. She got the hint and pulled out a few magazines and started flipping through the pages.

He thought about the call with Michael, and then about Amanda and Jake Bannon. Did he really think he would be able to stop all this from happening by simply sending those two into the middle of it? Not only was

Michael in danger now, he had put two more innocent people into the fray. *Why did I let it get this far?* But he knew the answer. He never thought it would happen. Deep down, he never really believed they would go through with it or that the day would ever come. Their plan to turn the Catholic Church on its head and to cause the world to take notice was inspirational when they first planned it. Now it seemed like the script from a book written by a psychopath.

It was so long ago. The pain was still there, but mostly for Michael. Michael was the one who endured, who had to put up with the messiness of the situation. Michael did it to protect him, and he had promised to help Michael. But through the years, it became less of his mission, and he learned there were evil people all over the world, not just in the Church. But maybe this still should happen. Maybe it was a necessary wake-up call. If he believed that, then why did he send the relic? He knew if they researched it, they would find that it wasn't real, and they would figure out what the symbol meant.

When Amanda's mother had called to let him know they were coming, his thoughts immediately went to all the stories her mother had shared about Amanda and Jake's involvement with solving mysteries and helping the police. He wondered how he could connect them to Michael. When Amanda's mother mentioned they had meetings in Chicago, and she hoped he could see them before they left Rome, it was a stroke of luck, or perhaps fate. He had the relic made just before they arrived in Rome. He did not want to tell them what was going on. This would get Michael in deep trouble. However, he felt if he sent the relic to Michael through them, Michael would call the whole thing off. Michael would know that the Bannons might figure out what was going on.

He now realized it wasn't going to work. Michael was no longer in control. He sighed heavily, and the girl next to him looked up from her magazine, but he closed his eyes and she went back to reading.

He would have to be the one to stop it. He only hoped it would be in time.

CHAPTER 31

GAVRIEL WAS CONVINCED THAT THE NINE DAYS BETWEEN December 12, 2012, and December 21, 2012, symbolized the nine Lords of the Night, also from Mesoamerican mythology. Each lord was associated with a specific fortune, and each night was ruled by one of the lords in twenty-nine-day cycles, based on their calendar. He read through his journal and noted all the specifics of the nine lords and how they would work into the plan.

He had waited a long time and finally the days of epic retribution would begin. He was tired of planning and putting up with the toxicity of this world. Worse was watching the people justify the workings of evil by celebrating it through worship or ignoring it altogether. *Open your eyes and see what you have done.* He shrugged it off. *People are sheep, so now they go to the slaughter, unknowing and unseeing.*

He was a believer once, too, when he was a young boy. He thought working for a greater good by giving himself to religion would ease his pain and the pain of others. He would be able to gain some grace, some kind of ability to push his pain aside. His prayers went unanswered. The pain only intensified, and a dark cloud formed over his heart. He vowed then to do what was necessary to honor his brother and expose the nonsensical myth of hope based on religion. *There is no hope, and there is no religion. There is only here and now, and what we do in the next nine days will forever be inscribed in the history of the world.*

He liked that, so he wrote it down in his journal dated 12/12/12. The fire was easy, just a bit of a smoke bomb more than anything else. He had meant to leave it in the restroom of the Waldorf, but it would have been much more difficult. He couldn't believe his luck when following the Bannons that she would be going to the Cultural Center. He had done community service there for a few months after getting busted for smoking a joint in a public bathroom. He knew the building well. He also knew that very little was happening there on Wednesdays, especially at lunchtime. It would be the perfect time to start the fire, but not before he left a message for the Bannons and the rest of them. "Blessed are the meek, for they shall inherit the earth." The meek wouldn't inherit it. They would take it back.

He slammed his journal shut and leaned back against the wall on the single bed in his apartment. He had moved there long ago. There was a second bed against the other wall. Anthony's bed. But Anthony never made it. He never had the chance to sleep in peace, in comfort. He never had a chance to dream nice dreams that weren't full of nightmares and monsters.

Gavriel looked over at the nightstand. The clock showed 4:00 a.m. It was time to get some sleep. The first day was over. They still had nine more to go. His thoughts lingered for a few more minutes on Anthony. He worked hard to bring the image of his younger brother's face to the front of his mind. It was getting more difficult as the years went by. He had no pictures. He only had memories, and the memories were horrid.

Anthony, he thought. *Anthony is dead, and God didn't save him.*

CHAPTER 32

CHECKING HIS GIVENCHY TIE, STANFORD LEANED IN TOWARD THE mirror. He pulled his tweezers out of the holder and selected a tiny nose hair and yanked quickly. Today he had a meeting with Laurence Fend, a very wealthy southerner who came from old money. Fend was not a self-made man like Stanford, who loathed these meetings. Fletcher could easily handle them on his own; however, he always reminded Stanford that relationships build business. In order for their clients to feel cared for and important, the CEO must be present at these initial meet-and-greets, and Fletcher, of course, was right.

He would support Fletcher in these meetings, but Fletcher would do all the talking. Stanford loved to watch him. He was sure that by the end of their meeting Fletcher would convince Fend that Newman and Company had only his family's best interests at heart, and unlike the other firms out there, they were successful because they treated their clients' investments as if they were their own. Stanford also knew that their company's reputation for solid returns and the testimonials of their current clients would surely put Laurence Fend at ease. Stanford was considering which names to drop when he caught a glimpse of something dull on the immaculately clean granite counter of the bathroom. A small brownish smudge, just at the edge where the sink started.

He peered closer to see that it was dried blood, probably a tiny spot he missed after he cleaned up the leather strap before watching the news last night. How did I miss that? Hmm . . . might have to start wearing those darn glasses.

He didn't like the notion that his eyes were becoming weak; however, he knew it was a natural thing at his age to don a pair of reading glasses. Looking at small objects or trying to read a menu at a restaurant in low light was becoming a problem. He went to the linen closet and pulled out a small hand towel. Using hot water he scrubbed at the smudge, and it vanished. *Too bad I can't do that with her.*

He gazed out into the room at the closed door. He had to take the plastic with him, to dispose of it, as he usually did prior to getting to the office. He didn't like having to carry the plastic and place it in the back of his spotless Cadillac, nor did he like having to carefully pull it out, making sure it didn't touch any part of his immaculate attire, or to throw it into the Dumpster that was five miles out of his way. Usually the blood was dry at least. She really didn't bleed that much. After all, it was a simple punishment—just a little strapping, no worse than what kids used to experience at school before everyone got overprotective with children. He agreed that you had to have rules or things could get out of hand, but discipline was necessary. It really was nothing to gather the plastic and dispose of it, but he still felt disgust, like having to clean someone else's toilet.

He reached for his briefcase that rested against his nightstand. He had planned to read over the Fend profile again last night before the meeting today, but Elise ruined his whole evening. *Bitch.* He thought he might still have time to run through it this morning. He sat on the bed and flipped open the soft Louis Vuitton case. He loved this case. Josh had pointed it out one time when they were looking online for a birthday present for Josh. It was under a section called "For the Man Who Has Everything." Josh was curious to see what kinds of things were on a list for someone who had it all.

There were all sorts of strange and useless items, but Josh had pointed directly to the LV attaché. The perfectly stitched graphite color, with the well-known checkered design, was stunning.

"That's so you, Stanford!" Josh was being facetious, but Stanford didn't recognize that. And after Josh left without choosing anything at all for his birthday, Stanford went back to the site and ordered the briefcase for himself. *Why not?* After all, he deserved it.

He sifted through the neatly filed pages of the folder in the briefcase and stopped when he noticed the corner of an envelope protruding out. He remembered the envelope then—the one he found in the garage with Josh's scrawl, which was a shade away from illegible. Why would Josh be sending a letter? These days Josh spent all his time on his iPad or smartphone, as most kids did. It didn't make sense to send snail mail when he could reach someone instantly. *Who the heck did he know in Florida?*

Stanford was torn between simply leaving the envelope on the kitchen counter for Josh or opening it up and finding out what it was about. There was no need to mistrust Josh. Now, if it were Elise, that would be another story. He couldn't understand why Josh would write a letter, but perhaps he had made friends with someone who didn't have access to technology. Highly unlikely, but not impossible. He decided to hold on to the letter and ask Josh about it to his face. That way he was not invading his privacy, and his curiosity would be satisfied. Josh always had a good answer, or a good enough one anyway.

His Patek showed 7:05 am. No time to read the profile at this point. Stanford reluctantly turned his attention back to the cleanup and made his way over to the dark room.

CHAPTER 33

THE NIGHTMARE WAS SUFFOCATING. HE COULD SEE ALL THE FACES of the children melting like wax dolls, expressions of shock and fear frozen in place as their skin slid down to reveal bone and flesh. Smoke stung his eyes, and red tears rolled down his cheeks and dripped from under his chin onto a small cross that hung from his neck and rested on his chest.

Father Kristofferson bolted upright in his bed. The stench of burning flesh made him gag, as he swung his legs around and placed them on the cool stone floor of his room. He switched on the night table lamp and reached for the cross he wore regularly. It was a small wooden piece Samuel had given him many years earlier. They collected these small carvings and other objects. It was only a hobby at first. Then they began in earnest to find some items of significance. They wanted to donate their collection as part of a legacy project, once they both felt they had fulfilled their commitment to the Church. But that was before, when they were truly in love with the Church and its teachings. Before they realized that the Church was just another cover for greed and corruption.

He stood and stretched. Then he turned the clock radio toward him. It was after 7:00 a.m. He usually woke around 5:30 in the morning. The old clock radio's alarm hadn't worked for several years, yet he never needed it. His internal clock rarely failed him, but it had today.

It was difficult to tell what time of day it was, as his room had no windows and was shrouded in darkness, except for the artificial light of the lamp and some candles he would light on occasion when he wanted the warmth and ambience of soft light.

He opened the top drawer of the nightstand and pulled out a small flashlight—the kind pilots hung around their neck. He imagined a large airliner going into complete blackness, and the pilots clicking on these miniature lights and trying to figure out what instruments to point them at. *Like bringing a knife to a gunfight, right?* He checked that the light was working and then walked over to the desk and slid his fingers under the top until he felt the familiar switch. The panel made a click, and he could see the dark slim line appear beside the panel. He slid it open and stepped through.

He felt the immediate drop in temperature as he held the flashlight and cautiously descended the stairs. Only as he descended did he realize he had no shoes on. The stone steps were smooth enough, but when he stepped onto the dirt floor, small bits of gravel and dirt prickled his feet. It was uncomfortable but not enough to make him go back for shoes.

How many hours had he spent down here in the rooms with the children? Talking them down when they were upset? Helping them to understand their anger could be directed at a bigger cause? They had purpose and meaning in this world, and he would show them how they could take all that pain and do something that would change the world.

Gavriel was one of his most triumphant successes. The boy was completely broken. Back in those days Father Kristofferson was purposely scanning the north end of town for lost souls. He didn't think about why he did this, only that someone had to, and it gave him solace to know he was not the only one who had experienced great pain in his life. Even then, as he and Samuel were planning ways to expose the Church, Michael Kristofferson still had to find a way to tame his anger, which was a bitter and raw anchor around his neck, a constant reminder of his past.

When he first found Gavriel years ago, he was clearly stoned, sitting on the sidewalk in the midday sun. Few people walked the streets during the day in this part of town, and gangs roamed mostly at night. Father Kristofferson took to wearing his priest's robes when he ventured here. For some reason even the ugliest of characters seemed to veer away from a priest with a cross around his neck. His shadow fell over the young man for a few seconds before Gavriel's head bobbed a couple of times and then turned upward to the priest. His eyes were partially closed due to the sunlight, but the priest could see that his pupils were dilated. Moreover, they were dead eyes, with no life in them at all. Tattoos flanked the upper part of both arms and continued up under the sleeves of a black T-shirt. His jeans were dirty, and he had an odor that reminded Father Kristofferson of a low-end hospital, medicinal but unclean.

The weeks that followed were difficult. He tried to help Gavriel, who often left for days without a word, and then showed up curled on the ground at the back door of the church in a pool of vomit and urine. It took nearly a year to get him clean and to convince him to stay clean. Now, years later, Gavriel was the one who would lead them out. Even as he thought this, Father Kristofferson felt a pang of bittersweet anxiety. He wondered if this were right, using his pain as a catalyst to sacrifice so many. *Was it justice?* He shook the thought out of his head. *You didn't come this far. You didn't make believers out of them. They believed it before they came to you.*

He had made it to the small chamber, where the Inner Circle gathered, remnants of their last meeting apparent. He closed his eyes and saw the melting faces from his earlier nightmare. *What would happen at the end? Would the meek inherit the earth, or . . . ?* In his mind, he could see the verse. Isaiah 53:7: "He was oppressed, and he was afflicted, yet he opened not his mouth: he is brought as a lamb to the slaughter . . ."

CHAPTER 34

WHISTLING AN UPBEAT MELODY, PROFESSOR ORLOFF MOVED around his meeting room, which had been converted into a high-tech lab, and reviewed the information he had for the Bannons. They would be there shortly, and he wanted to make sure he hadn't missed anything in his opinion about the piece they brought to him. The fact that his opinion mattered so much to them gave him a warm feeling. They seemed like nice people.

He was looking forward to seeing them again. Frankly, he didn't get a lot of visitors or business these days, and he felt like he was starting to get a little slow in his assessments due to lack of practice. He loved the research part, but when you had nothing to research you started to work on other less meaningful projects, and it dulled the mind. He moved his glasses up onto his forehead and rubbed at his eyes with his fists, looking like a child just waking in the morning. He heard a light tap behind him. He spun quickly, and the glasses simultaneously plunked down on his nose, giving it a hard tap and causing his eyes to sting and water. Although blurry from the tears, he could make out the slight shape of Amanda Bannon and, directly behind her, Jake.

"We're sorry to come directly back here, but there was nobody in the front reception—"

Professor Orloff interrupted her by waving them in and shaking his head. "No problem at all. Don't apologize. My mother takes Thursdays off to shop. It's really the one thing that keeps her alive these days. I think she is a shopaholic. Is that what they call them these days? Anyway, come on in. I was just going over these notes I made for you."

"Professor, we are very interested to hear your thoughts on the relic, or whatever it is. We are a little mystified right now with what this can all be leading to." Jake wanted to get right down to business.

"Yes, Jake. Come on over, you guys. Take a look at this." They moved into the dimly lit area, and Professor Orloff pulled over one of several scientific lamps. "Infrared?" Jake asked.

"Not required," responded the professor.

He switched on the lamp and held the piece under it. "From what I understand this is supposed to be a very old piece or relic with religious significance."

Amanda moved in closer to get a better look. While the professor continued, "This piece is made of mahogany. Until about the 1700s almost everything was made of oak. Then the use of walnut and mahogany became popular. And this piece is not handmade. See the smooth lines all around? And how perfectly symmetrical it is? Feel it around the edges."

Jake took the piece and plopped it into Amanda's open palm. She felt around the edges.

"Feel any nicks or scratches?"

"None." Amanda looked up curiously.

"First of all, most religious artifacts are handmade, and I am not saying this one wasn't. However, if this were carved, for example, it would not be perfectly symmetrical and smooth. This was cut by machine. With small pieces, uniform diameter is difficult to do by hand."

Jake jumped in, saying, "That's true, Professor, but didn't they have wood-cutting machines as early as the 1800s? So wouldn't this still be considered a relic or antique?"

"True, Jake. And when you look at the finish, which is a varnish and not shellac, it means that it had to be after the mid-1800s, probably closer to

1860 or '70. Then, if you take into account that this piece has been around for that long, it would definitely have . . ."

Now it was Amanda's turn to cut in, "Scratches or nicks around the edges, of which there are absolutely none."

"Correct." Professor Orloff's eyes looked huge through the thick lenses of his glasses. "And from the type of varnish used, I would even guess this was made sometime in the past few years."

"Well, that doesn't make any sense now, does it?" Amanda was trying to piece things together, and her mind kept wandering back to the dinner conversation she had had with Jake.

The professor was going on about types of varnish and how even wax was used back prior to the 1700s. He was sharing the details of French polishing when Amanda felt a sudden dizziness. She stumbled and dropped the piece. Jake moved in quickly to grab her as her stomach cramped. She could see flames and a wooden cross hanging around someone's neck. Children were screaming. They were on fire, and she was reaching out to grab them, to pull them from the fire, but it was too hot.

"God no!" She was panicked and hyperventilating. She was sitting on the floor. Amanda could see the large shoes of Professor Orloff a few feet away. Jake was stroking her hair gently, brushing her sweat-matted bangs off her forehead and out of her eyes. "You okay? Can you stand?"

Amanda nodded, but she didn't feel okay. Her legs were shaky, and she leaned all her weight into Jake as he helped her up.

The professor was staring, making his large eyes seem even wider. Amanda was embarrassed. "Um, I was having a—" She choked and coughed on her words, and Jake rescued her.

"Professor, my wife has a condition. She has visions, and quite often they predict the future. They take a lot out of her, and she cannot control when they come." Jake did not feel an apology was necessary. However, he knew it would be difficult for a man of science to understand.

"I have heard of these things before." The professor seemed to be weighing the authenticity of Amanda's bout in his mind. "Do you mind sharing?" His gaze shifted to Amanda.

At first Amanda wasn't sure what he meant. Then her eyebrows went up knowingly. "Well, if you can keep an open mind, Professor."

He nodded, "Of course, please . . ."

Amanda took a deep breath. She noticed the concerned look on Jake's face that said she really didn't have to if she didn't want to.

"I saw a church on fire, and children were caught in the fire. I was trying to help them, but it was too late . . ." Her voice was a whisper at the end. Jake put his arm around her shoulder and gave her a squeeze.

The professor was mulling it over. "Anything else?"

"Oh yeah, a cross made of wood. It was hanging around someone's neck, but I couldn't see his face."

"My rule of thumb is that we consider all options and leave no stone unturned. If your vision is related to the current circumstances, it gives us some advantage to understand what's behind the curtain before it rises."

Jake considered what the professor was saying, "Professor, our problem is we don't know what any of this is about. Yes, we are getting some insight indirectly to what could happen, but we have no idea what the bigger picture is. So how do we stop these things from moving forward?"

"That, my friend, is the question. Isn't it?"

CHAPTER 35

JOSH COULD HEAR STANFORD MOVING AROUND. HE LAY ON HIS BED staring up at the ceiling, waiting. He didn't want to get out of bed or leave his room until he was sure Stanford had left for work. He dreaded those mornings running into him and having to talk uncomfortably about his life. His father never lectured him anymore. He used to when he was younger. Stanford would tell him about being a straight shooter and looking right at people. He'd speak on the importance of being firm with his handshake and having confidence in himself—all that macho guy stuff. Yet it had made Josh feel, at the time, like his father really cared. Now he was on a different level with Stanford. It was as if Stanford were waiting to see if all those years of lessons and chats would result in something amazing.

Of course Stanford was proud of all Josh had done to date. He was top of his class, a great athlete, and had his choice of universities. Josh knew that Stanford took the credit for how he turned out. And yet to Josh, Stanford seemed like he was always walking a tightrope when it came to discipline. Josh could never really do wrong. The few times he was caught coming in past his curfew, it resulted in Stanford changing the curfew rules, and then there wasn't really a curfew at all. Elise was not happy about this, but she had no say in it, or in anything, for that matter.

Josh could feel the old familiar emotions coming back, and he pushed them into the farthest part of his mind, where he sometimes went only to glimpse the past: He and his mother were laughing, eating cereal out of a box on Saturday morning while watching *Looney Tunes* and *Merrie Melodies*. His favorite episodes were Wile E. Coyote and the Road Runner. However, as he got older he disliked the Road Runner more and more. There was something sadistic about how the bird continually and purposefully put the Coyote in danger. By the time he was no longer interested in cartoons, Josh believed that the Road Runner was a sinister character that depicted the real evil behind human behavior. The Coyote had everything backfire on him. He worked hard and achieved nothing, while the Road Runner simply won. Nobody was that innocent.

He could hear the garage door opening and jumped out of bed. *Wonder what Elise is up to? Licking her wounds and waiting for the next round? How long . . . how long until she cracks?* Josh could picture it in his mind. To him it didn't matter. He would be long gone by the time it happened. It was too close to Christmas for Elise to lose it. It was the one time of year that Elise seemed to be happy. She spent hours putting up the Christmas decorations and the tree on Christmas Eve. Stanford didn't want the tree up any sooner, and he wanted it taken down before the New Year. Stanford didn't care much for Christmas, but he always brought home Josh an amazing Christmas gift. It was wrapped professionally and usually something that none of his friends seemed to have but wanted desperately.

Josh was aware that Stanford spent most of his young life in an orphanage. Growing up he sometimes heard bits of conversation between his parents that suggested a tough upbringing for his father. Josh figured those Christmas times weren't too memorable for Stanford. He didn't want to be reminded of his youth. This seemed to be the most obvious reason that Stanford didn't take to the season. Deep down though, Josh had an inkling that the real reason for Stanford keeping Christmas to a quick and meaningless event, at least these days, was because it was something Elise looked forward to, and Stanford had stopped wanting happiness for Elise many years ago. Josh shrugged the thoughts away. Why waste time thinking about all this? Looney Tunes and Christmas—none of it mattered anymore. Christmas was as much of a farce as anything. It was nothing more than a money grab for retailers and bribing children into good behavior. Suddenly everyone was good for a few days of the year, and then we all went back to whom we really are.

He took a quick shower and changed into clean black jeans and a black T-shirt. Gavriel had given him the rundown on today's program. He would have to be quick and careful. He had to make sure he survived at least until the final day. Eight more nights, and it would be done. He felt relief. He wanted this to be over. He wanted everything to finally be over.

CHAPTER 36

BEFORE HE LEFT, STANFORD HAD COME IN AND EXPERTLY PULLED UP the plastic off the floor, rolled it up, and stuffed it into a large black garbage bag. Elise was already up and sitting in the dark at the back of the room. He didn't look up, but she knew he could feel her presence. *Can you feel the heat from my eyes burning through your skull, you fucking maniac?* Even just thinking this while Stanford was in the room made her heart race. She feared he could hear her thoughts, read her mind, and if she weren't careful it would instigate another night in the dark room. She quickly turned her thoughts to other things. *Did she have any meetings today? What day is it?* She was frustrated. Everything was starting to blur together, like a giant TV screen that has lost its picture and all you see is the white fuzz on the screen. *Snow. Yeah, that's what they call it on the TV. Snow.* Elise wished it would snow. She loved Christmas, and it wouldn't be Christmas without snow.

She hadn't realized that Stanford was gone. He had scooped up the evidence and left, without a word. *What were you expecting? A quick peck on the cheek and a cheery "See you later honey, have a nice day"?* She laughed out loud at this and then quickly slapped her hand over her mouth, just in case Stanford was still in the house. Then she heard the Cadillac start and the garage door in full motion. Slowly she stood. The pain was now a dull ache. Her back was stiff, and she could feel some of the cuts reopening as she moved, causing small droplets of blood to trickle down her shoulders and back.

Although it was still dark outside, the room was not as black as the dark room. She made it over to the bathroom and turned on the light. After being in the blackness of the dark room, it always took a few seconds to adjust to the light, and her eyes were sore from crying. She slowly, carefully peeled off the dress and went to the back of the closet they shared. Even in here the evidence they were no longer a couple was overwhelming. Stanford's neatly pressed suits and shirts were lined up on the left and hers were on the right. *Never the two shall meet*, she thought, as she pushed her clothes over, making room at the end of the line for her torn dress. It hadn't happened yet, but she wondered how long before the torn dresses outnumbered the others. She quickly pushed back the clothes against the dresses, so they were not noticeable.

She looked in the mirror. Her face wasn't too bad—a small purplish bruise on her left cheek close to her nose. Her nose was a bit swollen. Although not broken, it still hurt terribly. She stepped gingerly into the shower and turned the water to hot. It took a few seconds to heat up. Once in, she turned to get the full sting of the hot water directly on her wounds and let out a small cry. The pain was brutal but not nearly as bad as what she had gone through last night, so she just stood and let it hurt. She used a soft sponge to gently rub Dial gel over her cuts to keep the wounds clean. Then, as if this were just a regular morning, she shampooed and conditioned her hair and stepped out. Toweling herself by gently patting her body, the towel came away with small spots of red on it. She tried her best to cover the cuts with antibacterial cream, but she couldn't reach all of them. The last thing she wanted was an infection. *You are an infection.* Stanford's words rang loud in her head. She stared at herself in the mirror, right into the depths of her own slate eyes. She could see her reflection in her eyes. She watched her own fist come up and punch the side of her head, like it was someone else's arm. She kept punching now with both arms, avoiding the face, hitting the side and the back of her head until her fists hurt. Elise slumped to the bathroom floor, sobbing uncontrollably.

CHAPTER 37

"I THINK UP UNTIL THIS POINT, WE WERE BASING EVERYTHING ON A preconceived notion. One that was simple, and this is no longer simple." Jake was rubbing his forehead with his thumb and forefinger as he spoke.

Amanda couldn't help feeling sorry for him. He never complained about all the trouble she got them into. It was seemingly innocent at first, but then a twist or a misinterpretation, or just random bad luck, usually brought them into something more dangerous. She was drawn to it, but poor Jake—he was dragged along for the ride. She again saw the image of Jake bleeding, calling for her, the nightmare that kept playing over and over in her mind like a bad commercial. The Adventures of Jake and Amanda Bannon. *A true life-and-death reality show. Thursday evenings at 8:00 p.m. Just like* The Running Man *book. What a terrible game.*

"Amanda would know the answer to that," Jake was saying.

"The answer to what?" She snapped out of her macabre thoughts.

"This priest you know." The professor addressed her directly. "How well do you know him, this Roland?"

"Well, I really don't know him all that well. My mother met him some time ago, at a convention. The Church was trying to get hip and reconnect with its followers by launching some brand marketing. They held a convention, the same way businesses hold industry conventions. The marketing seemed to work. From what I remember, there were over two thousand attendees. Samuel Roland was one of the keynote speakers. He was promoting and handing out copies of a book he wrote on culture and Christianity. After his session, my mother wanted him to autograph the book. He was impressed by her knowledge and dedication to the faith, and they ended up chatting and exchanging contact information. He has been a great comfort to her over the years. He is the highest ordained priest she knows personally, so it's kind of an . . . I don't know. I guess she feels he is closer to God than most, so she somewhat idolizes him. Like kids and their rock music heroes these days."

"Wow. She's a real believer then? I mean in the whole Catholic hierarchy and traditions and all?"

"Yes." Amanda sounded defensive. "She is, and I don't judge her. We all have a right to believe in what we choose. She is a good person with a kind heart."

"Oh, I am not doubting the faith of your mother or her good sense. I am simply trying to figure out what was behind Cardinal Roland's efforts to get this piece into your hands, or the hands of this Father Kristofferson. Where is the tie-in?"

Jake stepped in. "Amanda had this thought at dinner, and it's not out of the question, really. She hypothesized that perhaps Cardinal Roland was trying to either tell us or tell Father Kristofferson something by using this idea of a message through the relic. You have to admit the signs carved into the piece are not what you would expect."

"I couldn't agree more." The professor was rolling the piece over and over in his hand like he was expecting to extract the answer from the wood by rubbing it out like a genie from a lamp. "It seems the message here is anti-Christian, and this is not a normal symbol. These have been placed one over the other to form a new symbol—one that if you were inquisitive enough or had a good understanding of religious symbolism you could easily figure out. Have either of you chatted with Cardinal Roland and outright asked him?"

Jake and Amanda looked at each other. The most obvious solution and neither one of them thought of it.

"That's all right. Don't feel bad you didn't think of it sooner. You know, when you're in the jar, it's pretty tough to read the label." The professor grinned.

Jake had already whipped out his cell phone and was dialing. Amanda and the professor waited eagerly. It was the middle of the afternoon in Rome, so it shouldn't be a problem getting a hold of the cardinal.

Jake's Italian was fluid and quick, so it was hard for Amanda to keep up with his side of the conversation. Then she saw an eyebrow draw up. Uh-oh. What's wrong? She tried to penetrate Jake's thoughts by staring into his eyes. She couldn't make out what was going on by his expression.

"*Grazie mille,*" Jake was saying and ended the call. He looked up at Amanda and the professor. "He's gone."

Amanda was stunned. *Gone? What?*

"According to the Vatican secretary he left this morning...for Chicago."

"I guess there is more to this story and to Cardinal Roland than you thought . . ." Professor Orloff scratched the side of his head, messing the already tussled hair.

"I guess we can wait until he gets here and ask him to his face." Jake was matter of fact.

"No." Amanda was anxious. "I think we should stick to the plan and go see Father Kristofferson with the relic. I am not sure why, but I believe he may be part of the answer to all of this. It was what Cardinal Roland asked us to do in the first place, and we have waited far too long to meet him."

Jake had seen Amanda in this mindset before. "No use arguing," was all he said to Professor Orloff, who gave him that knowing look. The professor offered, "I believe you. And I'm coming with you."

"Professor, you've done enough. We thank you so much, but I don't think it's a good idea."

"Amanda, I may be able to answer some questions and back up the authenticity of the piece, if questioned by Father Kristofferson."

"We haven't told you everything, Professor . . ." Amanda hesitated, not wanting to sound like a jerk for not disclosing everything. For some reason she felt like the professor was now part of their team.

"There was a young man. I think he was a priest, too. Perhaps one in training, if that's what you call it. He was at the church when Jake and I went looking for Kristofferson yesterday."

"Yes, go on, Amanda." The professor didn't seem offended; he was curious.

"On the back of his left hand, he had a tattoo. It was exactly the same as the symbol on the piece."

The professor looked at the floor for a moment, then his large eyes moved up to Amanda's face. "Well, it seems like we may have someone who can definitely tell us what this is all about then. This is the most excitement I have had in years! Shall we go?"

Jake was cautious. "Happy to have you, but I am not sure how safe this whole situation is . . ."

"I understand there are risks involved, but I do believe I can be of some use to you, at least in a discussion about the piece and markings with the priest, don't you think? We're just going to a church to see a couple of priests. How dangerous could that be?"

Jake and Amanda knew that they wouldn't have gotten this far without him, so when Amanda nodded, Jake shrugged. "The more the merrier. Do you have a car, Professor? We're in a two-seater Benz."

"We can use my mother's. She takes a cab on her shopping day. She likes to have a few glasses of wine with lunch. It's parked in the lot at the back of the shop."

The professor locked the front door and the three of them walked around to the back lot. When they got to the car, it was worse than Jake could have imagined. Sitting in the back of the lot, covered in a blanket of dust, was a 1977 four-door Ford Granada with rust spots. Amanda gave Jake a quick glance, wondering if he would just flat out refuse to get in to the car.

She pleaded with her eyes, hoping he wouldn't embarrass the poor professor after he had so graciously offered the use of the car.

"Well, here she is." The professor walked around to the rear of the car and pulled a set of keys out from behind the driver's side back tire. He tossed them at Jake, who juggled them for a second before securing them. "Hey, wait a minute, I . . ." Amanda shot him a look, and he continued, "I . . . um, well it's your car. You should drive, Professor."

"Actually, as I said, it's my mom's car, and I can't drive. Can't get a license with my condition." He pointed up at his eyes.

Jake sighed deeply, walked around, and opened the passenger door for Amanda while the professor scrambled into the back seat. Amanda tried not to make eye contact with Jake. She was afraid she would laugh, and he would become really grouchy. He would suffer through it. She knew him well enough to know that.

He turned the car ignition over with no luck. He tried again when the professor tapped him on the shoulder. "Jake, it's a '77. You need to step on the gas to start it."

"Oh yeah, right." Jake fumed inside. He was at least ten years older than the professor, and here he was being told how to start a car. He wondered if this day could get any worse.

CHAPTER 38

FRANCIS AMATO PUSHED THE SWING WHILE THE LITTLE DARK-haired boy giggled. Francis laughed out loud, his face warmed by the sunshine of the August day. He was eight years old and off for the summer break. His little brother, only three, had a cast on his left arm, so Francis was careful not to push too high, even though he had put him in the swings for the little kids. The protective seat secured Anthony with a bar across the front, but not well enough that Francis felt he could push really high, since Anthony could only hold on with one hand.

His father would be home today from his business trip to New York. Francis couldn't wait, because Dad always brought a treat for both of them, sometimes chocolates, sometimes a toy. He had to explain to Dad about Anthony's arm. He knew his Dad wouldn't believe his lies, but if he didn't lie, then there would be more trouble.

Francis would play with Anthony for hours in the park. Sometimes he would forget the time and only when Anthony complained that his tummy was hungry would he realize they had played right through lunch. Today, however, Francis kept checking the Batman watch his father had given him for his birthday. He spoke to his dad before bed last night, and his dad explained that the plane landed at noon. This meant his dad would be home by 2:00 with the traffic. It was 1:30 now, so Francis had enough time to feed his brother and get cleaned up.

"We have to go now, Anthony."

"N-o-o-o. I like to swing, Frankie."

"I know, but Daddy will be home today. Don'tcha wanna see Daddy?"

Anthony's brown eyes grew big and round, and he tried to clap his hands, but the cast made it difficult for him. His little face crinkled as he concentrated to make the clapping sound.

"Okay, let's go then." Francis gently lowered him down from the swing and took hold of his right hand.

When they got home, they opened the back door gently. Francis put his finger to his lips indicating they had to be very quiet. Anthony imitated him with his tiny finger pressing so hard his lips were turning white.

Francis peered around from the kitchen into the living room. Their mother was lying on the couch on her back with a wet facecloth on her forehead. She was having one of her headaches and they had to be careful not to disturb her sleep.

Holding hands and tiptoeing back to the kitchen, Francis pulled out the peanut butter and made Anthony's favorite. The little boy's eyes lit up as he saw what Francis was making, but Francis quickly put his finger back to his lips and his brother nodded slowly.

He poured a small glass of milk for Anthony and set the sandwich and milk on a paper towel in front of him. He cupped his hand over Anthony's ear, "Try to eat quietly, okay?" Anthony nodded again. He was used to playing this game with Francis.

Just as Francis went back to make a second sandwich for himself, there was a small thud. He turned to see the glass of milk on its side, slowly rolling toward the edge of the table. Anthony, not used to the cast yet, had accidently hit the glass while reaching for it, knocking it over. Anthony's tiny face was frozen in horror as Francis bolted to try and stop the glass from rolling off the edge. The glass shattered loudly, and then they heard the creak of the couch.

* * *

Gavriel sat up. Beads of sweat were streaming down the sides of his face. It seemed like only minutes since he last looked at the clock at 4:00 a.m., but it was now 7:15 in the morning. The image of Anthony's face was still clear in his mind. He could still hear the echo of the creak made by the couch as if it had just happened. He remembered his mother coming into the room, her face contorted as she reached for Anthony, his small frame shaking while a silent scream formed in his tiny mouth.

* * *

Josh knew his mother wouldn't come out of her room until he had left the house. This was the ritual after she had pissed off Stanford. He could hear her sobbing and was ashamed at how numb he had become. He didn't really understand what happened in there. This was all he knew of family life, and he had always pretended it was normal. *Do I even know what normal is? What am I doing?* He walked over to the door of his parents' room. He stood outside for a moment and lifted his hand to knock, then quickly dropped it and turned away. He had to remind himself that what he was doing wasn't about him. It was for Father Kristofferson and the Inner Circle. This group was his only real family. He had convinced everyone in the circle that it was the right thing to do. He had to finish it.

He left the house. It was still early and dark outside. He couldn't take the bike. A light dusting of snow had fallen throughout the night, so he headed toward the bus stop with his backpack in tow.

There was a quick BEEP BEEP. Josh spun sideways to see a blue Hyundai Accent rolling up beside him and stopping under one of the light posts. The light had just shut off at sunrise, according to the auto-timing the city put in place.

"Hi, Josh." Emerging from the driver's side was Olivia Bennett. Her dark shape became clearer as the sun started to come up on the crisp December morning.

"Hey, Olivia. What are you doing . . . well . . . here?"

"Oh, you mean on the right side of the tracks?" Her smirk was apparent even in the diminished light. "I happen to have a friend who lives close by, and we had a sleepover. I was heading out when I saw you walking, which is unusual for you."

"Well, it's difficult to ride a bike when there's a half inch of snow everywhere." Josh sounded bitchy even to himself.

"What I meant," she said, ignoring his terseness, "was that I thought you might have a car."

"'Cause my dad could easily get me one, right?" He didn't know why he was becoming defensive and could feel the heat rising in his face.

"I didn't mean to piss you off. I just thought I'd say hi." Olivia started to inch back into the car.

"Don't worry about it. I am sure you need to head out. You must be tired from your sleepover. What's his name, your friend?"

"Fuck off." Olivia slid back into the driver's seat. Before she got the door closed Josh had already opened the passenger side and quickly jumped in.

"What the hell are you doing? Get out of my car!" Her eyes were blazing.

"Not until you tell me about your sleepover." Josh couldn't believe he was doing this; it was like he was having an out of body experience. This was definitely not him, not now. He didn't have time to play games. What was it about this girl that caused this reaction from him?

"Why the hell should I tell you anything?" she demanded.

"Because I can tell you like me. Why not admit it, and we can stop all these stupid games and innuendos. What do you say?"

"A little arrogant, aren't you? You think just 'cause every girl who sees you has the hots for you that I must be one of them. Well, I have much better taste."

"Yes, I saw your taste last night. A little rough around the edges for you, isn't he?"

"Are you talking about Ryan? He's your friend. I only stopped to ask him about . . ." Olivia stopped without finishing.

"About me? Don't tell me you're playing the field." Josh tried to sound mean, but it came across as hurt. And although he was clearly being an ass, Olivia's gaze softened.

"Where did you take off to last night? I saw you, and I know you saw me." Her voice was kind.

"I had to leave. I had something important to get to. Sorry, I didn't mean to make you feel bad." Josh couldn't believe the words that were coming out of his mouth. He wanted to jam his fist in there to shut himself up. His mind was reeling as his inner voice kept saying, *Shut up and get out of the car now.*

Instead, his arm shot out and grabbed her by the back of the head. He roughly brought her face toward his and kissed her deeply. When he let go, they were both breathing erratically and looking deeply into each other's eyes.

"I . . . um . . ." For the first time Josh didn't have a smart comment. His usual quick wit failed him.

"It's okay." Olivia's eyes held no offense. "I didn't mind at all." She smiled and looked absolutely radiant to him. "Can I give you a lift?"

"Sure . . . I mean, yes. I could use one. I am a bit late now." He grinned, equally happy and embarrassed by what just happened. "I'm heading to Old Town."

"Oh, the Church," she responded nonchalantly. "Yeah, I know the one."

Josh's heart skipped a beat and not because of the kiss. What did she know about the Church? What did Ryan say to her? He needed to find out. The last thing he wanted was for Olivia to get involved.

She pulled away from the curb. As she did, Josh cringed as thoughts of what would happen over the next few days flashed though his mind. He looked over at the beautiful girl beside him, and for the first time since he started with the Inner Circle, Josh felt a pang of regret. The danger was far too great, and she had no idea what she was getting into.

CHAPTER 39

"SHE PURRS LIKE A KITTEN, DON'TCHA THINK?" THE PROFESSOR was all grins, leaning forward between Jake and Amanda as they traveled at a leisurely pace toward Old Town.

"More like a sewing machine," Jake grumbled under his breath. Amanda gave him a stern look that he pretended not to see.

"Such a nice day for a drive. I don't get to do this much." The professor sounded tepid, as if he were afraid they might find this comment strange. Amanda felt sorry for the professor. It must be difficult having his handicap and feeling like you were at such a disadvantage. Even as intelligent as he was, it would still be discouraging.

She knew how he felt. With her visions often causing her more grief than joy, she wished she could just be like everyone else.

"Professor, there isn't much of a market for what you are doing these days, is there? I mean your line of work?"

"Nope, at least not in Chicago. But my mom lives here, and she loves it and still wants me close by. My dad died many years ago. I think it's been nearly twenty years now. She had kind of a nervous breakdown when he passed."

Amanda heard the tremble in his voice. "I am sorry to hear that, Professor."

"Oh, it was a long time ago, but I promised never to leave her. And I want to make sure she enjoys the rest of her life, so I moonlight on the side. Something quite secretive, government-type work."

"Oh yeah?" Jake interjected. "And what do you do on the side, Professor? Work for NASA?"

"Nope. I do work for the CIA, specifically the Counterterrorism Division."

"That's amazing!" Amanda spun in her seat to look at the professor more directly. She wanted to read his face and see if this were true. She could tell that he wasn't joking. This was real. "What's your specialty?" She was intrigued.

"Explosives, and I speak Russian. Not that that's any use these days. But the pay is good, whether you are actively working on something or not. But we are always working on something . . . I checked you guys out. You have some pretty high clearance yourselves, so I know you understand the importance of confidentiality with this information. Besides, if you say anything, I will have to kill you." He grinned at his own joke.

Jake was floored. This guy was a real nerd slash genius. "I only have one question for you . . ." Jake's left eyebrow shot up as he peered at the professor in the rearview mirror. "Why are we driving a Granada?"

"My mom likes it."

CHAPTER 40

GAVRIEL CLOSED HIS EYES, TRYING TO SQUEEZE THE CHILDHOOD memory into a little black hole in the back of his mind. He hated the fact that the images came back so clearly, like he was watching a horror film in high definition and there was no way to turn it off.

"What the hell is going on in here?!" The explosiveness of her voice was enough, but her eyes were afire with the look that both the boys associated with certain harm.

The scene was chaotic, especially to a nine-year-old. She went directly to the kitchen drawer and pulled out a metal spatula. At the same time, he remembered moving between her and Anthony. His useless impulse to protect his younger brother never seemed to work.

She spun. "Get out of the way, Francis. You know he is the devil, right?"

Poor Anthony. Tears were welling up in his eyes, but he tried to blink them away. He wasn't allowed to cry. He tried to mute all sounds, because crying made her angrier. He was trained not to make a sound, and Francis felt like he could burst with hatred for his mother.

Francis had been able to talk her down a few times, so he tried again. "Mama, do you know what time it is? Daddy is coming home today. He should be here any minute."

His mother froze mid-stride. She seemed to be searching for something in the back of her mind. Her eyes looked up and then from side to side and then back up. Francis prayed in silence that she would put the spatula down and go back to lying on the couch. Her hand holding the spatula was also frozen in a half-raised position. But almost in slow motion she raised it higher as her eyes came back to focus on Anthony.

"I said move, Francis. He is not clean, and you know better than to get in the way. You are too good, and you can't see what he really is."

When she was in these moods it was impossible to reason with her, and it happened mostly when his dad was away. His father would go and get her medication, but the medication only put her to sleep when she got the headaches. She had run out of medication two days earlier, and she was too sick to go and get more. She would say terrible, ugly things and see things that nobody else could see, and she always saw Anthony as something else, something bad and unholy. She claimed she was trying to protect Francis from Anthony, but Francis knew it was she who was evil. And no matter how hard he prayed in his head, God would not help.

That day was not the worst day of his life. The day Anthony died was. That was the day that his father never came home. While going through airport security prior to boarding the flight home to Chicago, his father, who looked very fit, but ate poorly and drank heavily, had a fatal heart attack. He dropped dead right after crossing through the metal detector, holding his chest. Francis found out about it a week later. That day he waited, checking the watch his father gave him and watching the 2:00 p.m. time frame come and go. He was devastated. That same day Anthony had been beaten so badly that Francis finally ran to the neighbors, who called the police. While Anthony was rushed to the hospital, Francis sat staring at his watch, each tick of the second hand like a knife through his heart. He knew then that his dad would never come home, and that things had changed in his life forever.

Anthony lived through that episode. He was in the hospital for nearly a week, and after social services investigated and ensured she was back on her medication, both boys were sent home with their mother. Francis was told quietly about his father's passing by the psychologist, who also determined that his mother was under a lot of stress with the news of her husband's heart attack and death. They assessed that the stress, along with being off her medication, had caused her to be unaware of the severity of her actions. With proper administration of her medicine and regular visits from the social service counselors, they were sure the children would be okay. But Francis knew it wasn't the news of his father's death that set her off. She wasn't even aware of what had happened to his father when she lost it on his little brother. He knew this wouldn't be the last time and that his mother was not any better. You couldn't fix what she had wrong with her. They were left to defend themselves against a greater evil.

Francis left home at an early age, quit school, and got a job. He was only fifteen, but he wanted to get a place and take Anthony with him. He rented a room for cheap from an old junkie who needed the money. The bed he bought his brother and neatly made up with clean sheets and a warm wool blanket would never be used in the small room he had rented. His mother was later diagnosed with bipolar disorder. The severe combination of depressive behavior and psychosis would result in her violent acts. She was treated at the Chicago Lakeshore Hospital's psychiatric ward until she committed suicide. When he heard, Francis didn't care. She was the reason that Anthony wasn't sleeping in the bed that Francis got for him. He had so many wonderful thoughts of him and his brother living together. They would hang out and go to the movies and be like a normal family. But that would never happen. Instead, he had recurring dreams of his brother reaching out, calling to him, dreams that would never go away. After Anthony died, he went on a complete self-abusing bender, drinking and doing drugs until he was completely numb while trying to block out the fact that he had failed his little brother. He had reached bottom when Father Kristofferson found him. And after many months, the two started to understand they had a purpose. They had both been stripped of their faith for different reasons. But they both wanted retribution, and they would get it. He changed his name then to Gavriel, the modern Hebrew name for the Archangel Gabriel. The messenger of God. He felt it was appropriate for their cause.

CHAPTER 41

SHE HEARD THE DOOR SLAM SHUT, AND SHE STOPPED MID-SOB AND held her breath. Had Stanford returned? Her eyes darted around the bathroom looking for something to throw on before he came upstairs. Then she remembered Josh was home. *He must have just left. He must have heard me crying and left.* All the same thoughts flooded her mind: *How did we come to this? What a shitty mother I must be. My only child is indifferent, and my husband detests me.* She shuddered as she rocked back and forth on the bathroom floor. Her head was pounding as she slowly pulled herself up off the floor and went to the medicine cabinet to get an extra-strength Advil. She pulled the bottle out and then saw the codeine from when she had her wisdom teeth pulled. She was late in getting them out. They were impacted and had to be broken into tiny pieces and then extracted. The surgery was pretty major. The older someone is, the more complicated things become. The prescription was for three weeks' worth of the painkiller; however, she only ended up using a week's worth. She was used to pain, and after a week, the dull ache was better than the nausea that often went with the pills.

She turned the bottle around with her fingertips, looking at it. There were about thirty pills left. *I could just swallow all these and the bottle of Advil. Would that do it?* She wasn't sure how much she would need to kill herself. The last thing she wanted to do was try and fail yet again at something.

And if she didn't die, she was sure this time Stanford would finish the job for her. Or would he? He was too selfish to get himself into a situation where he might end up in jail. He would just torture her for the rest of her life. Josh would see her as a coward if she killed herself. She wondered again how much he truly knew of the relationship his parents had.

Josh was important to both Elise and Stanford, but in different ways. She knew that Stanford saw Josh as himself, suffering with an inadequate mother. He was going to ensure Josh had every opportunity and a leg up in anything he wanted to do. This was his way of making up for his lost childhood. Elise wanted Josh to have a good life—one like she had had, growing up with great parents who set an excellent example and didn't hide their love and affection for each other. The kind of marriage she always hoped for.

Elise thought about how differently they wanted Josh to be brought up, although they both wanted the best of everything for him. If she killed herself, she would leave Josh completely in the hands of Stanford to mold as he pleased. The very thought made her cringe. He would destroy Josh.

Elise had no idea who Josh really was. But even so, she was determined not to leave him to become his father's son. She realized then what had to be done. Like seeing a beautiful sunrise after years of darkness, she grabbed the codeine and Advil and almost skipped from the bathroom into the bedroom to get dressed for the day.

CHAPTER 42

THE CHURCH LOOKED ABANDONED, BUT IT USUALLY DID. NOT TOO many people came in these days. It was only at Christmas and Easter that the pews overflowed for Mass. Father Kristofferson was still seated on the floor of the Inner Circle room when he thought he heard the faint sound of voices. *Who could that be? Is there someone here? In the church at this hour?* He tried to remember if he had made any appointments and then the Bannons came to mind. They would be coming back to see him, but they wouldn't find him down here. He had to get back up and not cause any suspicion. They were very observant from what he understood.

He listened intently. Perhaps he only imagined the voices. The nightmare of the burning children was still a clear image in his mind. Perhaps the voices were just in his head. *No, there they are again. This time closer. That can't be.* Father Kristofferson was starting to panic. What would happen if the Bannons found the entrance? If they found this underground labyrinth, the entire plan would be botched. He couldn't allow it. He looked around desperately as the voices grew louder. He wasn't sure exactly what he was going to do. But if they found it, he would have to make sure they never left. For him it wouldn't matter. He was going to go down with the ship regardless.

He quickly moved the flashlight around the room and then the light glinted off something metallic looking. Kendra's knife. The young girl kept it down here, because she couldn't carry it around with her. She wanted it to protect the Inner Circle. He could now see a dim light that was getting progressively brighter just outside the entrance of the room. He moved quickly across the room, grabbed the knife, turned his flashlight off, and stuffed himself into a dark corner of the room opposite the entrance. Hardly hidden, he knew someone would notice him there almost immediately, but there was really no other place to hide in the small chamber.

He prepared himself to do what would be necessary. The voices became louder, and the light filled the room as two people walked into the chamber.

"Father?"

"Oh, Josh!" The relief in Father Kristofferson's voice was apparent, and Josh walked quickly toward him as the priest bent over. With one arm around the priest's shoulders, Josh half-carried Father Kristofferson and placed him gingerly on a cushion on the floor.

"Father, what's wrong? Is everything okay?"

"Oh, yes. Sorry, Josh. I didn't mean to worry you. I . . . well . . ." He was about to go on about his concerns with Jake and Amanda Bannon and how they were to visit today, when he remembered they were not alone. "Who've you brought with you, Josh?"

"Oh, yes. This is Olivia Bennett, a friend from school."

"Oh?" Father Kristofferson's eyebrows went up, as he remembered the name of the girl they had spoken about just a day earlier.

"Yes, she is um . . . she knows about the Inner Circle and our mission, Father."

"Oh? Okay, and you were showing her the clubhouse?" "Clubhouse" was a code word they used when they weren't sure if the person was going to appreciate the true cause of the group.

"That's right, Father."

The priest nodded. "Well, I will leave you two down here to explore then."

He gave the young lady a kind smile, and then he moved quickly past them and headed back up the passageway to the doorway that led into his room.

"He seems like a very nice man." Olivia's brown eyes looked soft in the glow of the flashlight.

"He is very kind. He is my mentor and more of a father to me than my own." He couldn't believe he had said that out loud. For some strange reason this girl clouded his mind, and he let his guard down without even realizing it was happening.

"Listen, Olivia. I brought you down here for a reason. I need to know what you know . . . about the Inner Circle, besides what you hear at the Gathering."

"I know that you guys have a special group that works in secrecy for a unique mission, one that will change the world."

"Who told you all this? Was it Ryan?" Josh knew he sounded angry and maybe a bit jealous, but he had to find out how much she knew. Worse, he had to find out if Ryan was out there blabbing about their plans to the entire world. This could have a tremendous impact on the success of the mission.

"No. Ryan is even harder to get any information from than you."

Josh felt a sudden relief. Maybe Olivia wouldn't have to get involved after all. She had no reason to jeopardize herself, and he had no right to put her in that position.

"Well, this is just kind of like a clubhouse where we all just hang and talk. It's a forum for abused and neglected children, more or less. Father Kristofferson, over the years, has found us and helped us heal. We do things for him, to help his mission with the Church, as a thank-you for all he has done for each of us."

He smiled at her, hoping she was buying it. After all, in many ways this was the truth.

"So why are you here?" Her pointed question caught him off guard.

"What?"

"I said, then why are you here?" Her tone was matter of fact, but it held a slight hint of something familiar, almost an anxiousness that he also was feeling. "After all, you are the child prodigy, the best of the best. Your parents are known for their kindness, generosity, and success. You have everything you need and more. So . . . why are you here?"

Never before had Josh felt like he owed anyone an explanation or that he actually wanted to give one. Today there were a lot of firsts for Josh. His mind reeled with the thought of telling her, telling someone for the first time, everything he had been living with for all these years. He knew that it was nothing compared to the other tragic stories he had heard from the members of the group. But he also felt like he had the burden of all their pain rolled into his own life and that it was the only reality in his pretend world. How could he explain his ugly truth to this beautiful girl about how the Inner Circle had saved his life?

CHAPTER 43

"CAN WE STOP FOR SOMETHING TO EAT BEFORE WE GET THERE?"
Amanda could hear her stomach growling, and she found it difficult to concentrate on anything if she was hungry.

"That sounds wonderful!" Professor Orloff sounded like he just got invited to tea with the Queen.

"Where exactly would you like me to pull in?" They were in the middle of morning traffic, and Amanda could tell Jake was already getting annoyed with the motorists who were driving like they had lost their minds due to a little snow on the ground. "You'd think these people would be used to snow in Chicago."

"Okay, honey. Chill. We don't have to stop. We can find something in Old Town after we visit Father Kristofferson, okay?" She was talking slowly as if she were talking a jumper down from the ledge.

"Don't patronize, darling," Jake said with a smirk.

"You guys aren't fighting, are you?" The professor's head appeared between them from the back seat.

"No, we do this all the time. It's called sparring, but it never gets nasty. After all, we are married. It's too much work to think about ending it." Amanda was joking, but the professor seemed unaffected.

"Oh, yeah. Gotcha. It's kind of sexual, isn't it? You know, like teasing all day and then you take it out on each other later in bed."

Amanda's eyes grew large, and Jake cracked a huge grin.

"I read about it somewhere," the professor continued. "I hear it's quite healthy actually, as long as it doesn't get out of hand. Sounds like you guys are pros at it."

This time both Jake and Amanda burst out laughing. Amanda had tears in her eyes she was laughing so hard, but she quickly tried to contain them when she saw the puzzled and somewhat hurt look on the professor's face.

"Sorry, Professor." She calmed herself. "You see, that's a very interesting theory, and you know, I think you may be quite right."

The professor took her comment at face value and seemed to be content that he had been able to contribute to the conversation and maybe even teach them something new about healthy marriages.

"So tell me, Professor, what got you interested in explosives? It seems quite different from your current interest in historical artifacts."

The professor looked pleased to be center stage and cleared his throat with some authority before beginning. "Well, you see, it was actually the other way around. I went to school to become a chemical engineer, hoping to veer off and specialize in nanotechnology."

Jake and Amanda were impressed and urged the professor to go on.

"Of course, my eyesight made school difficult to begin with. But I got my undergraduate degree and then worked through to my master's, earlier than most. I was in college at sixteen. My father, as I mentioned, became ill and died, so instead of pursuing nanotechnology as I wanted, I got a job to help my mother. Like I said, she went through kind of a breakdown, and she was in a care facility for six months. I guess being Canadian you can appreciate we don't have the same kind of health care programs you do up there."

Amanda nodded. She was aware how in many ways they were lucky to be in Canada, especially when it came to unexpected health concerns. However, she also knew that, because of the socialized systems, the best doctors in Canada headed straight to the States to get work, where they could make a lot more money, with less stress and fewer hours, than what they would make in Canada. There was a catch to most things.

The professor continued his tale. "It was expensive care, and I had been working for a small government group that was looking at products made from alternative fuel and was able to design some very cool things that I am not allowed to talk about. They said I had some kind of a gift, but I'm really just smart, actually. They moved me into a subdivision of the CIA's Special Activities Division to work with explosives. After a few years there, we had the terrible events of 9/11, and I was asked if I would move to the Counterterrorism Division for some work that I cannot disclose. I enjoyed it very much, except for the sad reason that it had become such a priority."

Amanda could hear the sadness in the professor's voice, and she knew that for many Americans, and in fact for nearly everyone in the free world, the events of 9/11 would forever remind them that nobody is safe, anywhere. If the USA could get attacked on home ground, then any country could. Like most people, Amanda could remember exactly where she was and what she was doing when that first plane hit the World Trade Center. Jake had called her from out of town. She was getting on a plane that day to meet him. It was early in the morning, and in a somewhat shocked voice he asked her to turn on the television. It was like a movie. And right while they were watching the live coverage together, the second airliner could be seen coming in and crashing into the second tower. It was unbelievable, and she was still floored each time she visited New York City and those landmark towers were gone, along with everyone's belief that America was untouchable.

"So now I work for them, on and off, and it keeps me and my mom secure, at least financially, and I can travel with her. We love to go off and find these rare and unique pieces from around the world and bring them back. We research and collect together and sometimes swap and sell to other collectors. It's not a real job. It's more of a hobby."

Wow, who would have thought this guy with the Coke-bottle eyeglasses and the bow tie was an explosives specialist? Amanda was turning this over in her mind when Jake piped up, "Okay guys, we're almost there."

Amanda had not noticed the drive go by as she listened intently to the professor's story. Her stomach started to make funny noises again, and she put her arm across it, hoping it would mute the loud gurgling sounds of hunger, but it didn't.

They pulled up to the church. There was a blue Hyundai Accent parked on the side street. Amanda wondered if that belonged to Father Kristoffer-son. *Hope so. That means he's here . . .*

CHAPTER 44

THE CHURCH WAS QUIET. THERE WOULD BE NO SERVICES TODAY. He rarely had services anymore. The larger, more ornate churches now had most of the congregation and only a few services still happened in his small church. It was more of a place for a few old patrons to come and find solace or fall asleep, usually after a night of drinking. One or two regulars generally meandered out in the early morning, but today there was no one in the church. Father Kristofferson was relieved. He didn't feel like chatting or giving comfort. He felt more like he was actually the one who needed it.

He longed for the days of his youth. So long ago now, when Samuel and he were free and unburdened by the evil bishop. The bishop no longer held any control over them. In fact, he held nothing over anyone. They had gotten word that Bishop Solomon had died. He didn't know of what, but he heard it was a rare and unusual disease. Samuel had tried to convince him, after the bishop died, that they no longer had to worry and that they could release the quest, forget the mission. However, Michael Kristofferson refused to throw it all away just because the bishop was dead.

"No, Sammy, this is not going to change what we have spent all these years planning. It's not about Bishop Solomon. It's about everything he and this religion stand for. You and I both know that God would want us to continue, not to turn tail and take the coward's way out. This is a test, and we must finish what we started. It would be easy to walk away now."

He remembered the sadness in Samuel's eyes as he acquiesced and nodded, looking downward. Samuel had just been appointed to work at the Vatican, and they both knew this would be very beneficial to their work. They would gain more insight on the inner workings of the entire Roman Catholic system. He remembered getting the information on a regular basis from Samuel. Most of the time, it was exactly what he expected—a lot of pomp and ceremony, not really a lot going on to make a difference in the world. Basically it dealt with their holding all the power and the riches and keeping all the lambs at bay and loyal through their ignorance. Every once in a while, however, Samuel would report that some good work was being done, and Michael would respond with "Well, what do you expect, Sammy? They can't just not do anything. Christianity is the largest organized religion in the world, with approximately 33 percent of the pie. Of that percentage, Catholicism is the largest, with more than one billion followers. That means we have an opportunity to effect change in a large group, even if it is just a onetime effect. In fact, because of that, we have to make a statement, one that will open the eyes of world. It has to be impactful, even if it doesn't immediately change things. It has to start a revolution."

Thinking back on his words, Father Kristofferson slumped and slowly walked over to the first pew in the church and sat down. His words, strong then, designed to inspire change and foster buy-in, now seemed weak and empty. He stared up at the large crucifix hanging over the altar. His eyes scanned the pained face of the child of God, the forsaken one. *Why hast thou forsaken me?* He slumped farther in the wooden pew until he was able to fold forward, kneeling on the padded knee rest. He put his head in his hands and started reciting "Our Father which art in heaven, hallowed be thy name," over and over out loud.

CHAPTER 45

AMANDA, JAKE, AND PROFESSOR ORLOFF QUIETLY ENTERED THE church. It seemed the right thing to do, when you entered a church—be as quiet as possible. The church needed a good dusting, and the stained glass windows were dulled from the dirt that had not been washed off in what Amanda thought might have been years. They made their way up the center aisle, looking around, peering into the dark corners, as if spirits from the afterlife were about to emerge from the shadows. A quarter-way up they could hear what sounded like soft chanting, a rhythmic sound coming from the front of the church. They moved silently to avoid disturbing anyone who might be in deep prayer. And as they got closer to the front, they recognized the Lord's Prayer being recited out loud.

Father Kristofferson was deep in prayer, his head in his hands, kneeling with his head bent so far down it seemed only an inch off the floor.

"Father?" The sound of Amanda's voice was like breaking glass in the quiet church. She flinched at the loudness of it. Father Kristofferson abruptly stopped his prayer and slowly moved up and onto the seat of the pew. He didn't turn or acknowledge them. He simply nodded.

"Father, I apologize for the intrusion." Amanda was whispering now after the shrill sound of her initial start.

"Amanda and Jake Bannon, I presume?" The priest's voice sounded small and sore, like he had been crying, but when he finally turned to face the group he had a hard expression, nothing like what his voice depicted.

Surprisingly, Professor Orloff took the lead in this somewhat awkward situation. He walked around Amanda, stood in front of the priest, and stuck his hand out. "Professor Moriarty Orloff." Both Jake and Amanda were struck by the name as he continued. "Yes, my mother has a wicked sense of humor. She wasn't a big fan of Sherlock Holmes, always thought Moriarty was much smarter . . ." He trailed off, his hand still outstretched to the seated priest.

Father Kristofferson stood up and took the professor's hand. "Michael Kristofferson. I apologize. I was aware that the Bannons were coming. I was in prayer and the time got away from me."

The priest seemed to be addressing the professor as if Jake and Amanda weren't in the room, but then he turned and smiled, beckoning them to follow. "Please, come. I have a small meeting room in the back."

They followed the priest. And although his tone had changed, sounding far kinder, his body language and demeanor remained rigid and forced.

They entered the back of the church and turned right into a small alcove that opened into a room about the size of Amanda's walk-in closet at home. There was a round wooden table and four chairs. At the back was a small chest with books and papers piled on it. Although light spilled in from the window, the dirt on the stained glass kept the room quite dark. The priest flipped a switch on the wall, and a hazy yellow bulb gave just enough light for them to see each other once seated.

"Can I get you anything? A coffee or tea?"

Amanda couldn't help but feel the cordial invitation was meant to be turned down, and even though her starving stomach thought that a little tea to settle it would be fabulous, her mouth dismissed these thoughts. "No thanks, Father. We would rather just spend a few minutes chatting with you."

The priest nodded and joined them at the table. The professor was scanning the room, as if he would make some great discovery in the few measly sticks of furniture spread throughout.

Jake started, "Father, we have come specifically at the request of someone we know is very close to you."

"Yes, Samuel. He asked you to come and see me. He is worried about me, I am guessing. I have not been feeling well these past few months."

"He is very concerned," Amanda chimed in. "He wanted us to pass on his feelings of concern, along with a special gift we received from him while in Rome. He was hopeful that it would . . . um . . . I guess that it would give you some comfort. Professor Orloff, who has joined us today, studies antiquities and is also a bit of a symbologist. We thought you might have some questions, and the professor would be able to answer those better than we can."

Slowly, Amanda pulled the piece out from her jacket pocket and placed it on the middle of the wooden table. Father Kristofferson glanced at the piece, then reached forward and brought it toward him for a closer look. He turned it over and held it up to the light, his eyes slowly registering the symbol on the object. He did not seem to be surprised by the symbol. Instead, he kept slowly rotating it around and around, as if he were hypnotizing himself with it.

Then suddenly, as if he were snapped out of the trance, his eyes flashed down and looked directly at Amanda. His eyes, dark and ominous, seemed to stare into her very soul. "It is too late."

CHAPTER 46

OLIVIA'S STORY SEEMED INCREDIBLE. SHE SEEMED TO BE SO STABLE. Josh had started to give another version of the Inner Circle and how it worked, hoping to protect her from the truth, when she put her hand up. He stopped mid-sentence, and she started her story. Feeling lost for words was unusual for Josh, but that was how he felt while listening intently as she told her story in the quiet underground chamber.

"Yeah, my mom wouldn't believe me, you know? I think her mind just couldn't or wouldn't comprehend. She ended up leaving him, but not before he raped me two more times. I was eleven, and I hated my mom after that for years." Her eyes were brimming with tears, threatening to overflow any second. Josh looked away. He didn't want to see any more tears. He had witnessed them too many times down in this room from too many young kids.

"We only recently started hanging out and doing stuff together, like shopping. When you saw us at the mall, we were working to heal our relationship. I think she is living in her own personal hell over it, knowing that bastard should be in jail." She looked up and around the cavernous room. "She prays for me every night. I hear her in her room, but that doesn't change anything for me. I think it only makes her feel like she is doing something to make up for her mistake, if that makes any sense."

Josh was now grasping the real reason behind Olivia's sudden commitment to the Inner Circle, and her persistence now made sense to him. He walked over and brushed the hair away from her face, where some strands were sticking to her wet cheeks. He kissed the top of her forehead and then wrapped her tightly in an embrace. They were frozen together for a very long time when Josh finally broke away.

"Listen," he said, looking deeply into her eyes, "I'm going to tell you something. I'm going to trust you, and you can make a decision to be part of it, or not, but you can't disclose anything to anyone. Nobody. Do you understand? You have to keep it secret."

"Secrets are the only thing I know, Josh. It's safe with me."

CHAPTER 47

STANFORD WASN'T HAPPY. THE DEAL HE AND FLETCHER HAD BEEN working on for months seemed to be falling apart right in front of him. He listened silently, as he always did when Fletcher was coming in to close a deal. Generally Fletcher was flawless, but something wasn't going their way today.

His face felt like a furnace, but on the outside his demeanor was cool and confident, as always. He could tell that Fletcher was losing the match and Stanford had to intervene. Fletcher was caught off guard when Stanford put his hand up, but Fletcher knew he needed help at this point and stopped mid-sentence.

A genuine smile came to Stanford's face. He knew he had to be absolutely perfect in his delivery to put the odds back in their favor. "Laurence, I thought this was what you wanted. We have worked hard, as your partner, as a protector to you and your family. We built this." He gestured toward the portfolio sitting on the table. "We built it specifically for you to secure your family's future."

"I'm just not feeling it, Stan." The big man's smile was equally genuine. Stanford flinched. He hated when people shortened his name, presuming it was chummy. But his smile never wavered.

"Well, sometimes we have to keep emotions out of it. Why don't we go downstairs to the lounge and get a nice Scotch? They just got in some

Macallan 25. We can review the details again. We may not be presenting this to you correctly."

Fletcher knew this was a move of desperation for Stanford, since Stanford didn't drink and would have to actually slug one back for the team. He watched Stanford carefully. He usually learned a good deal from his boss in terms of negotiation. Stanford was one of the greats.

"Naw," the southerner drawled. "I don't need a nice scotch to make things clear, Stan. The management fee is what's botherin' me. Y'all are gonna make a fortune off this deal, ain't ya?"

Stanford's eyes met Fletcher's, who gave a slight shrug as if to say, the guy's got a point. Stanford picked up the portfolio and traced the logo on the front of the folder. The package was painstakingly put together and now hours of research and planning were all down the drain. He turned to gaze out at the stunning view of downtown Chicago, his city, his kingdom. He felt a slight bout of his asthma coming on. He had not used an inhaler for years. He had worked hard to overcome the need for it with proper meditation and a healthy lifestyle. He was having shortness of breath, and he loathed the southerner for it. These people expected you to do unbelievable work for a marginal sum, a small fee like some kind of petty ambulance chaser. He could feel the anger rising from the pit of his stomach, churning up through his chest and burning his throat like bile. He no longer felt the need for the inhaler. Instead, he turned back to face the two gentlemen. Fletcher's eyes widened. He had never seen this kind of look on Stanford's face. He couldn't quite describe it. It had an expression of something between hate and pain, and it was red and bloated. He looked like a completely different person.

Laurence Fend, seeing this transformation in a man known for his amazing grace under pressure, nearly jumped out of his seat. *This man is cool as a cucumber. What's this?* "Well, gentlemen," the southerner started, "I should . . ."

"You should what?!" The words came out in an animal-like snarl that even frightened Fletcher. He had worked for so many years with Stanford and had never seen anything remotely close to him losing his patience like this, never mind becoming this angry.

Fletcher, sensing this whole thing was going sideways, stepped in. "Stanford, why don't I finish up with Mr. Fend . . ." The southerner was nodding in agreement when Stanford, still gripping the portfolio, suddenly flung it to the floor, grinding it with his Prada loafer, never taking his eyes off of Fend. The sound of paper ripping could be heard as the two others stared in utter disbelief. Stanford was basically dancing on top of the package now. If not for the heinous look on his face, and horrible timing, it would have been comedic.

They were frozen in place while Stanford continued to kick and stomp. His behavior was that of someone who had obviously just snapped.

The whole time, Stanford had his glare focused directly on Mr. Fend. "My name is Stanford, not Stan, you big fat piece of southern shit." He was speaking through clenched teeth. "I earned every cent I have and built this company from scratch. I did it by providing unparalleled products and service, well worth the money you lazy, silver-spooned fuckers pay." Spittle was now flying from his mouth as he moved toward the southerner, and he was kicking papers up in the air as he went. Fend stepped back and fell into the chair he previously occupied, fear rippling across his face.

Fletcher was now too stunned to do anything. This was a first, and he was having trouble believing it was actually happening.

Now standing directly over the big man, Stanford bent down to lean in about two inches away from the southerner's face. Fend was gulping air like a fish out of water and looked like he was about to have a stroke.

"You can shove your high-end financial portfolio up that big crack of yours and see if anyone else will do this type of work for what you want to pay. Nobody is going to get you the type of returns that I would. You can fuck over some people, but you won't fuck me." These last few words came out in a slow growl, as Stanford straightened to his full height and walked out of the office.

After a full minute the southerner got up shakily, supporting himself on the chair arms, looking as though his legs would collapse at any moment. He reached tentatively for his cowboy hat on the side table and carefully placed it on his head, then moved toward the door leading to the elevators. He checked both sides of the hallway to ensure that Stanford was nowhere in sight before he ventured toward the exit.

Fletcher marveled at what had happened. In the end, Stanford did make a very good case, if you took out all the swearing and threats. Fletcher watched as the only client they had lost in the past five years walked out the door.

CHAPTER 48

THE PILLS WERE GRINDING UP NICELY INTO POWDER. THE PINK AND white were blending together to make a very pretty color; at least Elise thought it was a lovely shade. She had hummed a tune all the way down the stairs with the bottles of Advil and codeine hugged to her chest, feeling happier than she had in a very long time. She had no sense of unease about what she was going to do, just a calmness that surrounded her entire being. When she was given the prescription for the codeine, she remembered the doctor specifically speaking to her about side effects and risks. Codeine could affect breathing and, in fact, stop the breathing of people who had asthma. *Stanford has asthma. That has to improve the chances of death due to an overdose, right?* She kept grinding, using the marble mortar and pestle that Josh had gotten her a few Christmases ago. Stanford wanted her to start making her own spices fresh and to stop buying the bottled ones.

It was 10:30 a.m., and Stanford wouldn't be home for hours. Elise would look through her cookbooks and make some of his favorites. She had plenty of time to get a cab and do some shopping. *Yes, fresh—all fresh ingredients. He loves organic and healthy!* A small giggle escaped from her lips, and she quickly covered her mouth with her cupped hand, looking around the kitchen as if someone might hear her or learn what she was up to.

But she was alone in the big house, which was a common circumstance.

Josh had left earlier. How happy he would be. "Oh wow, Elise. You grew a set. Way to go!" She mimicked Josh out loud. "What happens when the police get here, Elise? What then? Are you gonna show them all the lovely dresses you have in the closet, covered in dried blood? Do ya think they will let you get away with it? Do you really, Elise?" Her imitation of Josh ended with her choking on her name. *What will I tell them? Maybe I should just leave* . . . The thought caused her stomach to churn with anxiety. *He would find me. He would hunt me down, and then I would be punished.*

No, it had to be done this way. Even if she left him and somehow managed to get away and never be found, Josh would be left here alone with Stanford. Although Josh seemed to be his own strong person now, who knew what Stanford would do to corrupt him. Or maybe he would turn against Josh and take her disappearance out on him. She shuddered, thinking of Josh huddled in the dark room, naked and bleeding. She screamed in her head until the image dissipated. Then it finally faded altogether and was replaced with thoughts of freedom.

She reassured herself. "This is the right thing to do. And this will be my gift to Josh. His freedom . . . and mine."

CHAPTER 49

THE PLANS WERE SPREAD OUT ALL OVER THE SMALL APARTMENT—
diagrams and floor plans, names, places, and dates. Everything was going
as well as could be expected, with just a couple of hiccups named Jake and
Amanda. Gavriel was on the floor going over the various confirmations they
had received from young followers who were loyal to the Inner Circle and
double-checking that the timing was right. He wasn't sure if leaving all communications to Josh was the right thing to do, but so far the kid had been
impeccable with his orders. So why would things change now?

He looked over at the empty bed across the room. He pictured Anthony
there as he had last seen him—ten years old, laughing at the corny jokes his
older brother was telling him.

"Whaddya call a dog with no legs?"

Anthony would roll his eyes at him and say, "I don't know, Frankie. What?"

"You can call him whatever ya want. He still won't come!"

Anthony would burst out laughing and roll off his bed. Gavriel smiled
as he remembered running over and tickling him until Anthony begged him
to stop. Then he would take him down to the corner store and buy him a
Creamsicle, Anthony's favorite ice cream.

It had been so many years now. The last time he saw Anthony, he was in
a box. They had tried to make him look good. He was wearing a nice white
shirt and dress pants, but you could see the stitches under the makeup. He

looked so small. He was always small for his age, but being in that wood coffin made him look absolutely tiny.

Francis had been at work, and his supervisor allowed him to leave for an hour, so he could pick up Anthony from school and walk him home. His mother was out shopping with friends that day, which was good. He felt safer when she was not home, and Anthony was pretty good at looking after himself for the few remaining hours that Francis had to work. He would get him in bed and then go back to his own apartment. As long as his mother did not have to deal with Anthony, and as long as her meds were working, things seemed to be okay. Only a few more weeks, and he could afford to bring Anthony over to live with him. He had just bought Anthony a bed and needed to get a few more groceries and enough money to bus him to school and back. He had it all planned out. He was about to get full-time work at the corner store where he worked. The supervisor was leaving and had asked the owner if Francis could take over. In no time he would be making enough money to take care of his brother. He legally wouldn't be old enough, but he doubted very much his mother would care one way or the other. In fact, she probably wouldn't even notice that Anthony was gone.

"Frankie, can I watch *The Simpsons*?" Anthony asked him that day when they got inside.

"Sure you can. Do you have any homework, though?"

"Not today, Frankie. We had a substitute, and she didn't know what we were supposed to work on. It's good, because Mrs. Wilson was going to give us a test." He grinned sheepishly up at his older brother.

"Okay, I'll set it up for you on the TV. I'll be back before you make it through all the episodes, okay?"

Anthony nodded as his older brother set up the VCR to play the set of *The Simpsons* shows, his little brother's favorite. "And if you don't make a mess, you will get a treat when I come back."

"Creamsicle?!"

"Maybe. We'll see . . . maybe a spinach popsicle instead."

"Ugh, are you kidding me?"

"Yep, I'm kidding you, kiddo. Now be good."

With that he had left Anthony quietly watching TV on the couch with a bowl of dry Cheerios and a glass of milk sitting neatly on a side table. When he came home four hours later, the bowl of Cheerios was flipped over onto the couch, the glass of milk lay spilled over on the table, and Anthony was missing.

* * *

The neighbors had called the police after hearing his mother's rants, and Anthony's anguished cries. She had gone into one of her rages upon coming home. She had dragged Anthony into the garage and, using whatever was at her disposal, beat him until he was no longer moving. At first they would not let him see Anthony in the hospital. They were working to save him. Later, after they had mended what they could, he was allowed to spend a few minutes with him. He gazed down at his brother, his bruised and battered face barely resembling the boy he had left only hours before. The Creamsicle, still in his backpack, had melted, and later that night his little brother stopped breathing while he held him. The medical staff had to pry him off his brother. His mother had been taken away earlier. The funeral happened in a haze of social workers and relatives. The costs were taken care of by some relative on his father's side. However, none of the relatives had wanted any responsibility for Francis and Anthony or to be connected with them since their father's heart attack. Their father had been the brothers' only tie to the extended family. Since Francis was already on his own, he was allowed to continue to work and support himself. Once in a while a social worker would visit, but soon those visits stopped.

He spent the next part of his life in and out of a drugged fog, and then Father Kristofferson found him.

* * *

Gavriel started reading through his notes again and looking over the plans.

This is for you, Anthony.

CHAPTER 50

STANFORD WAS LEANING OVER HIS DESK, BREATHING HARD. THEN, while calming himself by looking out at the majestic view and the midmorning Chicago sky, the day suddenly turned dark. As clouds rolled in, a chill ran up Stanford's spine. For the first time ever he had lost it in a meeting, and for the first time ever he didn't feel like staying at the office. The fantastic view, the gorgeous décor, none of it stirred the usual satisfying feelings of power and reward.

What the hell did you do? He wasn't sure what happened in the meeting, and he didn't want to discuss it with Fletcher, not right then. He could imagine that Fletcher had thought he lost his mind, or was having some kind of breakdown. Fletcher was loyal, though, and this would not get any further than the two of them.

He couldn't control the mouth of that fat fucker though. He was sure Fend would be out there blabbing away about how the Ice Man, as he was called in certain circles, lost his mind during a meeting and went berserk on a client. A very influential client. "Shit," he said out loud. Stanford closed his eyes and clenched his fists and raised them slowly. Then he slammed them both down on the desk in front of him. Nothing moved on the desk. It was solid, and his fists took the worst of the impact. He slowly rubbed his hands as he opened his eyes.

His thoughts went back to this morning and Elise. *This is all her fault. She is constantly destabilizing me.* He thought of her pathetic antics from the previous night and all the energy he had to put into dealing with her. It made him tired just thinking about it. Of course he was not prepared to deal with these important meetings after that. Her stupidity influenced his ability to do good business. It rubbed off on him. How could it not, after all, have an effect on him?

The more he thought about the dumb bitch, the angrier he became. Now he would have to handle the fallout of all this: wasting time on rebuilding his reputation among Fend's acquaintances, getting Fletcher comfortable with the outbreak. He would explain that it was just a reaction due to lack of sleep. Fletcher would understand that, or at least pretend to. Fletcher knew what side his bread was buttered on. Next, he would have to spend thousands to wine and dine all his top clients, so they could easily dismiss the rumors as they heard them. Most of his clients despised Fend anyway. He would turn the whole thing around, and Fend would look like the ass that he really was.

He would tackle all of this tomorrow. Right now, he did not feel he deserved the opulence of his office. He did not feel like he was the top dog. He needed to cleanse himself of the layer of ugliness that was brought on by his outburst. Even if his outbreak was called for, he knew himself to have so much more control and for that he had to accept some measure of accountability. But he knew deep inside, the real cause was sitting at home in a frumpy housedress, pretending to be a wife.

He grabbed his coat out of his closet and headed out, not bothering to answer or even look at Marie when she asked if he would be back today. It was not routine for him to leave when his calendar clearly showed that he had no meetings outside the office. Marie was used to knowing his every move. He would deal with her tomorrow, and she would be fine. He knew that she had been trying to get him into bed for years. She wore amazing form-fitting suits tailored by the best and tried to catch him in the gym when she had the chance to show off her firm body. He, of course, would never lower himself to those levels. However, every once in a while he encouraged her with comments that could have a dual meaning. He did this to give her some hope. She was getting on in age, and it wouldn't be the first time a successful businessman left his boring mess of a wife for a hot executive assistant. It was almost expected these days. But he would have none of that. He would string her along, so that she would remain just another member of his overpaid loyal crew.

Yes, everyone would be okay tomorrow. He would make sure of it. He realized the only person who was still struggling was him. He jumped into the Escalade and headed out, at first not knowing exactly where he was going, but then a smile played on his lips. *Of course you know. To get even with her. After all, it is her fault . . .*

CHAPTER 51

THERE WAS A STRANGE LOOK ON OLIVIA'S FACE, BUT JOSH ASSUMED it was due to the magnitude of the plan. Nobody would be ready to hear how a small group of children in Chicago would impact an entire nation, how all of this had transpired over many years, and that the communication had been done through snail mail as opposed to much quicker and newer technology.

"That is the key, Olivia. Nobody would expect anyone to communicate such a major plan without using social media these days."

"I get that, Josh. What I don't get is, why the Catholic Church? How is that connected to all the issues that bring the Inner Circle together?"

"The Catholic Church is the oldest organized crime syndicate in the history of the world. It has taken from its followers, abused its members, and reaped fortunes off the people for thousands of years. It is the epitome of hypocrisy, don't you see? We have to get rid of the platform that allows society to do bad things and then be forgiven; to hurt people, to openly use people, and then be given the right to be forgiven by the all-knowing, all-seeing. It's an organization that is powerful enough to save them and send them to heaven. It's a ruse, keeping us in just the right kind of fear. The fear of losing our souls. The souls of everyone we love—our family, our friends. People believe, because they don't know. They are ignorant of the truth, and having something to believe in is better than the unknown."

The words were gushing out of him like a waterfall. Josh couldn't seem to stop. "The reason people pray for forgiveness is because they want to go to heaven. If they don't go to heaven, the alternatives of purgatory or hell are unthinkable to them. What most people don't think about is that if there is no heaven, then there can't be a hell. By creating a heaven, they inadvertently create hell."

Feeling vulnerable, Josh stopped his rant as quickly as he started it. He fumbled Kendra's knife that he had picked up after Father Kristofferson left them and nearly cut himself. Olivia slowly slipped the knife from his hand and laid it back down behind them.

"You are truly a believer in this cause, Josh. I can see that, but you haven't told me why you. You don't have a personal connection with these people beyond your friendship with Father Kristofferson. You weren't abused as a child, were you?" Olivia wasn't asking a question. She knew. "So what's your story?"

Josh's eyes turned dark. "My story is simple. I'm the one that got away."

It took nearly two full hours to go over Josh's simple story. He tried to help Olivia see his observations of the bigger picture. That, although his mother was constantly abused, she allowed herself to be. Children have no choice.

"Children come into the world believing their parents are there to love and protect them. To take that trust and abuse it, to take the unconditional love a child has and mistreat it, is beyond reprehensible." He had never been touched. He was the golden child, but that made it even more important for him to make a difference.

Olivia found it difficult to believe that someone could be that selfless, but Josh insisted that he had no other motives except to help Father Kristofferson make an impact, one that would hopefully change how the Church functioned. An impact that would show them that they were not immune to accountability for their actions, or beyond reproach. He had made a commitment to Father Kristofferson, and he planned on fulfilling that commitment, no matter what the cost.

At the end, he was exhausted, drained from the purge of information that he had kept mostly to himself for so many years. Olivia moved closer and held him. Then she whispered into his ear, "I'm in."

CHAPTER 52

"WHAT DO YOU MEAN, IT'S TOO LATE?" AMANDA STOOD UP FROM THE table, her arms folded tightly over her chest, chin raised.

Jake knew the look. She was steadying herself for a fight as he gently placed his hand on her arm. "Amanda, sit down. Let's give Father Kristofferson a chance to explain."

She slowly moved back into her seat without unfolding her arms or taking her eyes off the priest.

Professor Orloff's eyes were dancing from Amanda to Father Kristofferson, as if waiting to see the start of a great sparring match. He continued to watch the two of them, when Amanda moved forward and then bent over the table. She placed her head on her arms as if resting, but it was apparent she was in some sort of pain.

"Amanda, are you . . ." Jake was squatting beside her. Amanda nodded against the table, and in a few seconds she lifted her ashen face. Small beads of sweat could be seen across the top of her forehead.

"Jake, Father Kristofferson is right. It is too late. Something has already been put in motion. Something we cannot stop. Isn't that right, Father?"

The priest's eyes softened. He looked away from the group around the table and his shoulders starting shaking up and down. He appeared to be laughing. Professor Orloff was about to ask what was so funny, when they all realized he was crying quietly. His entire body seemed to be shuddering with the realization of the situation. It was apparent that the priest was unable to cope with the magnitude of what was happening.

"Maybe you should just tell us what is going on, Father." The calm voice of Professor Orloff seemed out of place between the priest's shudders and the dramatic aftereffects of the vision Amanda had just experienced. When he received no response from the priest, the professor turned toward Amanda.

"Amanda, can you shed some light?"

Amanda looked up from the table, trying to catch her breath, and put together the pieces of the vision that had flashed before her. "I saw children, and churches, much like one of my visions before. There were so many different churches, and there was fire, and screaming." She stopped to think back and closed her eyes for a few seconds. "What or who is Gavriel?"

Father Kristofferson looked surprised at first, then just tired. He nodded. His shudders had stopped, although his words were jittery. "The gift you have must be difficult to manage. I can't imagine the responsibility you feel." His voice was almost a whisper.

"Actually, I think you can imagine what Amanda is going through right now, Father. You do have a conscience, don't you?" Jake was holding out the wooden object toward the priest. The symbol caught the small amount of light the room offered, and the markings seemed to light up. "Why don't you answer Amanda's question? Who is this Gavriel?"

"Well, I can tell you symbolically who he is," Professor Orloff jumped in to fill the void between the two men. "Gavriel is the Hebrew version of Gabriel. The archangel, one who brings light to darkness. The name means 'God's able-bodied one' or 'hero of God.' Is that who he is?"

Father Kristofferson placed both his hands palm down on the table and seemed to be trying to gain inner fortitude, perhaps trying to draw strength from the table itself. Jake walked over and placed the object on the table directly in front of the priest.

"Father, the symbols separated stand for Christ, or Christianity, and the end. Together, they could mean the end of Christianity. Is this something that God's hero would do, or is it the irony of the name that is being played here?" Jake was pacing behind the priest's chair as he spoke. "I am not sure this is something that Cardinal Roland is fully aware you are involved in."

The priest slammed his fist on the table, and Amanda's already racing heart jumped. "Keep Samuel out of this! He has nothing to do with any of this. He would never allow it to get this far. He has forgiven."

Amanda caught Jake's eye and raised eyebrow. She shrugged slightly, just enough for him to understand she didn't know what the priest was talking about.

"What about the burning churches? Is this something that is really going to happen? If so, how?" Jake continued his pacing. "And does this Gavriel person have a tattoo on the back of his hand, one that looks exactly like the carving on that piece?"

"As I have said, and your wife has acknowledged, it's too late, Jake. The events have already begun. We cannot in any way stop what is happening. The churches will burn, people will die, and it's the fault of those we all trusted in the first place. This is much bigger than you can imagine. I am only glad that . . ."

Amanda looked up, "Father, it's too late for that, too."

"What?" His eyes met hers.

"You were going to say that you were only glad that Samuel wasn't here to witness all of this. Or to understand the full scope of the situation, something to that effect anyway."

"How? How did you know?"

"Don't ask." Jake continued, "And she's right. It's too late. Cardinal Roland is on a plane, about to land very soon in Chicago."

The look on Father Kristofferson's face was a mix of confusion and terror. Amanda couldn't help but feel sorry for him. No matter how much he was involved in this disaster, the magnitude of which they still didn't fully comprehend, she could tell that he had once been a good man and probably still was.

She was watching him and thinking this, when the priest leaned forward to touch the wooden relic. And as he did, she caught a glimpse of an object hanging from a leather string on his neck. *A cross, a wooden cross. Oh, God.*

CHAPTER 53

ELISE WAS PUTTING THE FINISHING TOUCHES ON HER FACE, USING makeup to cover the bruise on her cheek and nose. *Nicely done!* She heard the sound of the garage door opening. Her hand froze mid-stroke. *It can't be . . . He hasn't come home at this time of the day for years. It's not possible.*

Just as she was thinking this, she remembered the crushed medication. She had left it on the counter to use when she returned home with the groceries. The thought that Stanford might come home this early never even crossed her mind. What could have happened to cause him to come back? Maybe he wanted to finish her off this time. The punishments, he decided, were not enough for the late dinner last night. Or he was just done with her overall. The thoughts were flying around nonstop in her head. What should she do? She could feel her mouth go completely dry. How would she explain the powder mixture? Maybe he wouldn't see it. Maybe it was Josh coming home. Perhaps he forgot something. Although that was almost less likely than Stanford skipping work.

Her thoughts were reeling to the point of dizziness when she decided it had been some time since the garage door opened. Maybe it was her imagination. She decided the only way to know for sure was to head down.

She finished by smudging some lip gloss over her dry cracked lips and grabbing a sweater. She quietly slid down the carpeted stairs, one at a time, until she got to the bottom. Then she inched her way toward the kitchen. Glancing from side to side she didn't see anyone. She moved fully into the kitchen and stared over at the counter where she had left the powder mixture. It was gone. Her stomach sank.

She felt more than heard someone directly behind her. She spun around quickly, slipping in her stockinged feet. She barely recovered to face Stanford. "Looking for this?" He asked as he held the small marble bowl in his outstretched hand. "Now, what were you planning to do with this concoction, Elise?" He put the bowl up to his nose and sniffed. "Smells medicinal."

"No . . . nothing . . ." She was stammering, "I wa . . . was just trying to take something to ease . . . th, the, headache, uh, pain . . . from my nose bleed. I read it on the Internet."

"I don't know, Elise . . ." Stanford sounded different to her. She wasn't sure what it was. His voice was strained. It was off pitch, higher than normal. "I think you have gone through an awful lot of trouble to just create a more potent dose, don't you? It seems a little overkill."

"I . . . I just wasn't thinking straight, Stanford."

"Oh, Elise. Please, don't even try. . . I mean, I found the bottles in the garbage. Don't you give me any credit?"

Elise glanced around the kitchen. *Was he actually waiting for an answer?*

Before she could think of what to say, he took three quick steps toward her. She put her hands up just in time to partially block the marble mortar as it came down against the left side of her head. Powder flew everywhere, and she stumbled backward, reaching up to feel the area on her head that was hit. There was a warm, sticky substance flowing between her fingers down the left side of her head. Her vision was partially blurred, as blood ran into her eye, and she felt dizzy. He had never hit her with so much force or caused so much damage before. She was confused and trying to grasp the reality of what was happening.

Her back touched the counter, as she continued to move out of his reach. The fridge was on one side and the sink on the other. She knew that directly behind her was the wooden knife holder, the kind with those really sharp blades you can buy on TV. *Is it Ginsu knives?* It seemed important to remember what they were called for some reason.

Stanford was coming toward her, the mortar still held up high. He wasn't done with her yet. *This is it. He's going to kill me after all.* All she could hear was Josh's voice in her head. *Stop being such a coward and fight for yourself. There isn't much time left. At least end it with some dignity.* She grabbed frantically behind her. Blood was streaming over her left eye, so she closed it and focused with her right eye. She pulled the knife out from behind her with her right hand as Stanford was now within striking range. He lifted the mortar high to bring it down hard. And as he did, she ducked to the right and speared the knife forward with all her might. He missed her head, but the mortar crushed down on her left shoulder. The crack was audible as her arm went limp. Her face was sprayed with blood as she crumbled to the floor. She lost consciousness.

It seemed like a long time before she was able to move, to open her eyes, and wipe the blood away. The blood had coagulated and was thick. She couldn't move her left arm or shoulder. She managed to roll and push herself to a seated position. As she looked down at herself, she realized she was covered in blood, a lot of it. The searing pain from her shoulder and head was unbearable, but she forgot the pain when she looked over and saw the eyes of her dead husband. His face turned sideways toward her, planted against the hardwood floor. His dark eyes could no longer see, and the knife protruded from under him. He was lying in a pool of blood that ran the length of the floor and was just starting to soak into the edge of the carpet leading into the living room.

CHAPTER 54

THEY HAD A WONDERFUL RELATIONSHIP. THEY WERE IN LOVE, and they spent almost all their time together. As young priests in the program, it was easy to justify their outings and service to the community. They felt they could be themselves and worked as a team to do good work. Because they were deacons in the church, no one questioned their commitment to each other.

Then came that terrible day, when everything changed. A visiting bishop caught them. It was a complete and terrible accident. They were in their dorm looking at the relics they had just started to collect. Their room door was slightly ajar, and Michael had reached over and stroked Samuel's cheek with his hand. Samuel caught his hand and gave it a kiss. They were startled by a cough in the hallway, and standing there, looking at them sternly, was Bishop Solomon.

They were summoned to his interim office. He was there for only a few days, but he came back on his own several times to visit them after that day.

"You realize that you both will be expelled from the Church for your sinful behavior today?" His eyes were slits as he looked at them with disgust.

"Please, Bishop," Michael started.

The bishop held his hand up to stop Michael. "I don't want to hear your story or excuses. I want you both to meet with me to discuss this further. I may be able to help you."

"We would be grateful. The Church is our life." Samuel's voice quavered as he spoke. Although he wondered how the bishop would be able to help them. What kind of help? He hoped it wouldn't be months of counseling regarding their sexual orientation. No counseling could change that.

The bishop wrote down an address and held the paper out to Michael, who took it. "Meet me here, tonight at 9:30."

Michael did not recognize the address but noted it was at the north end of the city, which was not a part of town he would expect the bishop to be staying, or even know of. They would have to take public transportation to get there. He wasn't sure why the bishop would want to meet there.

It was dark when they arrived at the address, which was a small, worn, seedy-looking motel. They were in street clothes, so they were not too out of place. They started walking toward the front office of the motel. There was nobody on the surrounding streets. The parking lot was empty, except for two run-down vehicles parked at the far end.

"Are you sure this is the place?" Samuel sounded nervous, even scared.

"Yes, and I know it doesn't make sense." Michael was starting to wonder what was really going on when they heard something close by. They both turned toward the sound.

A shadow moved out from the corner of the building. It was dark. At first they were afraid it could be a mugger or someone who meant them harm, or maybe a junkie looking to score. Then they heard the voice of Bishop Solomon.

"This way." He turned, and they followed him to Room 24. As they entered, they could see the bishop was in regular clothing as well. He locked the door behind them. Michael noted the room was dimly lit, and all the blinds were drawn.

"Bishop Solomon, I am not sure what is going on here, but I think we should—" The bishop cut Michael off. "Should what? Take this to the archbishop or the head of your school? You will both be expelled. Is that what you want?"

"No." Samuel spoke softly. "Bishop, please, no, my family, they wouldn't understand."

The bishop walked over to Samuel and put his hand on his shoulder. "It's okay, Samuel. I understand. We won't let anyone know about this. It's our secret, but you have to do something for me then."

Michael pushed the bishop's hand off Samuel's shoulder as he realized where this was going. "What are you doing? You're sick."

"No, I am trying to reason with you both. I will keep your secret, but I have my needs as well. Satisfy me, and you can go on with your little love affair and nobody will know a thing."

Michael was incensed. "What do you think you're doing? You call us sinful and wrong. What you are trying to do is far worse. Why wouldn't we just report you to the archbishop?"

"Michael, really? Do you think the archbishop will believe you after I put in a report of what I found the two of you doing in your room? Don't you think he would believe me when I say you are lying, since I caught you in the act?"

Samuel looked terrified, and Michael couldn't think of how he could make the bishop change his mind.

The bishop looked up almost kindly at Michael. "Listen, I have been an upstanding member of the church for over twenty years now. It's my word against yours. Think about it. This is easily solved."

Michael hung his head. He couldn't think of a way out. They were both so young. They weren't experienced in dealing with these kinds of situations and wouldn't know what their rights would or wouldn't be. He knew that everything about their relationship would be frowned upon and that their lives would never be the same if the bishop were to report them. The lives they had hoped to create, their commitment to the Church, it would all be over. They would be humiliated. Michael also knew how cruel and unfair life was. They had no choice. "Okay, but not Samuel."

Samuel looked over at Michael, shocked. "No, Michael. You can't."

"We have no choice, Sammy." Michael glared at the bishop, who was considering the offer.

"Agreed."

"Samuel, go home." Michael gritted his teeth as he said this.

"I won't leave you, Michael."

"Sammy, go now!"

The anger in Michael's voice stung Samuel. He slowly moved to the door and closed it behind him. He stood and stared at the closed door for an eternity, imagining the humiliation that Michael was being subjected to. He finally turned, as angry tears burned his cheeks, and started walking toward the bus stop. More thoughts of what would happen to Michael started to manifest in his head. He had to squeeze these thoughts out of his mind, or he would go crazy. At that moment he felt a searing hatred for the Church, for God, and everything in between.

* * *

Samuel Roland woke to the static-sounding voice on the overhead speakers of the plane. "We are starting our initial descent into the Chicago area. The flight crew will be coming through to collect any items you have for disposal . . ."

He sat up from his slumped position and realized his face was damp. He quickly wiped the tears from his face and dried his cheeks with a napkin, getting a concerned look from the young lady next to him.

CHAPTER 55

IT WOULD BE SIMPLE. THAT'S WHAT WORKED BEST. AS SOON AS A plan got elaborate, things started to go wrong. The domino effect worked because of the time zones. Everyone had their instructions. It was all confirmed via Twitter; "#done" was the code. There was one that was missing—no response—but they couldn't expect 100 percent. After all, mail can get lost. They had done the majority of the important communication via snail mail. But they had to coordinate the final parts of such a massive attack using something more immediate.

Gavriel allowed this thought to linger only for a second, about what might have happened to the one who did not report in. Were those instructions not received, or did they lose one of their disciples? How would that affect the outcome? It wouldn't affect it at this point. There was no stopping it now. Nobody was going to own up to being a part of this, and it was too far-reaching to stop it all, regardless.

The papers looked so delicate, suddenly inadequate for the massive responsibility they held, and Gavriel felt too small to be part of such a grand plan. What would this accomplish? A grudge of an old priest finally being played out against the Church? To quiet the cry of a small boy being avenged by a brother who couldn't save him? So now we save the world for him? This was not going to do that. He knew it, but it would at least make a statement. A smile played on his lips. He didn't plan on being around to take the credit. He was going to make it happen, and then he was going to be with his brother once more.

He glanced up at the clock. It was time to get going. They were using their smartphones for timing. No watches. They couldn't be off even by minutes. Not if he was going to use the old beliefs to make this work. The mix of ancient and new was interesting to him. The scheme would not have worked if they had no purpose, something every business school would teach you these days. In order to get your team to buy in and reach their goals, they had to have purpose. Yet purpose was still tied into the old-school belief of religion where people just had faith, believing in something they could not see or touch, but only feel within themselves. If you could successfully tie it all together in a gathering, then you had a following, a cult, a tribe. A true congregation. You couldn't break that loyalty.

How else could you get a group of seemingly innocent people to blow up churches? To put others in harm's way? To have a greater cause and believe that human life is secondary? This was where the years of gathering, sculpting, and planning came in. Josh was key. He had a natural ability to lead. The rest of the Chicago group was loyal to him, and he was loyal to Father Kristofferson. *Kristofferson is a marionette, and his strings are controlled. I make the ultimate call on this. I will make the ultimate sacrifice.* He looked up and slowly closed his eyes. *If there is a God, he is about to meet the brother of the little boy he took, without cause or need. If there is a God, he will regret his obvious ignorance and apathy toward Anthony.*

Gavriel opened his eyes slowly. He allowed them to adjust to the light while gathering the papers off the floor, rolling them up and fastening each end with a rubber band. He headed to the door, switched the light off, and felt a small sting in his gut. He stopped and wanted to turn around, to take one more look at the small room he spent so many years living in. To take one more look at the crisp sheets and warm blanket he had so lovingly put on his brother's bed. He blinked once and closed the door behind him. He didn't know if everything would go as planned. All he knew was, either way, he wasn't coming back.

CHAPTER 56

"WHAT DO YOU MEAN, YOU'RE IN?" JOSH MOVED TO PUT SOME distance between himself and Olivia. She didn't appreciate the tone or the stern look on his face.

"Well, I mean, I am in. I want to help, to be part of the Inner Circle. Tell me what I can do to help the plan be successful."

"Olivia, this isn't some kind of junior achievement high school project. This is the real deal. This is something that you can go to jail for, just for even knowing about it. Worse case, you can end up dead."

Olivia's eyes were glazed. She seemed to be looking at something else, something inside of herself. Josh grabbed her by the shoulders and gave her a gentle shake.

"Olivia, are you hearing me?" His voice went an octave higher. "This isn't a game, and I don't have time for this."

"Josh, I get it." Her gaze returned his with full force. "I know what you are saying, and I understand the risks. My life is not worth anything, if it's not worth doing this. I hate what I am, what they have made me become. If God exists, then he wouldn't want me sitting back and letting a few do what so many of us need to do. Spending my life with my mom is like living a lie. She doesn't want to face what happened, because she can't handle it. She would have to believe that our faith allows things like this to go unpunished, and that is okay. No matter which way she deals with it, it wouldn't be the right way, so she lives in limbo. I have to live with it, too. Every day of my life, and I am just done." Her voice trailed off, and Josh looked at her. Olivia's voice might have softened, but her expression was one of pure determination.

Josh nodded reluctantly. "The rest of the team has already been assigned their tasks. They are being deployed throughout Chicago. The remaining events will take place around North America, in major cities. We thought about a global rollout, but that was too dangerous, would take too long, and had too many moving parts. We thought smaller, but with greater impact, works better."

"How do they know when and what to do?" Olivia was now curious and surprised at the magnitude of the initiative.

"Believe it or not, handwritten letters." He could tell she was stunned.

"But that would have taken months to orchestrate."

"Actually years." Now he had her attention for sure. "Years ago, when we first started planning this, it was to make a statement against the Catholic Church. Somehow the best recruits ended up being young people, in some cases, children. More specifically, children who had a chip on their shoulder and needed to use all their pent-up anger to lash out, to get some kind of acknowledgment for their issues and feelings." She nodded, encouraging him to continue.

"Well, I told you about my situation, not nearly as gruesome as most. In fact, I can't even compare, but I understand. The real catalyst is Gavriel. He has some really rough history behind him, and I don't even know all the details, but I do know he is a true activist and is willing to do to what he needs to do to ensure the plan happens as it should. Gavriel is probably the best person to lead this." Josh's face darkened. "He is also the most dangerous, because nothing else matters to him."

"The letters?" she asked quizzically. "How did you know who to target and who would keep it quiet?"

"Well, we had to take a chance on a few things. We started it with a website. It was set up as a safe place for kids to connect with other kids from abusive homes. The site has been shut down for a couple of years now, but it allowed us to get profiles of hundreds of kids who needed an outlet."

He slowly rubbed his hands together. He took another look at her, wondering if he should disclose any more information. *Who is she, really? And more importantly, can I trust her? It really doesn't matter now anyway. It's done.*

"We profiled and filtered until we felt we had a good group from thirty-three different metropolitan areas. The number thirty-three is significant, because it has to do with Gavriel's beliefs in the Mesopotamian timing to 2012, the end of the clock, or the end of time. I know it all sounds crazy, but he has a plan. And frankly, I am not religious. I don't believe in any of it, but I believe in the cause, the bigger picture. I also believe that if it does nothing else, it puts the Church under some kind of microscope when it comes to who did this and why."

"You look tired." Her voice seemed to come from inside his head.

He nodded. "I am."

CHAPTER 57

"IF GAVRIEL IS LEADING THIS THING, THEN WE HAVE TO STOP
Gavriel. Isn't that the answer, Father?" Jake's voice seemed to boom through
the room. There had been a rather long and thick silence that followed the
realization that Samuel Roland would be in Chicago shortly. Things seemed
to be falling apart for Michael Kristofferson.

Michael raised his head slowly. "Why is Samuel coming here? Who asked
him to come? This is all wrong. He could get hurt. He was safe in Rome."

"Nobody asked him. It was his decision. He is very concerned about you,
Father, and I am sure you knew there was a possibility that he might come."

"No, well, I guess he would come. We were once very close, and well,
that was a long time ago. Is there any way you can meet him? Stop him from
seeing me? Anything to convince him to go back to Rome?"

"I doubt we have that kind of influence, Father." Amanda was getting
impatient. "We are running out of time here. What is the plan? You say we
are too late, but too late for what? Can you tell us where Gavriel is and what
his intentions are? Is this at all stoppable, or do you even want to stop it?"

"I don't know. I just don't know how we can. It is now beyond the
point of one person or even one city." He stopped abruptly, realizing what
he just revealed.

Professor Orloff stepped in. "Father, are you saying that something will happen in more than one city? Where? How many? Do you know if people will get hurt and if Amanda's visions are correct?"

Amanda's eyes strayed down to the wooden cross hanging around the priest's neck. If her visions were correct, Father Kristofferson would be part of the casualties. She felt terrible knowing this. There must be a way to stop all this.

"Why don't you tell us what you do know?" Jake was no longer in a mood to play games. "You know that this is wrong. You know that perhaps there is a way to stop all this. You don't want any more innocent people to be hurt. There has been enough pain, don't you think?" Jake was hoping to hit a chord with the priest. To reach something deep within him that might cause him to give this all up.

Father Kristofferson sighed deeply. "Then you are right. We have to convince Gavriel. I just don't think that is possible. He has his mind set. Over the past few months, I have had second thoughts about our plans, about what impact it would really have, and about whether it would it be worth the sacrifices that would have to be made." He paused to take a deep breath. "It was like talking to a statue. He did not blink when I mentioned that many innocent people and children would be hurt by our intentions. I don't think he is going to change his mind."

"Then it's not about convincing him, is it?" Professor Orloff gave them all a knowing look. "We just have to stop him."

They all knew the professor was right, even if it meant permanently stopping Gavriel, but they also knew they had to somehow stop the rest. The plan had already been put into motion.

"What about the police?" The professor was matter of fact. "Can't we have them arrest Gavriel and prevent all this from materializing? After all, there has to be a trigger or something, right?"

The priest looked up, "Professor, what would you tell the police? What proof do we have? What can you actually charge Gavriel with? The reality is that this is all going to happen, and it starts today with those fires. Then there are eight more days of tyranny, and perhaps some will be stopped but some won't. Don't you see the worst will happen today?" He seemed done, but then continued, "We have to stop the start. It's too late for the police. We have to stop it now."

"How do we do that?" The professor sounded hopeless, although he was trying to be positive.

"Josh could do it." The priest spoke in a whisper.

"Who's Josh?" The professor perked up.

CHAPTER 58

SHE TOOK HIS HAND. "LET'S GET GOING. WHAT NEXT?"

Josh stood and stretched. He felt like he had been sitting in the same position for years. He wasn't just tired, he was worn down. All this time he had a vision, a purpose; he had nothing to lose. He thought about Elise. "Mom." He said the word out loud, and Olivia gave him a strange look.

He turned to look at her. "My mom, Elise, she never had a chance. Since I was little I could see what was going on. I hated her for not being strong, for not standing up for herself. I should have helped her." He sat back down and put his face in his hands and cried. He couldn't remember the last time he cried, not since he was very small. He didn't remember when Olivia had put her arms around him, or for how long she had been holding him while he cried. The release felt good.

"I have to go home and tell her. Tell her to leave him. She only stayed because of me. She could have had a life. It's all my fault."

"We make our own choices, Josh. Even I know that. Let's finish this. It's too late for regret. Do it for your mom. God didn't help her either."

He looked at her and nodded. They had little time to get things in order. The rest of the Inner Circle would meet in this very room in a few hours. They were headed toward the door when they heard something. Someone was coming. They froze.

*   *   *

He was exhausted, and although he did manage to sleep a bit on the plane, his dreams were filled with memories of his awful past. His mind swam with pictures of the days with Michael, the bishop who ruined their lives, and the hardships that fueled their hatred for the Church. He thought of the many years they planned to get their revenge, and then how the hatred softened over all that time, in his heart at least. Time does heal, if one allows it to.

Samuel knew that Michael was not as determined to do the things they spoke of in the past. He, too, had let time do its thing. But there was something else or someone else that had control now. He heard it every time they spoke. He could read it between the lines of his emails. Michael was careful never to speak or write directly about his intentions, nor was he negative toward the Church during those communications, but Samuel knew. He heard it in the intonations, the fake laughter, and the underlying emotions of every syllable. There was a burden greater than he ever wanted to imagine, and soon he was going to find out everything.

He grabbed his bag from the overhead compartment and passed the young lady's bag to her. She smiled once more, enchantingly, perhaps longingly, at him. He gave her one of his best smiles. "I am sorry if I disturbed you. I have been having fitful dreams of late." His English was perfect.

"Oh, that's quite all right. I thought you only spoke Italian, or I would have been far more conversational. Sorry about that." Her eyelashes fluttered.

"Not at all. Thank you for allowing me to rest. I needed it."

"First time in Chicago?" She wanted to keep the conversation going as they waited to disembark. "I know a really great place for a late-afternoon cocktail, if you are interested."

She was really quite pretty, he thought. Perhaps he had been too unkind in his purposeful dismissal of her on this trip. It wasn't her fault she was attracted to him and was simply trying to be cordial. He gave her no indication of being unavailable. He had no ring, and he wasn't wearing his robes and collar. Should he tell her?

"I would love to, but unfortunately I am previously engaged for another appointment. However if I were to meet anyone for a drink, and perhaps more . . ." he said with a wink, "it would definitely be you. Has anyone told you how stunningly beautiful you are? You must hear it all the time."

She was beaming. He had done well. "Perhaps another time." She said it with the tone of someone who knew it was not meant to be but appreciated his comments.

"Perhaps . . ." he turned and started walking down the aisle with the rest of the departing passengers.

As he waited to pass through customs, he thought about whether it was right to act the way he did with the young lady on the plane. He felt obligated after being so unsociable during the flight, and he felt God would forgive the suggestions he made. After all, he left her in a much better mood than she would have been in if he had offered the truth or said nothing. That would have been a far less charitable way of handing the situation.

He only had his carry-on, as he planned to be in Chicago for just a few days. Just long enough to see Michael and put an end to all these senseless ideals.

They were going to expose the Church for all it truly was. The power it used to influence believers was the same power it used to abuse those who had committed themselves to the Church. For years, he and Michael had been collecting recordings of the abuse. They wrote down the types of encounters, times and dates, and on many occasions took tiny recording devices in. Yes, they had plenty of proof, and they needed to wait until one of them got to a position of power and influence, as Samuel had now. They were going to expose and embarrass the Church for letting these things happen and for turning a blind eye. They both knew the consequences would be dire. Especially because they planned to send it out to the media. They also planned to announce the fact that they were gay, and let that piece of news hit the Catholic Masses at the same time, especially since Samuel was working out of the Vatican.

But now it all seemed so inconsequential, and Samuel was determined to convince Michael that they had gone too far. It was no longer impactful and would be just an embarrassment. Yes, it would be an embarrassment to the Church but also to them. They would have to leave their posts and wouldn't be able to help anyone with the same resources they had now. They would, in fact, be doing more harm than good at the end of it. The Church was a giant. This was not David and Goliath. They wouldn't win this one.

Samuel knew, however, that something had changed with the plans. Something more was going on. He was no longer privy to all the information, and what he sensed was danger. Something more terrible than the original intent, and he just couldn't put his finger on it. The symbol on the piece he gave Jake and Amanda was their logo, in a sense, from when they first embarked on the mission to bring down the organization. He hoped that sending it with the Bannons would at least give Michael a reason to pause whatever else he might have in the works.

He had no issues at customs. He never did. Cardinals were often treated with little to no suspicion and would actually make quite good terrorists. He stopped dead in his tracks. *No, it can't be.* Suddenly, his blood ran cold. He had a dizzying feeling in the pit of his stomach that slowly started to rise. What was wrong with him? He couldn't imagine Michael getting involved in something that drastic. He suddenly felt sick. There was bile coming up his throat and into his mouth. He frantically searched for a restroom and spotted one twenty feet away. He ran toward it, getting there just in time.

CHAPTER 59

ELISE CRAWLED ACROSS THE FLOOR, CAREFULLY AVOIDING HER dead husband's body, and made her way into the foyer. *I have to get out of here. I have to find Josh . . . No, the police will come. How would they know?* Thoughts were flying around her head, and she was dizzy with the pain from her wounds. She could call the police. They would believe her. It was self-defense, or was it? She had planned to drug her husband and hopefully kill him anyway, so she really was the guilty one, no matter which way she positioned it. She started to sob. What was she going to do? What if Josh came home and saw his father dead, blood all over? What would he think of her then?

Oh, God! What have I done? I have to leave and then call the police! I need time to think.

Stanford had driven the Escalade, so it would be parked in the garage. She searched for the keys, but her left arm hung dead. It was useless, broken at the shoulder, she assumed. Her adrenaline had kicked in, and although the pain was intense, she fought through it. She had to.

She looked around. Draped over the chair in the foyer was his long coat and briefcase. This was an indication of how irritated he must have been when he got home. He never left his coat lying around. It was always hung up neatly in the closet. The keys must be in his coat pocket. On her knees now, she made it to his coat and rifled through the pockets. There was nothing. She glanced at the briefcase. Perhaps they were in there. She opened it and sifted through the contents, finally dumping it upside down on the chair. Falling to the ground and landing next to her was a white envelope. She picked it up and examined it closely. It was sealed. The address was handwritten, and it was going to Florida. Was it Stanford's writing? She didn't think so. It was hard to tell. Everything was done on the computer these days. She rarely saw anything handwritten anymore. The only exception for her was her journal. She didn't write in it every day, but on occasion she documented anything that was eventful, like birthdays, and if she had a good day with one of her charitable endeavors. But mostly she wrote about the dark room and the punishments. She hid the book in the closet above the torn dresses. She knew Stanford would not look or even be concerned with her personal items.

She was curious about the letter. Even with his dead body in the next room, she felt anxious at the thought of opening up his mail. "Fuck you, Stanford!" she yelled at the corpse. She was never allowed to open the mail. She was never part of anything he did, in business or otherwise. *What if this was a letter to a girlfriend? What if he was having an affair? I have a right to know.* She felt a huge justification, and freedom, as his blood continued to soak into her expensive Tai Ping carpet. She took the time to open up the letter.

As she read through, it she realized this was not from Stanford. *This was Josh. What did this mean?* She read further . . . *St. James Catholic Church . . . set bomb for . . .*

She couldn't believe what the letter suggested. *Not Josh. How could he possibly be involved in something like this? He wasn't capable of such destructive thoughts, was he?* Then she gazed over at her husband's limp body. *I guess we are all capable of something we could never imagine.*

She didn't know what she should do next. According to the letter there was still time. It was to start today at 5:00 p.m. Where could Josh be? He hung out at that church with that priest all the time. He might be there, or the priest would know where he was. She had to find him. *Where are those damn car keys?!* She glanced back over at Stanford. *Oh, God.* She realized where they were. Barely hanging out of his trouser pocket was a set of keys. She caught a glimpse of the Escalade fob. She made her way slowly back toward his body, dreading having to touch her husband one last time.

CHAPTER 60

"YOU KNOW HE'S LANDED, DON'T YOU?" AMANDA CALMLY STATED. "He will be on his way here to see you shortly."

Father Kristofferson looked like he had aged ten years in the last ten minutes. "We have to get to Gavriel before Samuel gets to us. We have to find Josh. He is the key to stopping the events that will unfold across the country."

"Do you know where either of them are?" Amanda sensed someone was close by. She just didn't know who.

"Come with me." The priest stood up quickly and headed toward the room across from them. They all stood up and followed. A little apprehensive, Amanda grabbed hold of Jake's hand. He gave her a quizzical look but held her hand tight. Her dream was coming back clearly to her: Jake bleeding and her screaming. She wasn't going to let him out of her sight.

The room was small and cramped, with little light. His bed was on one side. This was obviously where Father Kristofferson slept, perhaps lived, as Samuel Roland had described. The room was empty. What was he going to show them here? They were all thinking the same thing when the priest walked over to his desk and slipped his fingers underneath the edge. They heard a soft CLICK, and then the priest walked over and slid the door open.

A secret doorway. Great. Just when things couldn't get any more complicated. Amanda tried hard not to think of where this was leading. She only hoped she wouldn't have any more visions, unless they were good ones, which never seemed to happen. Her visions were determined to show her terrible situations, constantly putting her in a position of responsibility. All too often, it ended up being a matter of life and death. For once, she would like to see a happy ending. Not that those didn't happen, but it seemed she was not destined to predict good fortune. Instead, she was given an indication of things that could be changed. An optimist would look at it as an opportunity to correct a bad situation, but frankly, Amanda was getting tired of all these opportunities.

The stairs were immediately in front of them. The priest walked down without even looking. The rest of them slowly made their way, checking their footing to ensure they didn't slip on the narrow steps. Father Kristofferson had brought a small flashlight, and they followed him single file down the stone corridor.

"What is this place?" Jake asked in a hushed voice. He wasn't sure why they needed to be quiet. It just seemed like the right thing to do.

He was surprised when Amanda, not Father Kristofferson, responded. "It's a labyrinth of tunnels that runs under the majority of the city, about sixty miles of it. It was built in the early 1900s until the company constructing it for an underground system went bankrupt in 1909. The tunnels continued to be used as a means to transport coal and other goods for many years. In 1992, one of the tunnels was damaged during a flood, and most of the other tunnels became flooded and useless. Also, due to all the terrorist threats, the majority of the tunnels have been plugged and are believed to be inaccessible."

Jake was impressed. "Where did you get those tidbits of information?"

"The Chicago Cultural Center. Before I jumped. The pictures I took were of the tunnels. I thought it was interesting, because they ran all over the city, including from under the Cultural Center to right here under this church. It seemed coincidental enough not to be significant, if you know what I mean."

"Amanda's correct," Father Kristofferson continued. "Most of the system was damaged. However, a few of the tunnels stayed intact. And in some areas, there were more than just tunnels. A few were offshoots that opened up to the most beautiful and majestic caverns. Some of the world's best spelunking can be done there. Of course, nobody really knows about any of it. We have used them as an underground meeting place for years."

"Father, this specific tunnel runs in two directions. One branches off toward Lincoln Park and from there to the city, where it also has a shoot that extends to the Cultural Center."

The priest nodded in agreement with Amanda. "Yes, you are correct, and the incident at the center, which I am sure you have already concluded, was not an accident."

"I am guessing that was Gavriel's handiwork?" She didn't have to wait for an answer. It was apparent from the look on his face.

They continued down the tunnel in silence, making their way toward the meeting place of the Inner Circle.

CHAPTER 61

"DID YOU HEAR THAT?" OLIVIA'S VOICE WAS SHAKY. "IS THERE another way out?"

Josh had heard the faint click of the door that accessed Father Kristofferson's room. He was so familiar with the sound, he knew someone had triggered the secret entrance and was coming. Then they heard the voices, muffled, but definitely coming toward them.

He was sure he heard Father Kristofferson's voice, but he didn't want to take the chance and wait to find out. Perhaps the priest was trying to warn him. "Let's go." Josh grabbed her hand, and they headed into the next section of the cavern that led to the huge expanse with the large opening that dropped to nowhere. "We can take the tunnel back to Lincoln Park and try and meet up with the rest of the gang at the Gathering. That's where most of them would come from tonight anyway."

They were running at almost full speed down the tunnel. It was dimly lit with some battery-powered LED lights that he had installed a few months earlier. It had been too difficult to continue to maneuver the tunnels in complete darkness, even though they were quite wide at six feet across and seven and a half feet high. He had thought it would be safer, at least until the job was done, to keep the tunnels lit. They were moving along quite nicely when Josh stopped so suddenly that Olivia ran right into his back, and they both stumbled forward onto the hard floor. Josh's right knee made a cracking noise as they hit the ground.

Standing in front of them, and the reason Josh stopped so abruptly, was Gavriel. Gavriel was holding his rolled up papers in one hand and a flashlight in the other. He shone the light directly on the pair. Josh shaded his eyes with his hand.

"Josh, is that you? And who do you have there with you?" Gavriel's voice was steely. Dangerous even, Josh thought.

"Gavriel, it's me, and I have a friend. Don't worry. We were just heading to the park to meet up with the rest, you know, as planned." Josh hoped his voice didn't give anything away.

"Running awfully fast weren't you? Something got you scared?"

"No, no, of course not. This is an important night. I wanted to get there on time."

"And who is this again with you? A friend?" He shone the flashlight directly on Olivia's face. She closed her eyes avoid the bright light but didn't turn away. "Quite lovely. I think I would have remembered her if she were one of the Inner Circle."

He's just talking about the Inner Circle like everyone knows what it is. What the hell? Josh wasn't sure why Gavriel would say anything. Gavriel didn't know how much Olivia knew. He was compromising himself and the mission.

"I think we should head back to the church, don't you?" His tone didn't leave any doubt. There were no options here. He meant to take them both back to the cavern. Josh wondered if he should tell him about the voices, that he could get caught, that there were outsiders in the tunnel. As he was thinking about what course of action would be best, Gavriel walked up to him and pulled out a small pistol from his pocket. "Josh, I am not asking. You have been an amazing asset to our little project here, but now I see you with someone who is new, not part of the plan, and I start to wonder if perhaps your loyalties are waning. Perhaps you no longer think what we are doing is for the benefit of all."

"Gavriel, you know that's not true. I was part of this even before you." He kept an eye on the small handgun in Gavriel's hand.

"That's right, but your loyalty has always been to the priest and not to the cause. At least that's what I could surmise. You're a weak link, Josh, and now you have dragged an innocent bystander into the fray."

Josh countered, "You're just as loyal to Father Kristofferson. He found you. You were broken, just like the rest of us. He fixed you and gave you a reason to live."

"He gave me cause to live, yes, and I am about to fulfill that purpose, and neither he nor you will stop me. Is that clear?"

"That wasn't the plan, Gavriel. We are all part of this." Josh was believable. "Olivia is a new recruit," he said as he nodded toward her. "I was taking her to the park to meet up with the rest, so we could move forward with the plans. She wanted to be a part of it."

Gavriel seemed to be contemplating Josh's words, putting it all together, weighing the situation to see if it fit. He looked over at Olivia who was nodding in agreement with what Josh had said. "Okay, Josh. You go. Leave her with me. When you come back with the rest of the crew, we can move forward."

Josh wasn't expecting this, and he felt worse when he saw the look of terror on Olivia's face. She didn't know Gavriel, and he was glad of it. He might be even worse than what she was imagining. Gavriel seemed to have been somehow destabilized. Josh knew he was different—that he was deliberate and focused—but he didn't think Gavriel was a threat to his own side. Now they weren't sure about anything, including what they were doing. Revolutions had a bloody history. This was a known fact, but did they have to be that way to be impactful? There were other ways, peaceful ways. Josh thought about Gandhi and Mandela, Martin Luther King, and, more recently, Aung San Suu Kyi.

"Yeah, no problem," Josh said calmly. He walked with a limp toward Gavriel. His knee was bleeding from the fall. He didn't think it was broken. It was probably just a hairline fracture judging by the apparent swelling that had started. He held out his hand and Gavriel took it firmly. He gave it a squeeze.

"Don't forget, brother, one wrong move, and there's one less beautiful face on the planet." Gavriel glanced toward Olivia. "After all, soon there will be explosions all over the country, just like the Fourth of July." He waved the papers in his hand as a reminder of the plans they had made together. "We planned it that way." Gavriel's smile was more of a sneer. Josh tried to pull his hand back, but Gavriel held on. "Wait, give me your cell phone, please." Josh sighed and handed over his cell phone like it didn't matter, but on the inside his guts twisted. He hoped to call the police once he was out of the tunnels. Cell phones didn't work down in the tunnels, and they wouldn't help Father Kristofferson, who was down in the cavern. But then again, the priest hardly ever carried his phone, so it was probably a moot point. Josh knew the code to stop the systematic stream of explosions that would rock the nation, and it had to be sent through a private tweet. He needed a cell phone.

He watched helplessly as Gavriel, holding Olivia by the arm, guided her back toward the cavern, Father Kristofferson, and whomever he had with him. Josh still didn't believe in God, but he said a silent prayer anyway.

CHAPTER 62

ELISE HATED GRABBING THE KEYS FROM HER DEAD HUSBAND'S
pocket, but it had to be done, for Josh's sake. She knew she was a mess and
didn't want to scare Josh with all the blood on her clothing. She put on a
long trench coat, then headed to the main foyer guest bathroom. She took
a warm cloth to scrub at the spray of blood on her face and neck. The plush,
cream-colored hand towel turned an ugly brownish pink as she worked
away. The blood on her wounds had started to coagulate, but it was apparent her head had been hurt quite badly. She carefully placed one of Josh's
ball caps on her head. Elise went back to the closet. She looked at the large
Prada bag that Josh gave her a few years ago for Christmas. She knew that
Stanford gave him the money to buy it, but it was still from Josh. She hadn't
used it, because she really had nothing to put in such a large bag. She stuffed
some Kleenex and Tylenol she took from the guest bathroom in the purse.
Then she swallowed four Tylenol dry and headed out.

As she made her way to the garage, she passed by the liquor cabinet. She
hadn't had a drink in a very long time. She grabbed the Louis VIII cognac
that had been given to them by one of Stanford's appreciative clients. It had
never been touched.

Elise managed to unscrew the cap, holding the bottle up with her good
arm and using her teeth. She held it to her lips, took a big swig, and almost

spat it back out as the liquid fire slid down her raw throat. She managed to swallow most of it, spilling a bit on the trench coat. It burned on the way down and then warmed her up from the inside. She had been parched. *Yes, this will do nicely*, she thought as she slipped it into her Prada bag. *I will definitely be needing medication for the trip.*

Elise slowly made her way on shaky legs to the garage. Her shirt was soaked at the shoulder, and blood continued to run down her arm. But the trench coat hid it to some degree. Only a few drops fell every now and then from her fingertips. She felt nothing. All she knew was that she had to get to Josh, to find out what was going on. If the letter was even remotely real, then her son was in a very dangerous predicament. He could end up in jail for the rest of his life. How could he conceivably be involved with such a shocking act of terrorism? This was domestic terrorism, and it had to be stopped.

She threw her bag on the passenger seat and then managed to pull herself up into the Escalade, using her right arm. She shuffled over, smearing blood from her injured left arm all over the door and seat. *Stanford is going to be really upset that I messed up the SUV. Wait. Stanford is never going to get upset at me again, is he?* A grin appeared on her face, and she felt a calm that she had never felt before, a peace like no other. No matter what happens to her going forward, Stanford couldn't hurt her anymore. She thought the consequences of her actions were well worth it, both for her and Josh.

She managed to get the SUV door closed, and then pressed each of the buttons on the built-in garage door opener in the Cadillac until the garage door opened. *Let's see. I used to drive when I was younger, before I married Shithead.* She slowly backed out. "Oops!" She didn't realize how wide the vehicle was. The right side mirror of the Cadillac ripped off the side of the car and was hanging down by its wires. She didn't think she needed that mirror anyway, so she backed out the rest of the way, then put the SUV in drive, and floored it. Tires squealed as she peeled out of the driveway. She could only drive with one hand. She was grateful it was an automatic, although she was thinking the challenge of a stick shift would have been fun. She felt giddy. *Old Town. It's been a long time . . . I always knew I would be back.*

CHAPTER 63

JOSH RAN AS FAST AS HE COULD, SQUINTING WITH PAIN AND HIS knee hindering him. He had been limping and running at the same time for about five minutes when he heard voices. He slowed to see Ryan, Kendra, and others coming toward him. He held up his hand to them, then bent over breathing hard. Ryan ran up to him. "Josh! You okay, man? What's going on?"

Josh tried to speak between breaths. "Gavriel . . . this is . . . all wrong. We . . . have to . . . have to . . ."

"Have to what?" said Ryan. He and the group gathered around Josh, disturbed and concerned by their leader's current state of distress.

"We have to stop the bombings!"

The group was stunned. In all the times they had spoken about the events to take place, they had never referred to it that way. It was so blunt, so unlike the heroic scenario they had imagined. It was like the magician revealing how the trick was really done. In short, it was extremely disheartening.

They all stood and stared. Josh caught his breath and realized he had to be "Josh the Leader." He had to get buy-in again for the total opposite of what he had been preaching to these young people for years. He took a deep breath and started, "I know what you must be thinking, and, trust me, I would be thinking the same thing. But I realized today, that it's not too late to stop this. If we do what we have been planning to do, that makes us no better than them. It makes us no better than those people who hurt us, took our innocence, gave us up for something that was more important to them. It makes us ruthless, just like the people who hurt us."

They were listening. He breathed a sigh of relief and continued. "We all love Father Kristofferson and would do anything for him, and that includes saving him from doing the wrong thing. Whether there is a God or not, what we are doing has nothing to do with religion, and it has nothing to do with righting a wrong, or ending the horrors of child abuse. Those things will continue to go on, as long as people are selfish and ignorant."

"So what are you saying, Josh?" Kendra's voice rang out strongly for such a small girl.

"I am saying that by bombing these churches we may be killing people who can make a difference, people like us who could stand up for those who can't stand up for themselves. I am saying we have no right to make that kind of statement. Don't you think each of us—and what has happened to us— already makes a statement? We should use that to help people. We should talk about our experience. We should share it, so that we bring awareness, not death."

"Josh . . . " It was Kendra again. *When did she become the voice of the group? Good for you, little Kendra. I am so proud of you.*

Kendra continued, "We all love Father Kristofferson, and yes, he saved us. But you were the one who gave us something to hold on to. You gave us meaning. You gave us a purpose, whether it was an elaborate plan to rock the world of Christianity or simply build a Lego castle. The fact is that none of us would have made it through those first years if you hadn't been part of our lives." Her beautiful, big blue eyes were brimming with tears. "We are here for you, so if you say it's off, then it's off."

He dropped to his knees, and there was a collective gasp. He had been their rock for so many years. A few of the members started to cry. They hated to see Josh like this. They were a family. Ryan walked over to help him up, but Josh stopped him. "No, Ryan. Help me by doing something else. How far are we away from cell coverage?"

CHAPTER 64

THEY ENTERED THE EMPTY CAVERN. FATHER KRISTOFFERSON WAS leading the way. Suddenly, he stopped, startled.

"Surprised, Father?" Gavriel was standing in the center of the room with the girl.

"Bring in your friends, Father. Please, introduce me." Gavriel's voice was bitter, and the priest feared that he was at the point of no return. In fact, he had known this was the case for some time now. Why he didn't stop this sooner was way beyond him.

Amanda, Jake, and Professor Orloff all made their way into the chamber. They were a bit surprised to see Gavriel, but were wondering more about the girl.

"Why, it's the Bannons. Nice to see you both again." Gavriel even seemed cordial. "And who have you brought here with you?"

"Oh, my name is Orloff. Professor Orloff. I am just here out of professional interest. I study rare historical artifacts and the sort. And you are . . . ?"

"And I am . . . the messenger of God."

"So you must be Gavriel then. You didn't formally introduce yourself when we first met," Amanda retorted.

"That's right, Amanda. But neither did you. Where's the trust?" He shrugged his shoulders and spread his hands out, revealing his weapon. "I can't image what you were doing at the Chicago Cultural Center either. You seem to somehow always be in the wrong place at the wrong time." He put his arms back down by his sides, the tattoo a dark stain on outside of his left hand.

"You know that tattoo you have doesn't exactly mean what you think it does," Amanda blurted out. Seeing the gun made her instinctively want to start a plan to distract the potential shooter. This was a negotiating tactic she was hoping would work.

His gun hand remained steady, but she saw the twitch in his eye, and her senses determined a shift in the air. Encouraged, she continued. "That's right. You did the research and you know the combined image means end of Christ, or end of Christianity, but do you know who created that image?"

He said nothing, but she could tell he was curious. "Father Kristofferson, did you want to expand on the symbolism that was created by you and Samuel?"

Gavriel glared at Father Kristofferson and waited. He was suddenly very interested in the background of the tattoo.

"Gavriel," the priest said as he moved toward his fallen charge, who raised his gun slightly. "That was never the symbol we made it out to be. It was nothing more than a bitter drawing made up by two young priests who were hurt by the system. It was never a real sign of things to come or our specific destiny. Nor was it created to signify the end of the religious beliefs that people have or will continue to have for the rest of time." He stopped a few feet away from Gavriel and continued.

"All our planning will have little to no impact on what we want it to affect. At the end of the day it could, in fact . . . it will end up strengthening the hold that the Church has. People would look to the Church for comfort and support after the events take place. That symbol we created was nothing more than—" he paused— "for lack of a better term, a logo for bitter revenge."

"No . . . no!" Gavriel's face twisted. "Liar!" The gun was now aimed at the priest.

Amanda, Jake, and the professor tensed up.

"You told me . . . you taught me this was a symbol of the end, and with the end is our beginning." Then his face softened somewhat. "What has happened to you, Father? Have they turned you against me and everything you made me believe? Against all your own beliefs and thoughts that—"

"Those were the thoughts of an angry man," Father Kristofferson interrupted, "who wanted to blame the world for his own issues and not face them head on like he needed to."

Gavriel bowed his head. When he lifted it, tears streaked his cheeks. He looked childlike, heartbroken. "I loved you like a father." His eyes darkened. "But we are not stopping this. It will come to pass, and it will change the world. It's not over. We have to finish it."

A loud blast echoed through the chamber unexpectedly. Amanda screamed "No!" as Father Kristofferson fell to the ground, a bullet from Gavriel's Beretta hitting the priest directly in the chest.

Olivia was shrieking, her hands over her ears, like she could have blocked the sound of the gunshot after it had already happened.

Jake ran over to the priest and gently lifted his head. Father Kristofferson was trying to speak. Jake put his head down to the priest's lips. "Don't let it happen, Jake," he whispered, "and tell Samuel I'm sorry . . ." With that the priest let out his final breath.

Professor Orloff stared at the dead priest. "Some way to treat someone who was like a father to you." He glared at Gavriel. Amanda placed her hand on the professor's shoulder, trying to keep him calm. Any wrong move could set Gavriel off. She felt for Father Kristofferson, but even more so for Samuel Roland. She knew he was on his way, and she was hoping he would avoid walking into this horrible situation. It would be bad enough when he found out Michael Kristofferson was dead, but he could end up dead, too. At least something must have changed in her premonitions. She remembered a priest with that wooden cross on his neck burning. This was definitely different from her vision.

Jake was wondering why he didn't bring his piece. *Why would I need a gun visiting a church?* This day was just not turning out the way they thought it would. They had brought the professor, hoping to convince Father Krist-offerson that the relic was not a "sign" and that he needed to thwart his own plans to end Catholicism. And in the end, he knew that anyway. Jake had no idea they would end up in this predicament. Sometimes he wished Amanda's visions were a little clearer.

"Why don't we go up into the church? I think we all need to do some confessing about now," Gavriel said sarcastically. "But before we get back into cell service, please, everyone, throw your cell phones over here. You too." He looked at Olivia, who slowly pulled her phone out of her back pocket and threw it on the floor in front of her. Jake and Amanda reluctantly dropped their phones onto the floor, too.

"What about you, Orloff? Throw it down!" Gavriel was pointing the gun at the professor.

"Don't carry a cell phone. Sorry, just never got with the times. You can search me if you like."

"Never mind. Just get moving." Gavriel pointed the gun out toward the way they came in.

"Can we take him with us?" Jake bent down to lift Father Kristofferson off the ground.

"No! He stays here, where he belongs." Gavriel's snarl even startled Jake.

"Okay, no problem." Jake slowly lowered the priest and undid the wooden cross at his neck, scrunching it tight into his fist as he laid the priest back down on the floor.

"Don't try anything like running out of here. Unless you want to be responsible for the death of this young lady." He squeezed Olivia's shoulder, and she yelped in pain. "Stay right in front of me. Don't let me lose sight of any of you, or else . . ."

They did as he said and slowly moved in single file back through the tunnel, up the stairs, and into Father Kristofferson's room. Then they entered the church sanctuary.

"All of you get in the first pew. Down on your knees, please."

They did as they were told.

"Now, if all goes as planned, we are going to hear about this in just a few hours. It will be big news. Fox, CNN, and the BBC will cover this. Not since 9/11 has there been something so carefully put together over such a long period of time. It's interesting how technology, or the lack thereof, has been the enemy."

Gavriel was walking across the altar, back and forth between the pulpit and the lectern, swinging the gun in their general direction as he spoke. Olivia was sobbing, and Amanda tried to console her. At the same time, she was thinking how to get out of the mess they had found themselves in.

Gavriel continued his sermon. "And these plans have been in the making for years, so don't think that a couple of last-minute hiccups, like yourselves, are going to make any difference to the outcome."

Jake caught Amanda's attention. He nodded toward the far side of the altar. She spotted a large bible, a wine goblet, and other small items used during service. She shot him a sarcastic look, as if to say, *Really? You plan to club him with a bible and then take a swig of wine to celebrate?*

He shook his head and widened his eyes. She took a more serious look that way, scanning the entire area, then almost gasped out loud when she saw Samuel Roland crouched in the corner, watching Gavriel strut across the altar preaching the coming of Armageddon. *Oh shit. Not the making of another saint.* She had felt the presence of Samuel Roland, but she hoped it was only his arriving in Chicago. Now she realized he was much closer.

Would he stay put at least until she and Jake had a chance to figure out how to get the gun out of Gavriel's hand? She didn't know.

CHAPTER 65

JOSH HAD MADE A PLAN WITH RYAN AND THE GROUP. HE SENT THEM back the way they came, and he slowly made his way to the cavern, hoping to catch Gavriel by surprise. When he finally got to the chamber room, it was empty except for the figure lying motionless on the floor. Josh had to place his hand over his mouth to stop himself from making a sound. A silent scream and a helpless sadness spread through every inch of his body. He moved in slowly, hoping as he got closer that he would find out he was wrong about the body on the floor. He reached the dead priest and fell to his knees. He slowly cradled the head of Father Kristofferson to his chest and wept quietly.

After a few minutes the sadness turned to anger—a deep hatred, one that he had suppressed his entire life. It was the combined pain he felt for his mother's suffering, the disgust he had for his father, and all the years he had to pretend to be someone he wasn't. He had to be the best at everything. He thought maybe he would somehow change his father's behavior, but it did nothing. Now, he held the only father he really had, someone who expected nothing from him but who he would have done anything for. Gavriel did this. He had to be taken down. If it were the last thing Josh did, he would do it for Father Kristofferson. He walked over to the place where he and Olivia had sat and talked earlier. That seemed like so long ago. He found Kendra's knife.

He would not leave Father Kristofferson down here in this cold dark place. He carefully bent down and lifted the priest up and over his shoulder. He spun, picked up the knife, and slipped it into his belt, hoping he would not cut himself as he moved with the priest. His hurt knee was burning with hot pain, but the priest seemed very light to him, more like he was carrying the weight of a small child. He slowly made his way toward the sliding door. He knew he had to be quiet, so it took some time to get the priest up the stairs and into the bed. Josh laid him down like a parent putting a sleeping child down, careful not to disturb him. Blood from the priest's wound had soaked through part of Josh's shirt, but he didn't notice. He kissed the priest on the forehead and took the knife out of his belt, contemplating his next move. He studied Father Kristofferson's face. He finally seemed to be at peace. The furrowed brow was smooth. Small laugh lines remained around his eyes. Josh tried to pretend the priest was only sleeping, but he wasn't. The hatred for Gavriel was building inside him. Josh decided to make his move.

He was about to start out into the church when he heard the telltale click of the sliding door. Someone was about to enter the room from the tunnels, but who? At this point, Josh trusted no one and grasped the knife firmly in his hand, ready to stab, without hesitation, whomever walked in. The door slid open very slowly and quietly, and the tousled blonde head of Kendra peered in.

"Jesus, Kendra. I nearly stabbed you. Are you crazy? What are you doing back here? You're supposed to be with your brother and the others at the Gathering. What went wrong?"

"You know that it will take them awhile to get up there and into cell phone coverage. We were almost at the room when you ran into us. They won't make it in time," she whispered, but it sounded loud in his ears. "I will trade you my knife for a cell phone. Deal?" She had a sweet grin on her face, but then she noticed the blood on Josh's shirt, and she entered the room fully. As she glanced over to the bed and Father Kristofferson's body, the bullet wound and the blood were apparent. Her face started to contort, and Josh rushed over to her and embraced her tightly, stifling the sobbing as best he could. He hoped nobody could hear them but he knew it was impossible to stop her. He knew exactly how she felt.

CHAPTER 66

THIS IS IT. "OLD TOWN." ELISE SAID THE WORDS OUT LOUD. SHE KEPT saying them over and over. Then she started singing, "Old Town." It hadn't changed much in all these years. That was a good thing. She scouted around looking for landmarks that would help direct her to the church.

She passed a few of the old hangouts. Well, if you wanted to call them that. Stanford had taken her out for dinner a few times, and they would stop for a beer at the local pub, reminiscing about their college days. They used to go to the pub quite often when they were dating, but it stopped when she started to get looks from some of the guys hanging out for beers after work. She didn't think much of it then, but Stanford had always been jealous. She knew that now.

She was pretty back then, she remembered. She became fat, but it was not due to having Josh. She couldn't blame baby fat on how she looked. It was definitely an eating disorder, another benefit of being married to Stanford. It was the beginning of the end, Old Town was. And now she was back. How appropriate.

Oh, that looks familiar. Elise made a left and kept going. *I am getting close now.* She remembered Lincoln Park was close by. She loved going there and walking for hours with Josh when he was little. He would ask her what the names of the trees were, and she would make up names for them, like snow leaf tree and sunshine willow. He would laugh and say that those were "funny-named trees," like Mother Nature mixed up the weather and the trees. Then he would tell her what the trees were really called. He was so smart, even back then.

He helped her get through so many hard days when she thought she had nothing left to live for. She would look into his beautiful slate-gray eyes and see herself, her happy youthful self. *I have to save him. I have to show him that he can have an amazing life, and that he can't destroy it and give it all up.* She fully blamed herself for the mess he was in. He needed her to be strong, to stand up for both of them, and she had failed miserably. Now it was her duty, even if it were the last thing she did, to help deliver him from whatever he had gotten into. She would take full responsibility, she and Stanford. But he had done his part. He died. She stepped hard on the gas. The Escalade couldn't go fast enough for her.

CHAPTER 67

AMANDA WAS WONDERING WHAT TIME IT WAS. SOMEONE MIGHT accidentally wander into the church, and then what? Another innocent person would be involved in this very messy situation. But she was in no position to do anything about it just then. She noticed there was very little cell phone coverage in the church the first time they came by to visit Father Kristofferson. *What was it? One bar?* She remembered thinking how ridiculous it was in this day and age to not have a wireless setup. She had no idea how powerful it would have been to be able to text someone about their situation right now. But the cell phones were down in the cavern, so what did it matter? She actually was hoping the professor had been lying about not having a cell phone, but she knew he wasn't. She was having ongoing feelings of uneasiness. She still could see a burning priest in her vision, the wooden cross hanging from his neck. She closed her eyes and willed it to go away. *What about Jake?* She felt uncomfortable about the dreams and the blood. Those could just be dreams. Sometimes they felt like premonitions, but they were just bad dreams. *Cauchemar*, Jake would tease her in French. Next to her, this young girl. *Olivia . . . that's her name.* Amanda sensed that and knew she was right. She was feeling fuzzy. Another premonition. She hoped otherwise. Just then the professor moved and startled her out of her daze.

Professor Orloff stood up, and everyone turned to him, wondering what he was up to. Gavriel quickly spun around and pointed the gun directly at him.

"Gavriel, if I may call you that, or do you prefer messenger of God?" The professor wasn't being coy, and the genuineness in his voice took Gavriel by surprise.

"What is it, Professor? If I didn't know better I would think you were mocking me. Don't try anything funny. We are all waiting to see what will transpire in the next hour."

Jake quickly glanced at his watch. He had not realized how much time had gone by. It was after 5:00. He was still trying to put all this together. What was about to happen? What could be so impactful and horrible? They had only gotten some of the larger pieces of information from Father Krist-offerson. The finer details were not discussed, and Jake had a helpless feeling.

The professor nodded, as if he understood the seriousness of the situation and everything Gavriel was alluding to. "I am a man of science and history. I am not religious, so I am not influenced by the actions and suggestions you are speaking of." Gavriel said nothing, so the professor continued. "I really believe that we can figure out a better way to get your message across to those who need to hear it. Don't you?"

"No, there is no other way. It's too late. There is no way to stop the process at this point. It is the way it is supposed to be, the way it was meant to be from the start."

"But surely there is a way to stop it. Perhaps the same way it was started?" The professor was trying to reason with someone who was beyond reason, and he knew that. What he was really doing was stalling, so he could search the room for a way to perhaps get out of the church with his new friends, but how? *The back way through the tunnels perhaps. How about the front door?* All he had to do was get Gavriel to put down the gun or take it away from him. There was only one of him and four of them. Chances were that if he acted, Jake would surely follow, and Amanda would do what she could as well. He expected nothing from the girl, but you never knew. When your life was on the line, heroic and amazing things happened.

He did notice the shadow in the back and caught the unspoken exchange between Amanda and Jake. His assumption was that Cardinal Roland was in the house as well. Certainly he wouldn't sit back and watch while the others jumped this madman. He had a feeling the only way out was for him to be the first to act.

As the professor was contemplating the options, Gavriel turned toward the altar and pointed the gun toward the darkness and the back wall. "Come out, Samuel. Join the others. I know you are here. You should join us soon, before I choose to make an example out of one of them on your behalf."

From the darkness, Samuel Roland made his way out, and a sneer appeared on Gavriel's face. "Here to see your precious partner, are you?" Samuel slowly raised both hands, as he realized the gun was now pointed directly at his head. He knew the young man was delusional, but he had no idea it was this bad. He had heard tense voices and shouting, at which time he slipped into the dark shadows of the church. He had watched in utter disbelief as the troop came through at gunpoint. He knew he could not hide forever, so one way or the other he would have come out. He was hoping to do so by helping the situation, however, not by adding himself to the fray.

"Gavriel, what has happened to you? What is going on? Where is Michael?"

Amanda's heart quickened, and she cringed at the answer that was about to be given to Cardinal Roland. It was going to devastate him. Just as she was thinking of a way to distract Gavriel, two things happened. She felt a presence. Someone else was here, actually more than one person. She felt that others were in the back. But more so, she felt that someone was outside the front door. She took a sideways glance to see a crack in the main entrance doors and a sliver of sunlight that disappeared as quickly as it had appeared.

At the same moment, Professor Orloff, in one smooth motion, hopped over the bench and lunged toward Gavriel with uncanny speed. At first, Amanda thought it was Jake. This was a Jake move, not a half-blind professor move. Of course, Jake was not far behind, and she put her hand over her mouth as the vision of Jake covered with blood came back full force into her mind. Olivia screamed as Gavriel spun to see both men nearly on top of him. A loud shot rang out, and Professor Orloff's body spun like a marionette on strings, his legs giving out. He slammed hard into Jake who was right behind him. The professor knocked Jake backward. This caused him to trip and fall, juggling the professor's body until he hit the ground with the professor landing on top of him.

Cardinal Roland froze as Gavriel quickly spun back toward him. "No more heroics, Your Eminence. As you see, I will not hesitate to shoot. Please join the others behind the bench while I tend to these troublemakers." Samuel did as he was told. He did not want to provoke Gavriel into shooting more innocent people. He felt silly for not jumping him when he had the chance, but the professor's move caught him off guard.

The professor was shot through the lower abdomen, and the wound was bleeding badly. He was still breathing, and his eyelids were fluttering in disbelief, almost as if he were more surprised than in pain.

Amanda's eyes filled with tears as Gavriel walked toward the tangled mess of the wounded professor and Jake. The professor was still breathing. She could hear the rasping of his breath from where she stood, now straining to see Jake. Gavriel walked with the swagger of a gunslinger who was about to finish off his opponent in a gunfight. Amanda was concerned about Jake being pinned under the professor and whether Gavriel's thoughts were to kill them both while he had the chance.

"I am not sure what you think you are preventing by trying to stop me. The course of action has been set and has already begun, so taking me out is not going to resolve anything. We have spent many years planning this. Do you think a few idiots like you can undo it in a matter of hours? For example, this little church, do you think I would let it stand after everything we have planned and done here? Father Kristofferson is dead."

Amanda instinctively looked over at Cardinal Roland, who had a shocked look of disbelief on this face. He had been standing, and it seemed his legs gave out at hearing the news about Michael. He slumped down onto the bench, his hands shaking, and he mouthed the word "no," but no sound came out.

Amanda was certain her ESP was kicking into full gear. "So where is the bomb, Gavriel?"

He seemed amused that she was clever enough to know about the bomb. "You're the one with the special gift. You figure it out." He continued coyly, "By the way, it should be enough of an explosion to take out half the block. Hopefully no innocent people will be coming to church in the next few minutes. They will certainly meet their maker."

Jake looked over at Amanda, who nodded at him. *She knows where the bomb is. Good girl.* The professor's head was close to Jake's, and he was trying to speak.

Jake put his ear close to the professor's mouth, and blood was oozing into Jake's clothes from where the bullet had ripped into the professor. "If you can find the bomb," he whispered, "I can . . ." he paused to suck in some air but seemed to get none, "disable it . . ." His voice was nearly inaudible, but Jake knew the professor would do whatever he could to help, even in his current state. Jake was touched by the professor's commitment, but he had no time to think past the fact that he had to move. Gavriel was coming toward him, gun pointed at his head. He had to do something, because he knew if he didn't, Amanda would, and she would end up dead.

CHAPTER 68

ELISE THOUGHT BETTER OF PARKING HER DEAD HUSBAND'S vehicle close to anywhere the cops could find her. Not that it really mattered at this point, but for some reason she felt like she needed to buy some time to see her son, to tell him how much she loved him, and to thank him for giving her enough courage to set herself free. She hoped that by telling him he had made a difference, he would stop whatever he was planning to do. The letter was vague, but it was apparent something very bad was going to happen, and it was going to happen today. She didn't know if she would get there in time, but she was going to try to do something about it. She had never had the nerve to step up while she was with Stanford.

She parked nearly three full blocks down and two over. She didn't think the police could possibly know anything about Stanford's death yet, but just in case they were searching for her and the Cadillac, parking somewhere else might buy her some time. She was hoping to have a few minutes to discuss things with Josh to explain what happened. She got out of the SUV. Her purse weighed down on her good shoulder. Why did she bring the cognac? Now she felt silly dragging her purse with this heavy bottle of liquor to a church, of all places. She thought of tossing it and decided she needed the liquid courage. She walked as quickly as she could. When she passed a con- venience store, she didn't know why, but she went in and asked for a pack of smokes. "What kind?" The girl at the register seemed annoyed. "What do you recommend?" she asked quietly.

"Don't you have a brand?"

"No, that's why I asked what you recommend. I want to start."

The girl looked Elise up and down and made a face at the disheveled looking woman and the hair sticking out from underneath the baseball cap. She looked like a homeless bum in the long trench coat, and she smelled of booze. Then she noticed the red flecks on her face and wondered if the flecks were freckles and what this lady had been up to. The girl sighed and said, "Show me the money first, and I'll pick out a pack for you."

Oh shit, money . . . She was pretty sure she had some. Every purse had a bit squirreled away in it. She put the bag on the floor and rummaged through it with her good arm. The girl peered over the counter at the curious site. She held out a twenty to the girl. "Will this do? I don't know how much they are."

"Yeah, it's enough."

"Oh, and I will need a lighter, too. Do I have enough for both?"

The girl rolled her eyes. "Yep, you do."

"Okay then and oh, keep the change." Elise seemed pleased with the transaction.

"Will do," the girl said, shaking her head.

Elise thanked the girl and threw the smokes and lighter into her bag. She picked it up and headed out the door. The bag seemed heavier now, but important in some way. She felt like her entire life now resided in her big purse.

Boy, we get all kinds, the girl thought, as she noticed the thin stream of blood that followed the strange lady out the door.

Elise was pleased with herself. She stopped a block from the church and lit her first cigarette. She managed to rip the package open, using her teeth and her good hand, but ended up dropping at least half the pack onto the ground. *Oh well. It's not like I'm gonna smoke all those anyway. I may bleed to death first.* The thought made her sad as she inhaled. Then she choked for at least a minute on her first exhale. After two or three drags, she seemed to get the hang of it. Her lungs burned, but she didn't care. It felt good. She felt alive. She started toward the church, bag in hand, cigarette dangling from her lips.

She reached the church and wasn't sure if there would be a Mass or something going on. She had glanced at the clock on the convenience store wall. It had read 4:55. It had taken her just over ten minutes to walk to the church. *Nobody worships at dinnertime, do they?*

Elise made her way up the front stairs and dropped her Prada bag gently to the ground. She delicately opened the door, just a sliver, and tried to peer in with one eye through the crack. She nearly fell over when she saw the scene inside the church. She managed to just as quietly close the door, hoping she had not been noticed. *What is going on in there? Could that be right? A bunch of people held hostage in the church?* Then her heart skipped a beat. *Where is Josh? Is he in there?* She hadn't noticed him in the group, but she really didn't have time look around. For some reason she was certain this was where Josh would be, and that maniac in there with the gun had something to do with the letter she found. *What had Josh gotten into?* Then there was a loud bang. She knew it was a gunshot, and she nearly jumped out of her skin. The street was deserted. She prayed that the gunshot was some kind of a warning and that her son was okay. *I have to go in there. Josh may be in there, and I have to save him.*

CHAPTER 69

THE LOUD SOUND OF THE GUNSHOT JOLTED KENDRA AND JOSH OUT of their sad embrace. "Shit. Sounds like Gavriel has lost it. We have to do this now." Josh was in a panic. Kendra grabbed his hand and placed the cell phone in it. "Josh, you are the only one who can stop this now. You have to get out there into cell phone coverage." They both knew cell phones did not work well in the stone church, and he needed to get outside. They had less than an hour, and they still needed to get past Gavriel to do this.

"Give me the knife." Kendra was waiting. "You know I am better with it than you are." She was right. He handed her the knife, and they quietly slipped into the hallway leading to the main area of the church. As they got close, they could see Olivia with two others, a lady and Cardinal Roland. *What's he doing here?* Josh had met him a few times before when he visited Father Kristofferson. That all seemed like a very long time ago now.

They watched as Gavriel walked toward something, or someone, on the floor. It was hard to see from where they were. Everyone was watching Gavriel. It was time to make a move. He nodded to Kendra. She nodded back. Then she grabbed the sleeve of his shirt. Josh stopped and watched her make the gesture of texting on a phone with her thumbs. He nodded again, understanding the urgency. The cell phone read 5:13 p.m. He had about forty-five minutes to stop this thing. It was all up to him. They crawled toward the pulpit, unnoticed by everyone except Amanda. They continued toward the altar under the large wooden cross. Josh looked up at the Son of God mounted to the wooden frame and was heartbroken by the look of sadness in his eyes.

Amanda started to move. Gavriel swung toward her. "No, Mrs. Bannon. This is not the time for heroics. A martyr is someone who does something for the benefit of others, who gives up their life for much more. Saving one's husband is an act done out of love, for one. It is not a love for many. I urge you to consider the others in the room. Besides, in about forty minutes, it will all be over."

Suddenly Amanda knew what needed to be done, her intuition kicking into high gear, perhaps survival mode. She knew there were three other people here to help. There was little time to work through how the plan would unfold, but there was something more important at stake: a message had to go out and a bomb had to be disarmed before 6:00 p.m.

The boy. She wondered if it were Josh. He needed to get a message out, something that could stop the flurry of events that were about to take place—the screaming children burning in her dreams. She had to help him do this. She realized Jake was watching her to see what she would do. She shook her head, hoping he understood that she knew better than to jump in between him and Gavriel. In her heart, she knew Jake would understand and want her to do the right thing. She had to protect the boy and get him outside, so he could send a text. She wasn't sure how one text would stop everything, but she wasn't about to argue with the intuition that had served her well over the years.

As Gavriel hovered over Jake with the gun pointed at Jake's head, the only part of him that didn't seem to be covered by the professor's body, Jake made his move. The words "Sorry Professor . . ." came out in a rough huff, as Jake pushed the man over and rolled him down the stairs, a short but painful distance. Olivia gasped, not because of Jake's move, but because, just at that moment, Josh and Kendra darted out from behind the altar toward Gavriel.

With all the commotion going on, nobody noticed a figure in a trench coat carrying a Prada purse sneak in and close the door behind her. Elise was down on the floor behind the back row of pews to the right, facing the pulpit. She crawled along to the far right side, hoping she had not been seen. She looked up in time to see her son and a small blonde girl circle out from behind the altar. *Oh my God, Josh. Get out of there!* She wanted to scream the words as loud as she could but knew alerting the crazy man with the gun would be like signing Josh's death sentence.

Gavriel moved to the side to avoid Jake, who was coming at him, and stepped over the professor, who wasn't any threat in his current state. Jake was on his feet quickly and managed to grab the gun hand of Gavriel, who seemed to be somehow gaining unbridled strength. While they were wrestling, Amanda bounded out from the bench. Olivia had started screaming, adding to the already chaotic situation. Cardinal Roland held her and tried to calm her down. All he could think of was finding Michael. *Where is his body?* He was hoping he could see him one more time, but the sick feeling in the pit of his stomach told him otherwise. If things didn't go right in the next half hour, they would all be blown to bits in this little church.

Josh was running toward the struggling men, and Kendra moved toward them from another angle. The wooden cross Jake had taken off of Father Kristofferson fell to the floor as he wrestled with Gavriel. Jake had intended to give it to Cardinal Roland.

The cardinal stood up to help Jake. He moved out from the pew. In the meantime, Amanda grabbed Josh by the hand, half-dragging him toward the door and cell phone service. "I know what you need to do. You have less than twenty minutes to put an end to this." He nodded and was ready to send "Stop" to the private Twitter group. They were not to set anything in motion until 6:00 p.m. on the nose. He wondered how much faith he could put in the disciples not to hit the trigger too fast. They were halfway up the aisle when shots rang out. Amanda didn't want to turn back and look but was compelled to do so. Jake lay bleeding on the stairs of the pulpit, as Gavriel tied something around his own neck. She glimpsed what looked like the wooden cross Father Kristofferson wore, now dangling from Gavriel's neck, and her mind flashed back to the burning priest, with the cross around his neck.

Kendra threw the knife as Amanda watched. It sank deep into Gavriel's back. He arched and screamed but didn't go down. Instead, he pointed the gun directly down the aisle at them and pulled the trigger.

She heard the noise but didn't register the impact until Josh's hand slid out of hers as he fell to his knees. "He will not stop this. No one will!" screamed Gavriel.

Amanda bent down to help Josh. He was extremely calm for someone who had just been shot. "Take it." He placed the phone in Amanda's hand. "Just send it. Please end this."

Amanda took the phone, got up, and ran as fast as she could toward the outside world. It was 5:42 p.m. She could hear more commotion behind her but didn't stop to look. She had to do this and get everyone out of the church before the bomb went off. She wasn't sure if it were even possible at this point, and her heart ached when she thought of Jake, shot and lying there helpless. Her visions were all coming true at this point.

Behind her, Kendra and Olivia were running toward Josh, whose limp body was lying on the floor of the church. Samuel Roland was heading toward Jake, who was bleeding from the shoulder and seemed to be unconscious. Gavriel was somehow still standing, blood running from the knife wound in his back. He reached behind himself to pull the knife out and flung it to the side as he raised his gun.

"Samuel, stop there." Gavriel pointed the gun at the priest. "I see you want to join Michael in hell." The pain registered on Samuel's face as the reality of Michael's death hit him. Gavriel started down the stairs in a jerky walk toward Amanda.

"I have to stop that bitch from sending that message." Amanda was almost at the doors when a shot rang out, just missing her and hitting the door ten feet in front of her.

Elise had crawled all the way around, her limp arm dragging and making it a slower go than she wanted. She knew Josh had been shot. When she came around the back of the pulpit, she could see his body on the floor in a pool of blood and the girls running toward him. Her own blood was running cold; she didn't scream, or cry. She knew this was her chance to do something right for a change, to make a difference.

Her only child lay there. His six-foot-tall body was somehow compressed into a small and helpless mound. His words were ringing loud and clear in her head, as she moved forward with the bottle of cognac and the lighter in her good hand. *Stop being such a coward and fight for your life. There isn't much time left. At least end it with some dignity.*

CHAPTER 70

JAKE WAS COMING TO. HE HAD HIT HIS HEAD HARD ON THE STEPS AS he went down. The bullet went right through his shoulder and shattered the bone. But he felt nothing. He was in shock. All he could think of was Amanda running with Josh toward the door of the church. She knew something, and he trusted it was more important than anything, even himself. He pushed himself up, realizing he had no ability to use his right shoulder, and rolled himself down the stairs as he watched Gavriel heading for Amanda.

Jake panicked as he realized Gavriel was going to shoot her. Gavriel pointed and shot, just missing Amanda. Jake somehow found the strength to try and stand, and Cardinal Roland ran to help him. "Amanda knows where the bomb is," Jake told the priest. "We need to find out from her, so the professor can disarm it—if he lasts long enough." They looked over at the professor who was bleeding profusely, gasping for breath like a fish out of water.

As Jake and Samuel made their way to the professor, a figure emerged from the shadows and rushed past them. Jake couldn't believe it. *Who else was in the church?* Gavriel was unsteady. The wound in his back was having an impact. He stood only twenty feet from Amanda as she was getting ready to push through the doors of the church.

Suddenly a crash at Gavriel's feet startled him, and he looked down to see a puddle of brown liquid soaking into his robes. He was confused for a half second and turned his head to see a small-framed person at his feet in a long coat. Then there was a flicker of light. Before it all had a chance to register, the liquid and his robe were ablaze. The flames spread rapidly, and his lower body suddenly felt the searing of its flesh. He started to move, to try and peel out of the robe he had put on earlier to signify his ascent as the messenger of God, but realized it was too late. He pointed the gun at the small woman at his feet. She smiled at him as he shot her in the face. She fell over backward, her knees still bent underneath her.

Amanda was bracing herself for the next bullet and was surprised when it didn't come. Instead, she burst out into the full darkness of night. Sometime in the past hour the sun had set. The sky was clear, and the moon shed some light. She quickly took the phone and sent the tweet out. She had full reception on the phone and prayed it was sent in time. The phone's clock switched to 5:46 p.m.

She had heard a crash as she was heading out the doors and looked expectantly up at the church. *Please, please let them be okay.* Her next call on the phone was to the Chicago Police Department. She had to go back in. The bomb was still armed.

CHAPTER 71

SAMUEL HAD ALREADY GATHERED THE GIRLS AND HAD TO practically pull them off of Josh's body. They were sent back to the tunnels. If they could get into the tunnels, there was a good chance they could make it far enough away to avoid damage from the bomb hidden in the church. Gavriel was still somehow standing, holding the gun, robes on fire. Samuel wished he had a gun to put the burning man out of his misery. He had to get the location of the bomb from Amanda.

He didn't stop to look at Josh or the woman who had set Gavriel on fire. He had no idea who she was or where she came from, but he was grateful for her courage. He ran past Gavriel and outside to Amanda.

The relief on Amanda's face as Samuel came through the doors of the church was enough to light up the dark night.

"Did you get it done?"

"Tweet sent," she said. Cardinal Roland looked a bit skeptical.

"Let's hope it worked. We will know tomorrow."

Her eyes moved to the church doors. "We have ten minutes to disarm that bomb." They turned toward the church.

Just then, the doors of the church slammed open, and Gavriel's flame-engulfed body came careening toward them. Samuel stepped in front of Amanda, ready to take on this undying psychopath. A few pedestrians were out for an evening walk on the quiet streets around the church, and a woman screamed as the flaming figure lit up the entire churchyard. The flaming body moved toward the stairs and then tumbled down and lay burning in the light layer of snow that had blanketed the yard while they were inside. More passersby stopped to gasp and peer as sirens could be heard growing louder in the distance.

Samuel was yelling at the crowd to move away from the church as there was possibly a bomb. That news caused even more hysteria, as the crowd started disbanding in every direction. He just hoped they would make it far enough away before the blast went off. He himself had nothing left to live for, now that Michael was gone. He made his way into the church after Amanda. The body of Gavriel was charred but still flaming as he ran by.

Amanda didn't stop to ask who the woman on the floor was lying next to Josh. Instead, she raced up to where Jake and the professor still lay on the stairs.

"Professor, can you move?" He nodded. "Jake, are you okay?" Her voice quavered as she checked the wound at his shoulder, giving him a light kiss on the forehead. "Couldn't be better." He tried to make it seem insignificant, but they both knew better. "It's behind the pulpit." Amanda helped the professor move up the steps as quickly as possible. Samuel then grabbed the professor, half-dragging, half-carrying him to the pulpit. Amanda raced ahead, thankful that it was not a raised one and stood like a podium on the floor. Looking behind the pulpit, she found a small but deadly looking package taped to the back. The professor was placed gently next to it. It was 5:55 p.m. They couldn't see a timer or anything that signified that the bomb was set to explode at a specific time, but they all knew it would. Pulling the professor closer to the bomb, Jake hoped it would be quick to disarm.

"I can tell you how, Jake. But . . . you are going to have to do it." Jake nodded, understanding fully. "Are you familiar with . . . this type of explosive?"

Jake nodded. "Delayed action fuse set to go off with a trigger, most likely a cell phone."

The Professor coughed. "Yes, correct." Some blood dribbled over the professor's lip as he continued. "Okay . . . go to the wires." The professor coughed up more blood before adding, "We are in luck . . . this is not a pipe or chemical. Just explosives, very old-school . . ."

Jake's impatience was clear. "Professor, please . . ." They were running out of time.

"Three wires, Jake. You know them." The professor paused to cough up additional blood. "The primer, the reactor wire, and the wire that feeds the ignition timer . . . you need to cut them in the correct order."

"Shit! Cutting wires?"

Jake looked around helplessly when Samuel suddenly produced the knife covered in Gavriel's blood. "I thought we might need this." Jake could have kissed the priest.

"Okay, Professor. So if I am correct, it's this one first, right? Professor?"

The professor lay still. His eyes were glazed behind the Coke-bottle glasses that had somehow managed to stay put through the entire ordeal. Amanda was already missing the kind man.

The sirens were growing louder, and they could hear shouts outside the church as Gavriel's body was found and police were speaking to the few witnesses that had stuck around. Jake took the knife from Samuel. There were only a few minutes left, and he had no choice. His shoulder was on fire from the bullet wound, but he had to slice the wires. One way or another, this was all going to end in less than sixty seconds.

He was quick, and they could only hope there was no secondary setup. He didn't think so. Gavriel was too sure of himself and the original plan to think there could have been a chance of failure. Besides, Gavriel was counting on the others who were set to detonate bombs across the country, all at 6:00 p.m. Central Standard Time.

As the police burst through the front door of the church, Jake finished cutting the last wire. The professor lay dead, practically in his lap. Passing the two dead bodies in the aisle, the police looked toward the main altar and the pulpit of the church. It made for an interesting picture to the officers on the scene.

CHAPTER 72

"OKAY, LET'S GO THROUGH THIS AGAIN." THE DETECTIVE WAS relentless. They were in Jake's hospital room at Northwestern Memorial, the hospital Amanda had insisted on. The paramedic wanted to take them to Loretta or someplace closer, but she would have none of it.

"He's lasted this long. I am sure he will make it. Just dress it up, and if you can't take us, we'll take a cab." The paramedic gave Amanda a patronizing look before rushing them to one of the best hospitals in Chicago.

"I am not sure there is much more to tell." Amanda was exhausted and could not imagine how Jake must feel. While he had the luxury of being on morphine, and she didn't, she continued. "A friend of ours, whom you have had a chance to question as well, Cardinal Roland, asked us to pay a visit to his friend—the priest you found shot in the church." *Along with all the other dead bodies.*

"And what exactly do you know about Francis Amato, the young priest apprentice who did all these horrible killings?"

"We knew he was a pretty good shot." Jake smiled.

"Okay, honey. Why don't you rest, and I will answer the detective's questions." Amanda patted Jake on the leg, and he grinned and nodded.

"Okay, sweetie pie." He was grinning ear to ear. The morphine was having a fairly pleasant effect.

"He has a clean system. He doesn't put any foreign substances into it. It's hard to even get him to enjoy a great coffee unless he is in Europe. You understand, right?" Amanda gave the officer her best smile.

"Yeah, I get it. Now what were the two of you doing in the middle of this mass murder scene? Did you know that an entire family was eliminated?"

Both Amanda and Jake looked at each other, and then Amanda felt her intuition coming on. *No, not now! Why?*

She pressed her finger against her temple, and Jake suddenly sobered up from his giddy gush and happy morphine state. "You okay, kiddo? What's up?"

"Josh's dad, right? He is dead. That whole family . . . what a shame."

"I would like to know how you know this, Mrs. Bannon. None of it has been released yet, as we could not connect with any immediate family members. Little did we know his mother was with you."

"Sorry, Detective Chambers. I know this will be hard to believe . . ."

He cut her off. "Yes, I understand you have some clairvoyant abilities. We received some intel on you from our Canadian counterparts. But you understand that you just know an awful lot for knowing nothing at all, and we will have to ask you to stick around for a while, so don't leave town."

"I don't plan on moving my husband in his current condition, so I will be at your disposal. You know where to find us."

He nodded and walked out. A few minutes later, Professor Orloff's mother stepped into the hospital room. She looked out of place when not behind the messy reception desk at her son's office. Her expression of sadness hurt Amanda deeply. Jake and Amanda had become very fond of the professor and still hadn't had a chance to truly digest his heroic passing.

Amanda stood up and readied herself for a barrage of guilt-induced accusations. But the feisty little lady simply walked up to Amanda and put her arms around her in a tight embrace. Startled at first, Amanda just stood still until Jake gave her a light swat on her behind, which prompted her into placing her arms around the older woman.

Finally, the professor's mother pulled away, tears streaming down her face.

"I wanted the two of you to know that Morry, that's what I called my

Moriarty, Morry really enjoyed you both. He spoke so fondly of you, like you were this dynamic duo full of adventure and you had accepted him onto your team."

Jake was touched. "Yes, he was a great part of our team, Mrs. Orloff. We are so sorry about how it ended. He was a hero."

"He was always brave." Her voice trembled. "Even when he was little, he put up with a lot of bullying, you know, because of his eyesight and everything . . ."

The couple nodded. It seemed that Mrs. Orloff needed talk about her son, so they waited for her to continue.

"He always found ways to brush off the teasing, and I think in some ways it forced him to show everyone how brilliant he really was. I know it seems strange, since you only knew him for a short while, but I think he felt the two of you were like family. He didn't have any brothers or sisters. I hope you don't mind me saying that you both meant a lot."

Jake and Amanda didn't know what to say. They remained in silence for a minute, remembering the professor.

Amanda broke the silence. "It's an interesting dynamic, Mrs. Orloff. Sometimes you know people all your life, and you never really feel like you connect with them. Then you meet one truly authentic human being, one who is kind and genuine, and he can instantly become a trusted friend."

Jake added, "He played a key part in a much larger operation than just the one in the church, and he helped to stop that operation from unfolding. We may never know the size or scope of the devastation that was prevented with his help. It could have impacted many cities and lives across the country. Like I said, a true hero."

Amanda raised her eyebrow for a change. It was unlike Jake to disclose so much about the situation to anyone outside the authorities during an investigation. But it seemed the professor's mother had struck Jake's heartstring. Amanda and Jake had watched the news all day and were relieved that there were no bombings or tragedies that they could tie into the workings of Gavriel. The plans that connected all the information had burned in the pocket of his robe.

In fact, it was probably quieter than usual in the news world, or perhaps it just seemed that way after their harrowing ordeal. It was like the whole world was holding its breath, waiting for the next ugly event to take place.

Amanda understood Jake's intentions in giving the professor's mother additional information. Doing this was a way of offering her a legacy gift, one that put her son in a light that she could hold dear for the rest of her life. Her son was a hero. He lost his life doing a great deed, and it was his choice. It would help give closure to the situation, and she would remain a proud mother.

"Thank you, Jake. You don't know what it means to me to hear that. I hope that you are going to be okay. How long until you are out of this shithole?"

Amanda burst out laughing. Mrs. Orloff was a pistol.

Jake suppressed a grin and spoke with a seriousness he didn't feel when he gave her the rundown of the surgery to his shoulder and the reconstruction of his shattered bone.

Mrs. Orloff listened intently, taking all the information in, and mentioned something about various herbs she grew, and sometimes smoked, which worked as organic painkillers.

Amanda heard all of this as background noise. She had wandered over to the window. As she looked out toward Lake Michigan, she thought about all that had transpired over the past few days. She felt for the young people who were involved in the events, especially the ones here in Chicago. She had had a chance to speak with Cardinal Roland briefly while Jake was in surgery. He had found Father Kristofferson's journal. Everything was in there. From the days when they were younger, to the abuse he received from Bishop Solomon. Cardinal Roland had choked up as he told Amanda about that part. The journal chronicled everything, all the way through each young girl and boy Father Kristofferson tried to help.

Each one of the kids he helped had a section dedicated to them in the journal. It told of how he found them and what haunted them, or at least as much as they divulged to him. Sometimes there was nothing. Like in the case of Francis Amato. He was never able to crack that one. However, the police were able to find out quite a bit more.

Detective Chambers, who was in charge of the investigation, gave away nothing. But Amanda made a few calls to some close friends who had access. They were friends she had assisted by using her skills to help solve some cases. They were happy to pull up the file from Amato's childhood. To say the least, it was a very disturbing history. She could understand how this kid would end up thinking the way he did about society. It wasn't a justification for his actions, but rather a sad explanation.

As for the Gathering, she assumed it would continue. After all, it was just a place for kids to hang out and let off a little steam. It was the Inner Circle that had the power to be dangerous, but it also had the power to do good. Cardinal Roland mentioned that he felt comfortable after speaking to the group yesterday. Ryan and a very serious Kendra assured him that they would honor Josh by keeping the group together. They would seek help through proper channels and conveyed that they were committed to using what they knew to help others who were going through the same experiences they had. Nobody knew who the individuals were that Josh had connected with across the nation, but Amanda had sent a second message to the group that day.

"It's over. Disband."

Each of them only knew Josh and none of them were connected directly to each other. She wasn't sure if her tweet would work. Only time would tell.

Amanda was thinking about how easy it could be to continue down the same path and avoid dealing with the core issues. It all comes back to making the right choices and taking responsibility for one's own happiness.

"Amanda?" Mrs. Orloff shook Amanda's shoulder, startling her out of her reverie.

"Oh, sorry. What were you saying?"

"I was saying good-bye . . . and thank you. Thank you for what you gave Morry before he died . . ."

"And what was that?" Amanda was genuinely curious.

"A chance to live."

The older woman gave Amanda another hug and blew a kiss to Jake as she slipped out of the room, slowly closing the door behind her.

QUESTIONS AND TOPICS
FOR DISCUSSION

1. What was your overall impression of *The Congregation*? What did you learn?

2. What is your opinion of Amanda and Jake? Did you enjoy being with them? Where do you hope they travel next?

3. Do you think that Cardinal Roland will change the course of his life? Is it possible he will go to Chicago and try to make something good out of Michael's sad fate?

4. Why do you think Samuel and Michael stayed in the Church? Do you think younger priests of this generation might leave the Church after suffering the abuse that Samuel and Michael suffered? If so, why?

5. What made the Inner Circle think their proposed violent actions were appropriate in the face of their suffering?

6. Do you think the Gathering will continue? Now there have been monumental changes to members of the Inner Circle, what do you think the remaining members will do, if anything?

7. Did you identify with any particular character or characters? If so, which ones and why?

8. What did you think about the character of Gavriel? Was he someone you felt you understood? Why or why not?

9. After meeting Olivia, Josh changes. How are the character and role of Olivia key to the plot?

10. When her abuse started, we are told that Elise lost her confidence. How does her reaction differ from what the young people in the Inner Circle were trying to do? Why did she continue to take the abuse?

11. Toward the end of the book, Father Kristofferson is pictured with slumped shoulders. What do you think was making him lose his resolve toward the fateful day, even though he agreed to go along with Gavriel's plans?

12. How do you believe that Gavriel was able to take control of Father Kristofferson?

13. How and why do you think Father's Kristofferson pain become so distorted that it allowed him to believe it was OK for him to destroy others?

14. Did you find it interesting that Amanda has visions? Do you consider them a gift or a curse? Why?

15. What motivates Josh? Why would a young man from his background propose the actions that he does? And how is it that he seems cold and immune to his mother's abuse at the hands of his father but is very empathetic to the young people he wants to avenge against the power of the Church?

16. We are used to stories about abuse both inside and outside the Church. Did reading this book make you feel differently about these issues? If so, how?

17. What do you think about the theme of love as it is expressed in *The Congregation*? Which characters have love and which don't? How is this significant?

18. What did you learn about secrecy within religion and within families and its consequences?

19. Many of the characters in this book have been taken advantage of in some way. What do you think it will take for these victims to break the cycle of abuse?

20. Do you think there is any symbolism to the different paths and tunnels that are below the church in Old Town? If so, please describe.

21. Do you think social media and virtual worlds have changed society and young people in particular? If so, how?

22. How do you feel about the verse Matthew 5:5, "Blessed are the meek for they shall inherit the earth"? What was the significance of its use?

23. Do you feel American society has failed its youth? If so, in what way(s)?

24. What about the Church's attitude toward its young? Has it also failed its youth? If so, how?

25. Out of all the scenes in the book, which one or ones did you find the most powerful and why?

26. What did you enjoy most about Amanda and Jake? Was there any particular scene with them you enjoyed more than any others?

AUTHOR Q & A

Q: What was your inspiration for *The Congregation*? When did you first know you wanted to write this particular story? Was it something you had been thinking about for some time or was there a sudden motivation or drive to bring it to life?

DB: Growing up Catholic I have always had my thoughts on the Church and any group that is in a position of power. How does that type of organization transcend thousands of years and still stay in control of so many? Two things come to mind when people follow something religiously: fear and inspiration. I thought the fear was more prevalent in this situation, at least for me, and the story just came from that.

Q: From early on in the book, it seems your knowledge of travel is extensive. Do you travel a great deal? Has travel unexpectedly inspired any of your plots? What are some of your favorite places to travel and why?

DB: Travel is a huge part of my life. Visiting most, if not all, of the countries of the world is on my bucket list. I have been to thirty-three countries so far and that includes every place I write about. I think you have to experience and feel a place before you can write about it. Some of my favorite places are Australia, France, Italy, South Africa, England, Grenada, Hawaii, Turkey, and Sri Lanka. They are my favorites, because they are all so unique. The cultures are fascinating, and the people are wonderful.

Q: The setting of Rome seems very logical with regard to the subject matter of *The Congregation*. How did you choose Old Town in Chicago for the other setting? Does it have a special meaning to you?

DB: I love Chicago as a city, and it has some very special little places. Old Town just happens to be a really cool area, kind of like the French Quarter in New Orleans or the East Village in Calgary where I am from. Old Town is just not a place you would expect some scary stuff to be happening, which is why I chose it.

Q: What settings or activities inspire you to write? Do you like to write on a computer or do you use pen and paper? If you have a special room or office dedicated to your writing, what is it like?

DB: I generally like a setting where I can see water. It lulls me into a type of meditative state, and things are far more fascinating in that realm. Hawaii and my cottage at the lake are inspiring places to write. The water is right at my feet. I use anything I can when writing, because things just come to you. So if I have a piece of paper and something comes to me, I write it down, or I make notes or record it on my smartphone. I also sleep with a pen and pad of paper on my nightstand, in case inspiration strikes during the night.

Q: Do you have a strict schedule for writing that works best for you?

DB: Mornings work best, but writing is an art, and you really can't limit yourself or put restrictions around it. My belief is that a true writer doesn't come up with a story. The story comes to them, and then it's like watching a movie in your head.

Q: When did you know you wanted to be a writer?

DB: When I was five years old and was reading books that took me to other places, worlds, and lives. It was the most amazing experience I had ever had by just using my mind.

Q: In your novel, the Roman Catholic Church is referred to as the "blackest, darkest cult." Can you speak to your upbringing, education, or experiences, and the influence that the Church might have had in your life?

DB: Growing up Roman Catholic and going through the rituals from baptism to confirmation, I thought the rules didn't make much sense. I went to Catholic schools that endorsed segregation and twisted words in the bible in order to get away with unspeakable things. Also, the strictness of the Church and how people were treated if they didn't believe in the same things seemed completely against what they preached. In my mind you cannot be hypocritical in religion if you want people to adopt your philosophies. I don't think religion is bad. In fact it's good for people to believe in something. I think the way religion is used by people to take advantage of others is what's not acceptable.

Q: "The one thing they had in common was that they had nothing to believe in, until now." Can you comment on this quote and its connection to the evolution of the story and characters of *The Congregation*?

DB: Children start with one thing in common, unconditional love for their parents, the people who create them. It makes sense. Why wouldn't you love and take care of something that was born of yourself? As a child, the day you realize you cannot trust the people who are there to protect and support you, you really lose faith in everything else. These children are looking for some kind of reason or purpose to be. Their connection to this one purpose gives them something to believe in. It makes them feel like they are significant and that they matter. That is a powerful influencer when you have felt like you were nothing before. We all want to belong to something.

Q: With regard to Matthew 5:5, "Blessed are the meek for they shall inherit the earth," can you give your insight into this verse and why you decided that it should play an integral part in the story?

DB: When I think of the meek, I think of those who cannot fight for themselves or have been taken advantage of. For me, it ties into the group of kids and into other characters like Elise and the professor. Gavriel writes this down as he is still avenging his dead brother whom he also saw as meek and frail. At the end of the story, there were many meek individuals who make significant contributions.

Q: Can you comment on the theme of love denied, specifically the contrast of the fully realized love between Amanda and Jake in contrast to the love that was denied to Samuel and Michael?

DB: I think this is something most people can identify with. Whether you are in agreement with gay rights or not, we all know how love can impact us to a point that we would do some crazy things in the name of "love." The love denied was a catalyst, along with the bishop's actions that launched the plans against the Church.

Q: *The Congregation* charts the stories of a series of interconnected people who seem to have lost their way in life. Can you comment on this and how you decided to create characters whose disappointment or betrayal led to a lost life?

DB: We have all gone through some kind of rough patch in our lives. For most, it is not this dramatic or impactful. However, there are many who have and will go through some pretty disturbing events. These things play out differently for everyone, but they contribute to the character of who these people become. This book may highlight more of the bad traits. However, I think it also shows how some of these people can shine and even become heroes throughout the story. Not all the lives are lost for good. I think we can all think of a time we felt lost, but we eventually found ourselves again.

Q: Did you base any of the characters in *The Congregation* on people you've known in your life? Who was your favorite character to write? And which character did not turn out as you had imagined or whose development surprised you during the course of the novel?

DB: All the characters in this book are based on my imagination, nothing more. I loved writing them. Like the countries I love to visit, the characters are all unique and different creatures. I think the person's character who tricked me a bit during development was Stanford. He turned out to be more sinister and dangerous than I had anticipated.

Q: Amanda's clairvoyance is central to her character. Can you comment on her gift (or curse) and how or why you decided to craft her with this power? Amanda is described as talkative with lots of energy. Is there someone in your life who inspired this character?

DB: Amanda's ability to "see" more than what is there comes from a lot of work I do with intuitive leadership. As a business leader, I mentor a number of young people with this skill to help them use it as a tool to improve their decision-making process. In doing this, sometimes we wish we could see more, or know more, to help us along the way. I think this is where that part of her character came from.

Q: With regard to Cardinal Roland and Father Kristofferson, can you speak to why Father Kristofferson seems to be lonely and beaten down, while Cardinal Roland does not seem to be particularly unhappy? Can you also share why the two men decided to stay with the Church even after their humiliation?

DB: Father Kristofferson was growing tired. The more he thought about the impact and what the potential outcome could be of the work he was doing with the Congregation, the more questionable it became. When they started the vendetta, they were young and full of anger about the Church. After planning for so many years and designing a way to get back, they both started to realize this was not who they were or what it was about. Cardinal Roland managed to distance himself from it when he was awarded a post at the Vatican. Whereas, Father Kristofferson remained in the city, which was a daily reminder of the ordeal they went through. They stayed with the Church, because they still believed in the fundamental purpose of enlightening its constituents. However, the type of enlightenment they planned was now daunting instead of helpful.

Q: Do you view Gavriel as being a prototype, and, if so, do you believe there are many other "Gavriels" out there in the world? Can you elaborate on his character as a leader at the Gathering and how it relates to online recruitment of young people to the terrorist activities that we hear of in the news?

DB: I am not sure if Gavriel is a prototype, but I do believe we are limited in our thinking as young people, just by not enough experience or exposure to the world and what's in it. This tunnel vision can be enhanced if something truly bad occurs in your life. It focuses on the negative and can be especially powerful if it touches someone you really love. Gavriel's brother was his purpose in life, and when he lost him, tragically, he filled that void with anger and resentment for a religion that talked of love and salvation and a mother who didn't protect, but hurt, her child. I think we see how small children can be influenced by a number of things. These influencers range from threats to their lives or others they love, to making them believe by way of propaganda and limiting their access to the truth, to torture and manipulation. These things go on in the world of terrorists and also in our own world. We just don't talk about it.

Q: Amanda describes herself as being spiritual, in contrast to her mother who is described as being religious in the traditional sense. How do you feel about the possibility and likelihood of young people, such as Josh and Gavriel, finding a spiritual path to a meaningful life?

DB: This is one of the positive messages I hope comes out of the book. You don't have to throw away your beliefs. There are spirit and purpose in a meaningful life. Young people need something to believe in. They need hope, and they need to be able to trust. When a person is young, they are malleable. We are the guardians of those precious years, and supporting young people in their dreams and aspirations is everyone's responsibility.

Q: The character and descriptions of Elise were extremely compelling and memorable. Can you share whether you think Josh would believe that she found the dignity he told her to seek?

DB: Unfortunately, Josh was not able to see the heroics of Elise. However, Elise realized she had this within herself and proved it. Elise found her dignity and that was her victory.

Q: Do you know, or have you known, a young man like Josh? Can you describe why you think his family situation led him to become ready to commit crimes against others?

DB: There are different types of abuse, and we sometimes get caught up with the physical aspect of it. The more traumatic part is the emotional or mental abuse that comes along with or without physical abuse. Regardless, we should not discount neglect or indifference. Apathy is not a good trait for parenting. It forces children to find other ways to matter.

Q: How was Father Kristofferson transformed from being someone who was committed to helping young people to someone who would let young people make plans to carry out violent acts against the innocent?

DB: Father Kristofferson lost himself in the dilemma of right and wrong and by the time he figured it out, Gavriel had already taken over the reins. His intention initially was to make a bold statement. He recruited, influenced, and made believers out of the entire group. Going back on his actions was another blow to these kids who had already been betrayed by their parents. He put himself in a no-win situation in his mind.

Q: The scene between Elise and Stanford in the kitchen was extraordinarily vivid and succeeded in portraying the character of Stanford in a very powerful and shocking way. Can you share the roots of the inspiration that enabled you to write such an unforgettable scene?

DB: Stanford was the one character that surprised me. The twist in his character from the cool, calm demeanor he originally showed just burst into the book. It was one of those times that the words just came as they did without too much thought or provocation.

Q: Have you personally experienced anything like the final scenes of the book when the bullets are flying? What do you think are the keys to successfully writing such an exciting scene?

DB: I have not personally been in a shoot-out, but I could imagine being in one and have seen enough real scenes of war to know it is not as graceful as the movies depict it to be. That's why mine was a bit messy and confusing, because I believe that would be more realistic in that scenario.

Q: Can you talk a bit about your favorite authors and favorite books? What topics or genres most appeal to you? Were you influenced as a young reader by any author in particular?

DB: I love so many authors and books. Steven King for his *Dark Tower* series, Wally Lamb for the humanness of *She's Come Undone* and *I Know This Much Is True*, and Robert A. Heinlein for his imagination and innovative style. Ann-Marie Macdonald is an inspiring writer all around. There are hundreds I could name.

Q: Jake and Amanda have a love of good food and wine. Do you have a favorite meal? What is your favorite wine?

DB: I love every kind of food, and being a sommelier has given me a real appreciation for wines of every kind. My favorites, of course, being wines from the Bordeaux region and Tuscany, but that changes often!

Q: Do you have to hold back on certain plotlines, ideas, or settings, knowing that there are more Amanda and Jake Bannon stories to come? Are there any stories or places you might like to give a sneak peek at or hint about?

DB: I have already started the outline of a third Bannon novel. I don't want to give too much away, but I think it will take place somewhere a little more exotic where the normal rules of society that Jake and Amanda are used to are not there to protect them. We will have to wait and see!

ABOUT THE AUTHOR

DESIRÉE A. BOMBENON, BORN IN COLOMBO, Sri Lanka, is a successful CEO and certified strategic leader. She is a member of the Young Presidents' Organization and has won multiple global industry and leadership awards.

In addition to her involvement in several businesses, Desirée spends her time mentoring young people, contributing to community and philanthropic projects, and traveling extensively. She serves on both business and nonprofit boards. Balanced by her husband, Marc, and two children, Janine and Joel, she lives on four acres just outside of Calgary, Canada. *The Congregation* is her second novel.

www.ingramcontent.com/pod-product-compliance
Lightning Source LLC
Chambersburg PA
CBHW030618120726
47904CB00006B/1945